THE OTHER WOMAN

BETSY REAVLEY

Copyright © 2025 Betsy Reavley

The right of Betsy Reavley to be identified as the Author of the Work has been asserted by them in accordance with the Copyright, Designs and Patents Act 1988.

First published in 2025 by Bloodhound Books.

Apart from any use permitted under UK copyright law, this publication may only be reproduced, stored, or transmitted, in any form, or by any means, with prior permission in writing of the publisher or, in the case of reprographic production, in accordance with the terms of licences issued by the Copyright Licensing Agency.
All characters in this publication are fictitious and any resemblance to real persons, living or dead, is purely coincidental.

www.bloodhoundbooks.com

Print ISBN: 978-1-917449-8-30

*For anyone who has ever fallen over
and got back up again.*

Our envy of others devours us most of all.
  — Aleksandr Solzhenitsyn

People lie. Behaviour doesn't.
  — Unknown

SHE

I stand by the French doors, gazing out over the emerald lawn stretching far and wide, manicured to perfection, not a blade out of place. The early morning sun casts a soft glow over the grounds, and for a moment, I allow myself the quiet pleasure of it all. This is mine.

I'm at the edge of it all, watching as everything falls into place, just as I intended. It's almost laughable how easy it is to manipulate people when you know their weaknesses. A whisper here, a nudge there, and their perfect little lives start crumbling without them even realising it. People are so fragile—every one of them. They all think they're in control, like they have a say in how things will unfold, but that couldn't be further from the truth.

They're puppets. All of them. And I'm the one pulling the strings.

She thinks she has the upper hand, doesn't she? Always angling for attention, trying to cement her place at the centre of it all. She's desperate to be seen, to be needed, and it makes her so easy to play. The more she reaches, the more tangled she becomes *in her own web. But she doesn't see that. She never does. Not until it's too late.*

And him—he tries so hard to keep everything balanced. To be the peacemaker, the one who holds it all together. But I've seen through that façade. He's weak, torn between guilt and the weight of all his choices. He cracks, just like the rest of them. The world he thinks he's building is already crumbling beneath his feet.

Then there's the other one. She's the most satisfying of them all. Always so close to breaking, even when she doesn't realise it. It took almost nothing to send her spinning into chaos—just a few small moves, and she's doubting everything, including herself.

But here's the best part: this is only the beginning.

Everything I've done so far? Just laying the groundwork. Subtle moves, little seeds planted in their minds. I've been patient, watching them destroy themselves piece by piece. But now? Now it's time for something bigger, something that will push them over the edge.

People like to think they know how much they can take. They think they can handle anything that comes their way. But when you start to strip away their defences, one by one, it doesn't take long for them to fall apart. They make mistakes, they lash out, they turn against the people they love. And that's when they become the most fun to watch—when they're at their weakest.

What I have planned next will tear them apart completely. It will seep into every corner of their lives, into their thoughts, their relationships, until they can't tell what's real anymore. They'll fight to hold onto the pieces of their lives, but it'll be too late. The damage will already be done.

They think they've struggled so far? They haven't seen anything yet.

I've been here the whole time, invisible, unnoticed. Watching. I know every secret, every lie, every buried fear. I've been patient, waiting for the perfect moment to strike. And now, the time is almost here.

It's like watching a row of dominoes fall—every move has been set in place, and all I have to do is push. Once the first one falls, the rest will come tumbling down in a beautiful, inevitable collapse.

They don't know it yet, but their lives are already mine. I'm in control, not them. They're just players in the game I've been orchestrating from the very beginning. Soon enough, they'll have no choice but to watch as everything they care about crumbles into dust.

A soft smirk curves my lips as I glance back toward the distant hedge. How many have stood in my way, telling me I was aiming too high, wanting too much? Each one has gone now, vanished from my life like dust brushed from my shoes. Those who haven't learned early enough have paid the price, some in ways they never saw coming. But that is the thing, isn't it? Power is sweetest when it is subtle, an art in which I've become more than adept. Those who whispered behind my back, questioning or conniving—they have underestimated me. They had thought me fragile. They were wrong.

I sip the tea, the warmth sliding down my throat as I look out over what I have achieved. No one will take it from me. Not now, not ever. I have claimed my place here, and anyone who dares challenge that will soon find themselves on the outside, wishing they hadn't crossed the threshold in the first place. Just like the people from my past. Just like the dead.

OCTOBER 20TH

Lila sat behind the flat-pack desk in reception, waiting for the next candidate to enter. Her stomach fluttered with a vague anticipation, though she wasn't sure why. It had been the same all week: a parade of beige, faceless men and women filing through the office doors. She had no reason to believe the next would be any different, but something in the air felt unusual today. Something she couldn't put her finger on.

The winter sun hung low in the sky, casting long shadows through the glass front of the office building. By the entrance stood a large plastic plant, its leaves coated in a layer of dust. She made a mental note to clean it before the day was done—a task that, like so many others in this job, felt thankless.

Her eyes drifted to the clock on the wall. Only 2.35pm. Two more hours, at least, of sitting at her desk at Wellington Marketing Management Ltd. It wasn't the job she had imagined for herself, certainly not after her vibrant life in London, where she and Owen had once lived as young, carefree twenty-somethings. Back then, they'd rented a tiny flat on the third floor of a Victorian building in Hackney. The flat was barely big enough to turn around in, with creaky floorboards and a bathroom that always seemed to be on the verge of falling apart. But it had been theirs—a snug, lively little space that felt like home.

She could almost smell the lingering scent of paint and coffee, a mixture that clung to the walls from her many late nights working on projects and Owen's caffeine-fuelled mornings. They'd decorated the flat with second-hand finds, bits and pieces that they'd scavenged from local markets. She remembered the thrill of exploring the city together, spending weekends cycling along the Thames, discovering new galleries, and lingering over cheap wine in dimly lit pubs that buzzed with energy. London had felt limitless, brimming with opportunity and excitement, and she'd felt so alive, with Owen by her side.

She missed that feeling. Life had been simpler in the early days, filled with laughter, impromptu adventures, and a kind of freedom she hadn't realised she'd one day long for. Lila had fallen pregnant with their first daughter, Ella, very soon after they first met. Both knew that everyone around them wasn't expecting it to last but they'd stayed together against the odds. Owen had been her partner in everything—whether they were cooking on their tiny hob or spontaneously deciding to hop on a train to Brighton for the weekend. They'd shared everything, their dreams and plans, believing that nothing could dampen their love or steal away their sense of fun. Now, years later, with the weight of their life in Cambridge, two daughters, and a thriving business to manage, she wondered if that carefree couple had vanished forever.

Her eyes drifted back to the clock. Only minutes had passed. She sighed, adjusting a stack of papers on her desk, feeling the empty monotony of her job pull her back to the present. Since marrying Owen and moving to Cambridge, she had slipped into the role of secretary at his company, helping until the business grew. She hadn't expected to be there four years later. Every day at Wellington Marketing felt like another step away from the woman she had once been. Sometimes she felt grateful for the stability they'd built, the lovely Victorian townhouse on a tree-lined street, their two beautiful daughters. But on days like this, she couldn't shake the feeling that a part of her had been left behind in London, buried under years of routine and responsibility.

She had already shown three candidates into Owen's office, and the fourth was due any moment.

The door opened with a gust of wind, scattering the neat stack of papers on her desk. As she knelt to gather them, she didn't notice the man who entered. By the time she straightened up and returned to her seat, he was standing there, watching her with a polite smile.

"Julian Richards. I've got an interview at three o'clock." His voice was smooth, and as she took him in, she noticed more than his words. He was attractive—tall, athletic, with striking blue eyes and a confident presence that immediately commanded attention.

She flushed slightly, embarrassed by the mess she had made with the papers, but quickly composed herself. "Please take a seat," she managed, her cheeks warming. As he settled into one of the grey fabric chairs in the waiting area, she couldn't help but steal another glance. It was rare that she noticed other men; her relationship with Owen had always been stable and content. But Julian had a presence that was impossible to ignore. There was something about him—an effortless charm that drew people in.

Owen's voice crackled over the phone when she called to let him know Julian was waiting. "Send him in in five," he said, barely finishing his lunch.

When she relayed the message, Julian smiled, thanked her,

and returned to his reading, calmly thumbing through an industry magazine. She watched him from the corner of her eye, wondering what it was about him that felt so different from the others. It wasn't just his looks—there was something else, something about the way he carried himself. A confidence she hadn't seen in any of the other candidates.

A few minutes later, she sent him through to Owen's office. As he disappeared behind the door, she found herself idly curious, almost hoping he'd be the one Owen picked for the job. It wasn't like her to pay attention to the interviewees, but today, she was bored, restless, and intrigued by this new presence.

Twenty minutes later, Julian and Owen reappeared, chatting easily as they walked back into the reception area. Julian shook Owen's hand with a warm smile, thanking him for his time. Owen nodded politely, but she could see something in her husband's expression—a subtle tension. He wasn't convinced. As Julian left the building, giving her a courteous nod, she felt a strange mix of disappointment and amusement.

"He seemed nice," she ventured, watching Owen as he poured himself a glass of water.

Owen shrugged; his tone clipped. "Nice enough. I'm not sure he has what it takes, though."

"He's got the experience," she countered, more out of habit than genuine conviction. These days Lila often found herself disagreeing with Owen for the sake of it.

Owen downed his water and crumpled the cup in his hand. "Maybe. But I'm looking for someone who can close deals. Someone who has that killer instinct."

"This isn't the jungle, you know. Can you drop the hunter-gatherer act for just a moment."

She saw the hurt in his eyes and let the conversation drop. There was no point pressing. Owen would make the decision, as he always did. Her mind was already elsewhere—on the holiday they still hadn't booked, on the escape she was desperately craving. She had wanted to bring it up, but Owen's mood had turned sour at the mention of it, and she knew when to back off.

With a sigh, she turned her attention to her computer, searching for potential holiday destinations. She needed to get away from Cambridge, away from work, away from the monotony of it all. But as the hours ticked by and more interviews passed, the possibility of escaping felt more distant than ever.

"Are we ever going to book that holiday you've been promising me?" She couldn't bite her lip any longer.

"Please get off my case, Li. I am working really hard to grow the business. We just don't have the time or the money to do that right now. We will, when the time is right but stop nagging me about it." His shoulders dropped as he turned and headed back into the sanctuary of his office.

The afternoon dragged on, interrupted only by the arrival of a final candidate: a slim woman with high heels, tight faux-leather trousers, and an oversized tote bag slung over her shoulder. She barely glanced at the massive sign outside the building, clearly lost.

"Is this Fairfax House?" the woman asked, her tone casual.

"Yes," Lila replied, masking her surprise at the woman's appearance. She didn't fit the mould as the usual marketing type, but something about her had intrigued Owen enough to arrange a meeting.

The woman smiled, introduced herself as Cass, and disappeared into Owen's office a moment later. The interview was brief, but when Cass left, Owen looked thoughtful, even impressed.

"She's full of energy," he said, slumping into one of the reception chairs after the interview. "Not much experience, but eager to learn."

"You're not seriously considering her?" She raised an eyebrow, knowing Owen wanted someone with experience to take on the workload. "You can't be serious."

"We'll see." Owen shrugged again, cryptic as ever. "She's very willing."

"What is that supposed to mean?" Lila knew they were dancing around the same conversation that had been at the centre of their relationship for some time, the lack of sex in their marriage.

It was late by the time Lila left the office, tension simmering between them. She slipped into her coat, eager to leave the day behind and meet Zara, her friend, for a drink later at their usual spot, The Rabbit in the Hat. As she left the building, she didn't look back, but the growing distance between her and Owen weighed on her mind.

Outside, the wind had picked up, and the sun was hidden behind thick, angry clouds that matched her mood. As she walked to the large concrete car park, she pulled out her phone and texted Zara:

> Going to need a large one tonight. Thanks for helping with the girls x

Within seconds, her phone buzzed with a reply:

> Bad day?? x

She quickly typed back:

> Scrap that. I'll need a few large ones... x

Zara's response came with two kisses. They would talk about it at the pub when they were in private.

Climbing into her forest-green Mini Cooper, she

immediately turned on the heater. It was cold for October. Resting her head against the steering wheel, she let out a long, weary sigh. She didn't like walking away from an argument with Owen, leaving things unresolved, but her frustration had got the better of her. Why was his business always more important than her happiness?

Determined not to go home in a stormy mood, she started the car, turned on the radio, and pulled out of the car park, leaving behind the concrete world of work.

OCTOBER 20TH

The drive to Humberstone Road, where their Victorian terraced house stood, took only ten minutes. The house, nestled on a tree-lined street, had been a project they were proud of—purchased cheaply and lovingly updated over the past few years. It was a quiet, lovely part of the city, and she had always felt a sense of pride when turning onto her road.

Parking the car, she glanced at the last of the autumn leaves swaying on the trees, clinging to the branches in the wind. She got out, pulling her coat tighter against the chill, and made her way to the red front door of number 22.

The moment she stepped inside, shutting the door behind her, she shook her head to calm her unruly red hair. The sound of little footsteps came rushing toward her, and Molly appeared, still in her school uniform, wrapping her skinny arms around her mother with an excited squeal.

"Mummy!" she cried, her face lighting up with joy.

She hugged her daughter back, the warmth of Molly's affection immediately soothing the tension she'd carried home. "Have you had a good day, girlie?" she asked, brushing a mousy fringe off Molly's forehead before kissing her nose.

"We had art," Molly declared proudly.

"What did you draw?" She slipped off her favourite winter coat, hanging it on a hook in the hallway.

"Autumn leaves. Big ones." Her daughter beamed, proud of her artistic efforts.

"How lovely," Lila said, feeling the anger she'd brought home from the office begin to melt away.

"Can I have some Halloween treats?" Molly asked without waiting for an answer, before dashing back into the sitting room, likely to indulge in more sugary snacks.

Zara appeared at the end of the corridor, standing in the kitchen doorway with a mug in one hand and a tea towel in the other. She blew her fringe out of her face and gave her friend a knowing look.

"Good day, I'm guessing?" she asked with raised eyebrows. From upstairs came the familiar thud of music from Lila's teenage daughter's bedroom.

"We'll talk about it later," she said, not wanting to discuss her frustrations in earshot of Molly.

"Cuppa?"

"That'd be great," she said, heading toward the landing. "Just going to nip upstairs and change. I'll be down in a sec."

"I'll put the kettle on," Zara called after her, retreating to the kitchen.

She climbed the stairs, knowing her eldest, Ella, was in her room, likely absorbed in a Snapchat conversation on her phone. She knocked lightly before entering. "Ella?"

Ella didn't bother to look up from her screen.

"Hi, Mum."

"Good day at college? What did you get up to?" she asked, surveying the mess of clothes strewn across the floor but choosing to ignore it.

"Fine," Ella replied absently, her eyes glued to her phone.

"What's for dinner?" she asked, looking up just long enough to show how important it was she got an answer.

"Pesto pasta and salad," Lila said, stepping out of the room.

"And garlic bread?" Ella asked hopefully.

"If there's some in the freezer," she called back, shutting the bedroom door behind her. She leaned against it for a moment, feeling the cold, hard wood press into her back. Besides Ella's bedroom, the house was immaculate. Their cleaner, Lisa, had been in that morning while she was at work, leaving everything spotless. The thought made her feel strangely disconnected from the home she had worked so hard to maintain. The idea of stripping out of her work clothes and into something more comfortable was a relief.

She took off her uncomfortable shoes and neatly lined them up in her wardrobe before pulling on a pair of leggings and a soft grey mohair jumper. The change of clothes instantly lifted her mood.

A quick glance in the mirror revealed the tiredness gathering under her eyes, dark circles that felt like quicksand dragging her down. She ignored them, slid into her slippers, and headed downstairs. They were only a reminder of why she no longer felt sexy or wanted by Owen.

In the kitchen, Zara was waiting, sitting at the pine dining table with two steaming mugs of coffee. "Rough one, was it?" Zara asked, standing to give her a hug.

"I'll fill you in," she said, rolling her eyes as she settled into the chair across from her friend. "How are things with you?"

"All right," Zara replied, slurping her drink. "Mum had another fall, but nothing major. Just spent a bit of time at the care home."

"I would never have asked you to pick up Molly if I'd known. You should have said." She instantly felt guilty.

"It was no bother," Zara assured her. "She's fine. Probably doesn't even remember falling."

Zara, in her mid-fifties, was a lively and unconventional presence in her life. A brilliant historian by day, Lila let loose around her friend, embracing her quirky, eccentric self. Since moving to Cambridge, it had been hard for Lila to find people she truly connected with, but with Zara she'd never had that problem.

They had been friends since childhood. Lila was a shy child who lacked confidence. Until she met Zara. The two connected after Lila was put into care and an unbreakable bond was formed, that had remained unshakable ever since.

Zara provided support whenever Lila needed it, and they shared laughter and advice over countless cups of coffee. Her vibrant personality filled a space in Lila's life that no one else could, and soon, Zara became part of the furniture—a comforting, reliable presence Lila couldn't imagine being without.

"You've gone purple this week?" she noted, eyeing the streaks in Zara's hair.

"Yep." Zara grinned, running a hand through her colourful locks. "Felt like a change."

"It suits you," she said, though she wasn't entirely sure if it did.

"Is it too much?"

"I don't think so," she replied, glancing into her coffee mug.

"What time is Owen coming back?" Zara asked, pulling her pink-and-black fluffy cardigan around her as she sat back down.

"No idea. We had a bit of a tiff," Lila admitted, checking the time. It was just after five o'clock.

"Sounds like you need to talk," Zara said with a knowing smile as she placed her empty mug in the sink. "Got any cake?"

She smiled. Zara's sweet tooth always won out, despite her

constant battle with dieting. "I think there are some mini rolls in the cupboard above the microwave."

At that moment, the front door opened, and Molly's excited voice filled the house. "Daddy!"

"Hello, piglet," Owen's voice replied, as familiar as ever.

"I'll go and start the car," said Zara, slipping out of the French doors as Owen entered the kitchen, kissed his wife on the cheek, and set his bag down.

"So, do you feel there are any promising candidates for the job?" Lila asked, trying to ease the tension.

"Possibly," Owen replied cryptically, pulling a cold bottle of beer from the fridge.

"I'm heading to The Rabbit tonight. Won't be late," Lila said, grabbing her bag and changing into her shoes, "especially on a school night." She was still stiff from their earlier argument.

"When did you plan this?"

Lila responded silently with a shrug.

Owen took a long drink of his beer. "What shall I give the kids for dinner?"

"Pesto pasta, maybe garlic bread if we have some in the freezer," she said without looking at him, still holding on to some of her frustration.

"Right," he said, rolling up his sleeves. "Have a good time. I want to run something by you later, Lila. It would be good to talk tonight."

"I'll be back by nine," she promised, kissing him goodbye. She softened, unable to stay angry with him for long.

FEBRUARY 9TH

Despite Lila's initial concerns, in the two months since Cass had started working at Wellington Marketing Management, since handing in her notice at her previous job, Lila had found herself increasingly drawn to the vibrant energy her new colleague brought into her life.

From the moment Cass had first breezed into the office, a whirlwind of confidence and charm, Lila had felt threatened and insecure. She didn't like the idea of sharing Owen with another woman. But before long Lila was in awe of her. At first, it was subtle—Cass taking on more responsibilities, impressing Owen with her quick thinking and easy manner. But it wasn't just Cass's professional capabilities that captured Lila's attention; it was something much deeper.

Cass was unlike anyone Lila had ever met. She was magnetic, with a presence that filled every room she entered. The office had always felt like a grey, monotonous place for Lila, but with Cass there, everything seemed brighter, more exciting. Days that had once dragged on were now filled with shared laughter, secret glances across the desk, and whispered conversations that felt like they were in on a private joke no one else would understand.

Outside of work, their friendship had blossomed even faster. It wasn't long before lunch-breaks turned into after-work drinks, which in turn led to weekends spent together, much to Owen's delight. Owen, who had been fond of Cass from the moment he interviewed her, had no qualms about the women bonding. In fact, he encouraged it, perhaps believing that Cass's bold nature could bring out something in Lila. But Lila couldn't help feeling there was more to their connection—something that went beyond work or social convenience.

Cass seemed to bring out a different side of Lila, a side she hadn't realised she'd lost. Cass made her feel younger, more spontaneous, more alive. There were moments when Lila found herself looking at Cass in awe, completely captivated by the ease with which she carried herself, how effortlessly she could shift between being carefree and deadly serious. Cass was everything Lila wasn't—bold, confident, unapologetic—and that magnetic allure had only deepened their bond.

On that early February day, the two women strolled arm-in-arm through the park on their lunch-break. The sun was unusually warm, casting a golden light over the city, and for the first time in months, Lila felt like she could breathe again. Cass's presence beside her was comforting in a way she couldn't fully explain. They had spent nearly every day together for weeks, not just in the office but outside it too—shopping trips, lazy afternoons at cafés, long walks through the park.

"I think he's at it again," Cass murmured, chewing on her lip as they walked, her usual confident façade cracking just enough to let Lila see a glimpse of the vulnerability beneath.

"So soon?!" Lila's voice came out higher than she'd intended, startled by the sudden shift in the conversation. "With who?"

"Dunno. Some slapper he met at the pub or something probably." Cass shrugged, though Lila could see the strain behind her nonchalance.

"Oh, Cass…" Lila trailed off, unsure what to say. This wasn't the first time Cass had hinted at trouble in her marriage, but it always felt like a tightrope walk—Cass would mention it, then quickly dismiss it, as though revealing too much would weaken her somehow. Although Lila had never met Cass's husband, Mark, she felt as if she knew him inside out. And she didn't like what she knew.

"At least if he's shagging her, I get a break," Cass joked bitterly, but Lila knew better. She could see through her friend's bravado. It also reminded Lila of the lack of sex in her own relationship.

"I don't know how you do it. Owen and I hardly ever have sex anymore." Lila bit her lip, worrying she'd said too much. "Do you want to stay with us for a while? You know you're always welcome," Lila offered, wanting to do something to help, anything to ease the pain she knew her friend was hiding.

Cass smiled, her face softening for a moment. "Probably not, babe. But thanks."

"We could have a girls' movie night. Doesn't sound so bad, does it?" Lila encouraged.

Cass tilted her head up to the sky, letting the sunlight kiss her skin. For the first time that day, she looked genuinely at peace. "It sounds like bliss, honestly." Cass stopped walking. "You're such a good friend, Lila. I don't know what I'd do without you."

"You're my best friend," Lila replied, feeling a swell of emotion she hadn't expected. "Owen wouldn't mind if you crashed with us for a few nights. He's fond of you too, you know."

Cass grinned, though there was something unreadable in her eyes. "You're making me blush."

"He seems like his old self when you're around," Lila admitted bitterly.

"Are things not good with you?" Cass asked casually, their arms still linked.

"Not great, if I'm honest." Lila wanted to say so much more but stopped. She knew Cass was also Owen's friend, as well as his colleague and she didn't want to put her in a difficult position.

They continued walking, heading toward their favourite bar, the easy rhythm of their conversation picking up again. Despite the heaviness of Cass's revelations, the moments of lightness and laughter returned, as they always did. That was the thing about Cass—she never let herself linger in the darkness for too long.

As they settled at their usual table, ordering lunch and drinks, Lila found herself studying Cass more closely. She was always so put together—impeccable make-up, flawless clothes, an effortless grace. And yet, beneath it all, there was a fragility that Lila hadn't fully understood until now. Cass made it look easy, this balancing act of life, but Lila knew it was far more complicated than that.

Cass, ever the one to notice small details, was quick to shift the mood. "I'll bring a bottle of wine over tonight for us. Owen can join. I'll stop by and pick up cake for the girls. While they stuff their faces we can drink and put the world to rights."

"You've got yourself a deal," Lila said, impressed at how Cass could remember even the smallest of preferences—like which of her daughters liked chocolate cake and which preferred carrot. It was those little things that made Cass feel so... perfect, like she had everything figured out.

For Lila, Cass wasn't just a colleague or even a friend

anymore—she was someone to admire, someone to emulate. Cass had become the person Lila wanted to be more like: confident, untouchable, in control of her life in a way Lila had never mastered, despite the fact her marriage was clearly in tatters.

As they shared their meal, Cass leaned in, a sudden coldness flashing in her eyes for just a moment. "Thing about me, Lila, is, I'm nice... until I'm not."

The comment hung in the air, an odd contrast to the warmth of the day. Lila's stomach fluttered uncomfortably, but before she could respond, Cass smiled brightly, the moment passed. They laughed, and everything felt normal again, but the weight of Cass's words stayed with Lila.

Cass had let her guard down just a little, shown a crack in the armour she wore so effortlessly. And for Lila, that glimpse of the woman beneath the surface was enough to deepen the admiration she already felt. Cass was human, after all—flawed, hurting, but still, she was everything Lila wished she could be.

Cass had been busy on her phone, texting for most of lunch. Her eyes gleamed, reflecting the bright screen as she ran her tongue over her teeth repeatedly. She barely ate anything, and barely spoke. Just kept texting. It wasn't like her and it left Lila feeling flat.

Lila enjoyed an iced coffee, a mozzarella, tomato and spinach panini, followed by a blueberry muffin, flitting between watching Cass on her phone, and the people who floated by the café window going about their business, as a breeze began to pick up, pulling at people's clothes, and playing with rubbish from the street. She watched transfixed as an old crisp packet danced in the wind. Lila didn't know what it was, but something made her feel uneasy, as if a storm might be around the corner.

Wiping her mouth with a napkin to make sure any trace of the blueberry muffin was removed, she folded it neatly in half and tucked it into the paper wrapper that had contained her panini. Cass triumphantly dropped her phone into her Michael Kors burgundy leather bag and grinned at her.

"Sorted," she boasted.

"What is?"

"Our added fun for tonight." An over-the-top wink, and a nudge from her elbow followed.

"Sorry, I don't follow." Lila could feel the blank expression on her face.

"I'll tell you on the walk back." She looked like the cat who got the cream.

"Okay," Lila said as they both stood. "I thought it would be nice if I asked a friend over to join us for a drink tonight. The more the merrier."

A look of bitter disappointment, twinned with disdain crossed Cass's face.

"Is that a problem?" She pulled her coat on and put her bag on her shoulder.

"No, doll. Not really a problem. Just," she shrugged, "thought it would be nice for the three of us to spend a night in together."

"I'd like you to meet Zara." The statement hung in the air because deep down Lila knew they were opposite, but not opposites who would ever attract. They were like two sides of the same magnet, pushing against each other. Neither would be unkind or rude to the other, but Lila knew there would be an instant dislike of one another. Lila had been relieved when Zara had been unable to make it to the drinks party Owen and Lila hosted to welcome in the New Year. Lila had been hoping to meet Mark on that occasion, but he too had been unwell and Cass came alone.

"I'm sure she's nice," Cass chewed her plump bottom lip and rubbed her pointed boot back and forwards on the floor, "it's just I think it would be good if it was just us."

"You're worried she's not cool." Lila spoke over her shoulder as she waved a thank you to the man behind the counter and they left the café. "Aren't we a bit old for those games?"

"Nah, it's not like that." Suddenly her accent changed, and Lila didn't recognise the voice coming out of her friend's mouth.

"She's an academic. She gets her kicks in other ways. She's not like you and me." Lila could feel her defences rising and she realised that she wished she hadn't invited Cass to spend the evening with them.

"Look, doll," Cass's accent returned to normal, "it's your house and she's your friend. I'm just not sure she'd approve."

"Approve of what?"

"Approve of the delivery I have just arranged for us."

"Cass, what the hell are you talking about!" Her patience was wearing thin.

"Ever heard of a little thing called *cocaine*...?" She linked her arm through Lila's and smiled like the Cheshire Cat, as she lifted her sunglasses onto her face to hide the glint in her eye.

FEBRUARY 10TH

Lila woke the next morning to find herself lying across the sofa, still fully dressed. The chemical taste in her mouth was vile and the booze from the night before left a fuzzy layer on her tongue.

Reaching for a glass of water, she wondered what time it was she had passed out the previous night. She had a vague recollection of sitting at the kitchen table, drinking red wine, and chatting in a drunken haze with Owen and Cass. Everything else was a blur, except she remembered telling Zara her plans had changed.

Lifting her head and wriggling out from under the blanket that someone had draped over her, she sat up and was struck by a sudden unpleasant head rush. The water was room temperature, but she didn't care as she greedily drank the contents of the pint glass.

At that moment Cass appeared, standing in the doorway, her hands wrapped around a steaming mug of coffee.

"You look rough, doll." She slurped her drink, half smiling.

"I feel rough." Lila rubbed the back of her neck, which felt stiff.

Cass stood watching her, while it dawned on Lila that she was wearing one of Owen's shirts, and not much else.

"I hope it's okay," she smoothed the pinstripe cotton with her long fingers, "but I didn't have anything to wear in bed, and Owen offered."

"Sure." It was strange for Lila, looking at another woman wearing her husband's shirt, her long bare legs on show beneath it. "What time is it?" She stood, not making eye contact with Cass, feeling frustrated with herself that she didn't tell the truth, that seeing Cass wearing his shirt did bother her.

"Seven forty." Cass examined the fine gold watch that hung loosely round her skinny wrist. "The girls are up. I woke them." Lila was shocked by her smugness.

"Thanks." She felt instantly like a terrible mother. "I'm going to have a shower."

"Maybe brush your teeth too!" Cass snorted and Lila slipped past her.

When she went into their bedroom, she found Owen getting dressed. The smell of his aftershave flooded her nostrils and made her stomach flip.

"I need a shower." She caught a glimpse of her unruly hair and remembered she was still wearing yesterday's clothes. The bags under her eyes told their own story.

"You really were putting it away last night." Owen buttoned up his shirt, not looking at her.

"I feel bad enough as it is," she rasped, her throat dry.

"Why did you let her bring cocaine into our house? What are we, eighteen years old?!" he hissed back.

"Well, it was awkward, wasn't it. I couldn't say no. You looked like you were having a pretty good time yourself." Lila's words dripped with spite.

"I will not have drugs under the same roof as my daughters." He checked his reflection in the mirror before turning to her. "Is that clear?" She nodded like a chastised child, agreeing with him but remembering he was the one who'd spent the evening being flirty and cooing over Cass.

Stepping into the en suite, Lila peeled her clothes off and stepped into a steaming hot shower, hoping to wash away some of the guilt and the unnerving feeling she had in the pit of her stomach.

When she returned downstairs, wearing clean clothes and feeling more human, she was greeted by Cass sitting at the kitchen table with her girls. She was plaiting Ella's hair and for a moment Lila felt like a stranger in her own house.

"Better?" Cass asked, looking up and smiling.

"I'm fine." Lila busied herself making coffee, while Owen stood silently, leaning against the work surface, watching Molly pick at her breakfast.

"Big day today." Cass carried on, apparently oblivious to the tense atmosphere in the room.

"Huh?" Lila turned to face her, nearly spilling black coffee down her white blouse.

"The Kenneth Grahame meeting at eleven," she said, winding a hair band around the bottom of Ella's neat French plait.

"Shit." Owen scowled at his wife when he realised she'd forgotten.

"We've got this." Cass looked over to Owen and winked. "He'll be putty in our hands."

For the second time that morning Lila felt left out in her own home.

Kenneth Grahame was a multimillionaire and the chairman of The Cambridge Food Co, a group that owned several restaurants and bars around the city. Owen and Cass had been pitching to take on the marketing. Today was the day when they'd finally find out if they'd won the project. It was worth a substantial sum to Wellington Marketing Management and meant a great deal to Owen, who'd been working hard on it for months. He had spent many late nights in the office, working overtime and spent less time at home with his wife and the girls. Lila hoped, if they were awarded the project, that he would be able to return to working more normal hours.

"Make sure we've got the good biscuits in," Cass said, turning to Lila as she patted Molly on the top of the head.

"Yes. Of course." Lila did not appreciate being spoken to like a minion but couldn't find the strength to stand up for herself. She felt beaten down by the guilt of her own behaviour.

"I'm going to head to the gym before work. See you there at nine." Cass grabbed a piece of toast and took a bite before she tossed her bag over her shoulder and left the house.

"Is she staying again tonight?" Molly stirred the milk in her bowl of cereal.

"I'm not sure," Lila answered, hoping she wouldn't.

"Why is she staying?" Ella asked, twirling her hair in her fingers.

"She's a friend. She just stayed to have dinner and talk to mummy and daddy about work." She narrowly avoided telling them that Cass's husband was a cheat, and their marriage was on the rocks.

The door clicked shut behind Cass, and for a moment, the kitchen was enveloped in an uncomfortable silence. Lila could feel Owen's eyes on her, but she couldn't bring herself to look at him. Instead, she busied herself, pouring more coffee even though she had barely touched the first cup.

"I'll take the girls to school," Owen said, his voice clipped.

"That's fine," she replied, not looking up from the mug in her hands.

She could feel his irritation simmering beneath the surface. There was a regular undercurrent between them—a gulf that kept widening. Lila knew it was there but had no idea how to fix it. Every conversation felt like stepping onto a minefield, and she was too tired to keep dodging the explosions.

"Look," Owen said suddenly, his tone softer now, "about last night…" His expression was tight, like he was weighing up his words.

"What about last night?" she asked, her voice harsher than she had intended. The sharpness of it startling them both.

"You know Cass isn't a problem, right?" He folded his arms, his gaze flickering to his daughters as they chatted over their cereal, oblivious to the growing tension between their parents.

"I didn't say she was," Lila muttered, though the knot in her stomach told her otherwise. The sight of Cass in his shirt was still burned into her brain, and no amount of pretending would make it disappear.

"You've been giving me grief for weeks now. What exactly is the problem?" His voice was low and laced with frustration.

"I've been giving you grief?" She couldn't help the bitter laugh that escaped from her throat. "She's in our house, wearing your clothes, calling the shots, and I'm the one being difficult?"

Owen let out a heavy sigh, pinching the bridge of his nose like he was trying to hold back a headache. "You're blowing this out of proportion."

"Am I? Or maybe I'm just seeing things for what they really are," she shot back, her pulse quickening. The room felt smaller suddenly, the walls closing in on them both. "You're never here anymore, Owen. Late nights, overtime, this project with Cass—everything seems to matter more than what's happening in this house."

"That's not fair." His tone grew sharper, more defensive. "You know how important this project is. We're close to landing the biggest deal we've had in years."

Lila crossed her arms, feeling her body stiffen as the

resentment she had been trying to bury bubbled to the surface. "And what happens when the deal is done, Owen? Will you still not have time for us? What excuse next? Another project? More late nights?"

He didn't answer immediately. His jaw clenched as he looked out of the window, as if hoping that outside might hold the appropriate answer.

"You don't get it, Lila," he said finally, his voice tight with frustration. "This is for us. For the girls. If we land this, things will be better than they've ever been. We'll have more money than we dreamed of. We'll be able to…"

"Be able to what, Owen? Be a family again?" She was unable to keep the tremor from her voice. "Because right now, it doesn't feel like that. Right now, it feels like Cass is more a part of this family than I am."

Her words hit him like a fist to the face. His eyes flashed, and for a split second, she thought he might say something cruel —something he couldn't take back. But he didn't. Instead, he just shook his head and turned towards the door, grabbing his keys from the table.

"I don't have time for this," he muttered, "Cass and I are meeting the accountant at the office. I don't want to be late." It wasn't the words that hurt Lila, it was the finality in his tone.

He left the kitchen without another glance in her direction, the door swinging shut behind him. The girls didn't seem to notice the tension that hung in the air as they finished their breakfast, but Lila felt it, thick and suffocating. She stood there for a moment, gripping the edge of the counter, trying to steady herself, but the lump in her throat refused to go away as she fought back tears. She needed to speak to Zara. Zara would know what to say.

Cass adjusted her sleek blazer, glancing around Owen's office with a practiced eye. The space was impressive, all polished glass, chrome, and dark wood—a carefully constructed environment of authority and success that she had redesigned since joining the company. Cass's heels clicked sharply against the floor as she made her way to the large glass desk where Owen stood.

"Cass," Owen said, a faint hesitation in his tone. "This is John Rotherham, my accountant."

John extended his hand politely, his expression neutral but assessing. He was a middle-aged man with thinning hair, glasses that seemed to magnify his sharp, analytical gaze, and an air of quiet professionalism. He wore a well-fitted grey suit, understated but precise, a man whose life was shaped by numbers and meticulous order.

"Nice to meet you," Cass said smoothly, extending her hand, her grip firm. She flashed a small, composed smile, taking in the figure before her. She had heard a lot about John—a detail-oriented man who kept Owen's finances in line, someone unwavering when it came to numbers.

"Likewise, Miss," John replied, nodding. "I've heard a lot about you." His voice was measured, his handshake brief. He withdrew his hand, clasping it lightly in front of him.

"Please, call me Cass." She took her seat, crossing her long legs and maintaining a polite but distant smile.

Owen cleared his throat. "Cass, John and I were just going over some of the company's finances. There are things we're trying to clarify." He gave her a glance that Cass knew was more than a little pointed. This was the last thing Owen needed before the most important pitch of his career.

She nodded, wanting to remain neutral. "I see. I'm sure John is just the man to figure it out."

John gave a short nod. "Well, I certainly hope to. We have

some expenses and discrepancies that need clarification, ones that could potentially raise concerns if left unaddressed."

"I'm sure you're exaggerating, John. Owen is very careful with his accounts," Cass said, waving a hand while she watched him closely, her smile faltering slightly. Her tone was friendly, but there was an unmistakable hint of something else beneath it.

"Of course," John replied, his expression resolute. "However, as Owen knows, the company's finances are more complex than ever, and it's my job to ensure everything is in perfect order. If we don't want to raise questions with the authorities."

Owen's jaw tightened, and he nodded. "I'll look into it, John. I'll make sure everything is sorted."

"Well, if I can be of any help, don't hesitate to let me know," Cass said.

John gave her a polite nod. "Thank you, Cass. I'll certainly keep that in mind."

Owen's gaze moved between them, and for a moment, silence filled the office. The sense of formality between Cass and John was palpable, the unspoken tension lingering in the air.

"Shall we continue, then?" John asked, his gaze returning to Owen as he opened a file with marked precision, each item meticulously noted.

Cass watched them both, her gaze narrowing slightly as she studied John's impassive face.

"Now is really not a good time, John." Owen stood from behind his desk. "There is a lot riding on today and I can't be distracted by this right now. Send me an email later this week and we'll address it then. It's only a few lunch receipts. It will be fine."

Owen left no room for negotiation.

"Very well." John stood, extending his hand. "If you'd rather, I can deal directly with Cass on this matter."

"I'd be happy to help. In fact, I think you should hire a finance director, Owen. It would take so much pressure off you." She smiled, showing all her teeth and leading the accountant out of Owen's office, while he remained and prepared for the most important presentation of his life.

SHE

I crouch beneath the hedge, cold seeping through my jeans as I press my knees into the damp earth. The sharp scent of wet grass fills my nose, mingling with the faint tang of wood smoke drifting from their chimney. Through the window, the golden glow of their living room spills out, illuminating the perfect little world they've built for themselves. My breath fogs in the air, and I try to keep my teeth from chattering. I don't want to risk the noise.

Inside, they are laughing. The sound floats out, muffled but unmistakably warm, and it cuts into my chest like a thorn. She leans into him, her hand resting on his arm as he pours wine into her glass. Their heads are close, foreheads nearly touching, and she smiles at him the way women in magazines smile—practiced, pristine, unbothered by the weight of real life. His face mirrors hers, that easy, natural contentment that makes me sick to my stomach.

I curl my fingers into fists, nails biting into my palms. What do they know about hardship? What do they know about losing? About hunger—not just for food, but for affection, for stability, for something to make the gnawing emptiness go away? They sit there, basking in their perfect little life, as though they've earned it. As though it's their birthright.

The curtains are drawn halfway, and I edge closer, careful not to rustle the leaves. The chill in the air bites through my thin jacket, but I don't care. It's better to feel cold than to feel nothing, and besides, I'm not leaving. Not until I've had my fill.

He's standing now, his shirtsleeves rolled to the elbows, exposing strong forearms that catch the light. He moves to the kitchen, out of view for a moment, and she follows him, her long legs silhouetted against the warm light. She's barefoot, of course—carefree and comfortable in the home they share. Her laugh rings out again, and I can hear the clink of dishes, the hum of a life that isn't mine.

But it will be.

I can see it so clearly, it almost makes me giddy. The mess I could make of their lives. The cracks I could carve into their perfect veneer. I've been patient, haven't I? Watching. Learning. Knowing exactly where to push, exactly where to make them bleed. She doesn't deserve him. Doesn't deserve this. I'd take better care of it, wouldn't I? I'd appreciate it. I'd savour every second of it.

Her shadow crosses the window again, and I feel a surge of loathing so intense it takes my breath away. She doesn't even realise how fragile it all is, does she? How easily everything she has could crumble, reduced to dust in the blink of an eye. And when it does—when I've taken it all from her—I'll be there to pick up the pieces. To make them mine.

The wind stirs the hedge, and I pull my jacket tighter, inching even closer to the house. They're in the kitchen now, standing side by side as they chop vegetables, an image so nauseatingly domestic I can barely stand it. But I keep watching, my breath hitching as I map out the details in my head. The next steps. The lies I'll tell. The chaos I'll unleash.

The wine is poured. The firelight flickers. And inside, they think they're safe.

They're wrong.

FEBRUARY 12TH

The bar was dimly lit, the warm glow from the hanging lights reflecting off the half-empty glasses scattered across the table. It was near closing time, but the staff didn't seem to mind—Owen had greased a few palms to let them stay, and besides, tonight was a celebration.

Cass lifted her glass of champagne and grinned, her eyes gleaming with satisfaction. "To us," she said, her voice low and smooth. "And to landing the biggest deal Wellington Marketing has ever seen."

Owen clinked his glass against hers, though his smile didn't quite reach his eyes.

"To us," he echoed, though the words seemed heavier as they left his mouth. He took a long sip, letting the bubbles fizz on his tongue, but it didn't do much to lift the weight off his shoulders.

Cass leaned back in her seat, her gaze fixed on him.

"You should be thrilled, you know. This is everything we've been working for." She tilted her head slightly, her long, dark hair spilling over her shoulders as she gave him that familiar, teasing smile. "You don't look thrilled."

"I am," Owen replied, but even he knew the words lacked conviction. His mind was elsewhere—back at home, with Lila, who had barely said two words to him before he left the house that morning. He could still hear the sting in her voice that had wrapped around their conversation like a noose, thanks to the argument that still hung in the air from earlier in the week.

Cass must have sensed his hesitation because she leaned forward, her fingers lightly brushing against his on the table.

"You're thinking about her, aren't you?"

Owen stiffened slightly but didn't pull his hand away. He glanced at her, caught off guard by how close she was, her eyes locked onto his with an intensity that was hard to ignore.

"It's nothing," he muttered, though the knot in his chest told a different story.

"It's not nothing," Cass said softly, her voice barely above a whisper now. She moved her hand to cover his, her thumb gently stroking the back of his fingers. "I see the way you've been lately, Owen. The stress, the late nights... all the pressure you're under." She paused, biting her lower lip before continuing. "And I can't help but wonder if she understands any of it. She seems unhappy too."

Owen's jaw clenched, but he didn't reply. The truth was, Lila didn't understand—at least, not in the way he needed her to. And they were unhappy, although neither of them knew why, Owen felt Lila had changed. She wasn't the woman he'd first met and fell in love with. She was frustrated, angry even, but it wasn't just about the hours or the work. It was something deeper, something neither of them knew how to fix.

"I mean..." Cass let out a soft sigh, her fingers lingering on his hand. "It's not easy, balancing everything. The business, your family... but she doesn't see what we've built here. She's not part of it the way I am." There was a tenderness in Cass's voice that made Owen's throat tighten. She leaned in closer, the scent of her perfume filling the space between them. It was warm, floral, intoxicating. "I get it," she murmured. "The pressure, the late nights, all of it. I've been right there with you through every step of this."

Owen's gaze flickered to her lips for a moment before he quickly looked away, taking another sip of his drink.

"It's not that simple," he said, though his voice had softened. "Lila... she just—"

"She doesn't get it, Owen," Cass interrupted, her voice firm but gentle. "She can't. How could she? I know what it's like to work under this kind of pressure. To have everything riding on you."

Owen's heart raced in his chest. Cass was close now, too close. Her knee brushed against his under the table, sending a jolt through him that he didn't want to acknowledge. He could feel the pull between them—had felt it for a while now—but he wasn't sure if he was ready to admit what it meant.

"I'm just saying," Cass continued, her voice soft again, almost a whisper, "you don't have to carry all of this on your own. You've got me. You'll always have me." She smiled, a small, knowing smile that made his stomach twist. Owen stared down at their hands, her fingers still lightly resting on his. It felt good to be understood, to have someone who didn't expect him to explain everything, who could just read the tension in his shoulders and the exhaustion in his eyes.

"I don't know what I'd do without you, Cass," he said quietly, and for the first time that evening, his words felt honest.

Cass's smile widened, and she shifted closer to him, their legs now fully touching beneath the table. "You don't have to worry about that," she said, her voice low and sultry. "I'm not going anywhere."

For a moment, the air between them hung thick with unspoken words, unacknowledged feelings. Owen's pulse quickened, and he could feel the heat radiating from her body. The urge to lean in, to close the distance, was almost unbearable, but something held him back.

Cass tilted her head, her lips dangerously close to his ear. "You deserve someone who really sees you, Owen," she whispered, her breath warm against his skin. "Someone who knows how hard you work. Someone who's there for you, no matter what. Someone who can help you relax."

His breath caught in his throat, and he felt a surge of something—desire, or guilt, or both—wash over him. He swallowed hard, forcing himself to pull back, though it took every ounce of willpower he had.

"We should probably get going," Owen said, his voice hoarse as he pushed his chair back and stood, suddenly feeling the weight of the decision he hadn't yet made.

Cass's eyes followed him, her smile never faltering. She stood up slowly, her hand trailing lightly over his arm as she stepped back.

"Of course," she said softly, though the look in her eyes told him this wasn't over.

Owen nodded, grabbing his coat and tossing a few notes on the table to cover the drinks. He turned to leave, but he could still feel her gaze on him, burning into his back as he walked towards the door.

As he stepped out into the cool night air, the rush of guilt hit him harder than the chill. He wasn't sure what was happening anymore, but one thing was clear: the line between him and Cass was blurring, and he wasn't sure if he could stop it.

Half an hour later Lila was glancing at the clock for the third time in as many minutes. The candles on the table flickered softly, casting a warm glow over the carefully laid-out dinner. She'd gone all out, making Owen's favourite—coq au vin—hoping it might offer them a brief respite from the tension that had taken root between them. Besides, Valentine's was just around the corner.

She checked her phone again. No messages.

Sighing, she poured herself a glass of wine and leaned against the counter, her mind drifting back to their argument earlier that week. It was like everything they said to each other lately had an edge. There was no softness anymore, no space for understanding. She knew the business had been weighing on him, but it felt like he was slipping away—distracted, distant. Cass's presence didn't help, either. There was something about her that made Lila feel off-balance, like she was on the outside of her own life, looking in. One moment she thought Cass was the most wonderful friend, the next she wondered if she really trusted her. Not knowing how she felt about this big presence in her life made everything feel uneasy.

Just as she was about to text Owen, she heard the familiar click of the front door opening. Her heart leapt for a moment, and she quickly straightened up, smoothing her dress. But the second voice she heard behind his made her freeze.

Cass.

Lila swallowed hard, her grip tightening around the wine glass. She hadn't expected company. Certainly not *her*. She forced a smile onto her face as she stepped out of the kitchen to greet them.

"There she is," Owen said, giving Lila a quick smile that didn't quite reach his eyes. "Hope you don't mind, but Cass came along. We were just finishing up after the meeting, and I thought..." His voice trailed off awkwardly as he caught sight of the candle-lit table and the meal she had so clearly made for just the two of them.

Lila felt her stomach knot. Of course she minded. But what could she say?

"Oh... right," she managed, her smile tight, her eyes flicking to Cass, who stood by the doorway, an unreadable expression on her face.

"I hope I'm not intruding," Cass said, though there was a glint in her eye that made Lila wonder if she knew exactly what she was doing. She wore a sleek black dress, her hair artfully tousled, and she looked effortlessly put together, as always.

"Not at all," Lila lied, her voice a little too bright. She turned towards the kitchen. "I'll, um... I'll just get another place setting," she said as Owen cleared his throat.

"Yeah, sorry, love. I should have called." But he hadn't. And he wasn't sorry. At least, not enough to have made a different choice. Lila moved quickly, rearranging the table, the clink of plates and cutlery the only sound filling the heavy silence that had settled in the room.

The three of them sat down at the table, the awkwardness palpable as Lila poured wine into Cass's glass, then Owen's, and finally her own. The tension that had hung in the air between her and Owen seemed to have tripled, now that Cass was sitting across from her.

"This looks wonderful, Lila," Cass said, picking up her fork and examining the meal. "Coq au vin—Owen's favourite, right?"

Lila forced a smile as she sat down. "Yeah, I thought it'd be nice." She felt her stomach twist. How did Cass know that?

Owen took a bite, nodding his approval. "This is great. Really." The words were empty, and Lila could feel it. He wasn't *really* there. His mind, his attention—it was somewhere else, or worse, with someone else. She glanced up to find Cass watching her, those sharp eyes not missing a beat. Lila forced herself to take a sip of wine, though it tasted sour in her mouth now.

"So," Lila started, trying to steer the conversation into more neutral territory, "Big news, right?"

"Yeah, we got it. The Kenneth Grahame account. It's going to be huge for the company. A lot of work, but worth it." Owen nodded, finally engaging a little more.

Cass beamed. "It was a team effort, really. We've both put in so much effort to get it over the line. Owen's been amazing through it all."

Lila felt her pulse quicken. The way Cass said *we*—so casually, so intimately—it was like she was claiming something that wasn't hers to claim. And the way she smiled at Owen, like they shared a secret Lila wasn't part of... it made her want to scream.

"That's great," Lila said, her voice sounding hollow even to her own ears. She took another sip of wine, hoping it would drown the bitterness rising in her chest. "You both must be relieved."

"Oh, definitely." Cass took a sip of her wine and smiled, almost indulgently. "Though I'm sure the pressure's only just beginning. We've got a lot of work ahead of us, right, Owen?"

"Yeah," Owen said, though his voice was distant again, his eyes focused somewhere else. "It's going to be intense for a while."

Lila swallowed hard, staring down at her plate. She couldn't shake the feeling that she didn't belong at that table—that somehow, over the past few months, she had become the outsider in her own home. She glanced up at Owen, hoping for something, some small reassurance, but he was too busy nodding along with whatever Cass was saying.

Cass looked over at Lila again, her eyes softening slightly as if she was offering sympathy, though it felt more like pity.

"I don't know how you do it, Lila," she said, her voice dropping just enough to make it sound like a private conversation, even though Owen was right there. "Balancing everything. The kids, the house... and then dealing with all this pressure on top of it."

Lila didn't respond. Her throat felt tight, and she didn't trust herself to speak without her voice breaking. "But," Cass continued, leaning slightly towards Owen, her smile sweet, "I guess that's why we work so well as a team. Owen and I get the business, the grind, you know? The long hours, the deadlines—it's tough, but we're a great team."

Lila's grip tightened around her wine glass, and she couldn't help but glance at Owen. He didn't correct her. He didn't say a word. He just kept eating, nodding, as though Cass's words weren't stabbing Lila in the heart.

"Yeah," Lila said, her voice barely a whisper. "I'm sure you are."

The rest of the meal passed in a blur. Every word felt like it had a double meaning, every glance between Owen and Cass like a private conversation she wasn't part of. And all Lila could do was sit there, smiling, pretending everything was fine, even as the foundations of her marriage crumbled beneath her.

When the plates were cleared, and Cass excused herself to leave, Lila stood by the sink, washing the dishes with trembling hands, while Owen disappeared upstairs without a word. The sound of the front door closing behind Cass was the only comfort she had, though the emptiness it left behind felt even worse.

Lila stared at her reflection in the kitchen window, the faint outline of her face illuminated by the dim light above. She barely recognised herself. And in that moment, she realised that what she feared most wasn't losing Owen to Cass—it was that she might have already lost him.

SHE

The air is thick with smoke. It clings to my skin, burns my throat as I breathe in deep, ragged gulps, my lungs screaming for clean air. But there's none left. Only the stench of fire, of burning wood and flesh, wrapping itself around me like a living thing, like it's feeding off the fear thrumming through my veins.

I can't see them clearly through the flames, but I know they're there. I know it's them. The screams. My family. They're burning. I'm watching them burn.

I try to move, try to run toward them, but my legs won't obey. They feel heavy, like they're sinking into the floor. My hands— why can't I feel my hands? I try to reach out, but my arms are a dead weight, numb. Everything is slowing down. Too slow.

The house is crumbling around me, blackened walls cracking and splitting like a living thing, hissing and snapping as the fire eats away at them. The flames are licking the ceiling, curling up toward the sky, bright orange and red, like hell has opened up right here, swallowing everything I love.

I can hear the crackle of the fire, the sickening pop of wood breaking under the heat, but it's their screams that rip through me. Molly. Ella. I hear them crying out for me. I know their voices. God, I know their voices, and they're screaming for me, but I can't—I can't move.

I feel my heart pounding in my chest, so fast it feels like it might burst. My head is spinning, disoriented, trying to make sense of the chaos around me, but nothing makes sense anymore. Everything is wrong. Everything is burning.

I try to scream. My voice comes out a strangled choke, hoarse and weak, like my throat's been ripped open.

Something cold drips down my forehead. Blood. I can see it now, thick and dark, running down my face, sliding over my eyes, making everything hazy. It drips onto the floor, forming pools around my feet, and I don't understand where it's coming from. It doesn't hurt. I don't feel anything.

I blink, wiping at my eyes, trying to clear the blood away, but the more I wipe, the more it seems to pour. I look down, and my hands are stained red, slick with it. The floor is soaked, a sea of crimson pooling around me, and I'm sinking into it, the sticky warmth creeping up my ankles, pulling me down.

There's so much blood. Too much. It's everywhere, spreading, rising. It shouldn't be like this. There's no way there's this much blood in a body. No way. But it keeps coming, keeps rising. And I realise—I'm drowning in it.

My breath comes faster, panic clawing at my throat. I can feel the blood climbing higher, up my calves, over my knees, thick and warm, pressing in on me like a vice. I can't move. I can't get out.

I'm going to drown.

I try to scream again, but the blood rushes into my mouth, filling it, choking me. It's in my nose, burning, making me gag. The taste is metallic, sharp. My vision is going black. I can't breathe. I can't see.

I hear a voice—distant, distorted—but I can't tell where it's coming from. Twisted. It echoes around me, bouncing off the *walls of a house that is no longer standing. This must be a dream. Wake up. Wake up.*

My mind is fracturing, spinning out of control. I don't know what's real anymore.

My heart pounds harder, my body shaking with panic. I can feel myself slipping, losing control. The blood is up to my chest now, warm and suffocating. I push against it, but my arms are like lead. I can't breathe.

I see faces in the fire, twisted and contorted, their skin blackened and blistering. Their eyes looking at me, wide and glassy.

I thrash against the blood, against the fire, against the smoke. Everything is pressing in on me. Everything is too much. I'm trapped inside my own body, like I'm watching this happen to someone else.

I try to think, try to make sense of what's going on, but my thoughts are jumbled, tangled in fear and confusion. The fire, the blood—it all feels so real. But there's something... something wrong. Something off.

I blink again, the blood sliding over my eyes, blinding me. I hear another voice. Louder this time. But I'm here alone. Like I always have been.

I blink again, and for a second—just a second—the fire flickers, almost like it's not there at all. Like it's a trick. My heart skips. My pulse stutters. I reach out to touch the flames, but my hand passes through them, the heat fading into nothing.

I blink again, harder this time.

The blood. It's gone. The fire too. I'm standing in the middle of the room, but it's not burning. The walls are intact, solid. The air isn't thick with smoke anymore.

The voices aren't screaming.

"It's not real," *the voice says, gentle but firm.* "You're okay. You're safe."

The room tilts, spinning for a second before it steadies again. I blink, and suddenly, the world is back. The blood, the fire, the screams—they're all gone. Replaced by the cold, sharp clarity of reality.

I'm not in a burning house. There's no blood. No fire.

My hands trembling at my sides, my breath coming in shallow, broken gasps. The walls are closing in, and I can still feel the echo of the nightmare in my veins, the panic still clawing at me.

But it's not real. It was never real.

I close my eyes, a wave of shame washing over me. I let it in. I let it consume me.

And then I wake up. I'm dripping in sweat. I'm in an unfamiliar room and my throat is so dry, it's as if it's raw from the imagined smoke I was just choking on in my nightmare.

MARCH 1ST

Lila sat in the corner booth of the café, stirring her coffee absent-mindedly, watching the steam rise in lazy spirals and dance around the loose strands of her bright-red hair that was pulled into a bun. The early-afternoon light streamed through the window, casting a warm glow over the tables, but it didn't touch the icy feeling in her chest. Zara slid into the seat across from her, her eyes immediately locking onto Lila's.

"You look terrible," Zara said, her voice laced with concern as she tossed her bag onto the bench beside her. She reached for her own coffee, but her eyes never left Lila's, scanning her face as if she were reading all the things Lila didn't want to say out loud.

"What's going on, Lila? I know something's been off for a while, and I'm worried about you. You should be celebrating and enjoying your new-found wealth."

Lila tried to smile, but it felt brittle, like it might crack under the weight of everything she'd been holding in. "I'm fine, really. It's just—" She hesitated, unsure of where to begin. It all felt too big, too messy to put into words, but she knew if she didn't say something soon, she might implode.

Zara tilted her head, her brow furrowed, waiting patiently for her to continue. She was always good like that—knowing when to push and when to just sit in silence. But this wasn't something Lila could keep quiet about anymore.

"It's Owen," she said, her voice small and uncertain. "And Cass."

Zara raised an eyebrow. "Cass? The one from his work? The big marketing deal or whatever?"

Lila nodded, feeling her chest tighten. "Yeah, her. She's been... around a lot lately." She stared down at her coffee, avoiding Zara's gaze. Zara didn't say anything at first. Lila took a deep breath, her hand gripping the edge of her mug so tightly she thought it might crack.

"It's like... I don't know, Zara. It feels like she's everywhere. At first, it was just for the project. It's business, right? But now she's in our house all the time, staying over, being there with the girls. It's like she's... slipping into our life. Like I'm not enough anymore. Like she's replacing me. She's meant to be my friend but now..."

"Hold on—staying over? Since when has she been staying over?" Zara's eyes had widened, her mouth opening in disbelief.

"The first time was just after she had an argument with her husband. She needed a break, and I didn't think anything of it, but now... it's more than that, Zara. She's making herself comfortable, you know? Wearing his shirts, hanging around like she's part of our family." Lila nodded, swallowing hard as Zara's expression darkened. She hesitated, biting her lip. "I don't know. I mean, he says it's nothing, that I'm overreacting. But there's something... different about him lately. He's distant, Zara. Not like himself. And it's not just the work. It's like he's... I don't know, like he's not really here with me anymore."

Zara was quiet for a moment, her fingers tapping the side of her mug.

"Lila, you need to talk to him. Really talk to him. This doesn't sound right—none of it does. Are you still planning on the move?"

"Yes, we are. We should be completing soon. Thank God there isn't a chain. It makes life so much easier." She looked down at her wedding ring. "I want to talk to him but I'm worried he will dismiss it. Say I'm imagining things, that I'm reading too much into it. I bet he'd say it's all for the business, and I'm being paranoid. But I can't shake this feeling, Zara. I see the way they are around each other. The looks. The way they talk like they've got some shared secret." Lila let out a frustrated sigh, her hands trembling slightly as she tried to keep it together. Zara leaned back, her eyes narrowing with concern.

"Do you think they're…?" Zara trailed off, leaving the rest of the question unspoken, but Lila knew exactly what she meant.

Lila stared into her coffee, the murky liquid swirling in the mug as her thoughts raced. "I don't know," she whispered. "I don't know if it's gone that far. But there's something going on between them, Zara. I can feel it. And the worst part is… I think they both know I feel it. Like I'm the one on the outside, and they're just waiting for me to… what? Give up? Confront it? I don't even know anymore."

"You need to trust your gut, Lila. If something feels off, it probably is. And if Owen's not willing to have a proper conversation with you about it, then that's even more of a reason to push him on it." Zara reached across the table, grabbing Lila's hand, her grip firm but comforting. Lila nodded, trying to blink away the tears that were threatening to spill over.

"It's just… it's so hard. I don't want to believe it, you know? We've been through so much together, and I just… I don't want to lose him. But it feels like I already have." Lila's voice cracked, and she quickly brought her hand to her mouth, trying to hold back the sob threatening to escape.

Zara's face softened, her grip on Lila's hand tightening. "You're not the one who's losing him, Lila. If he's doing this, if something's happening with Cass, then he's the one making that choice."

Lila took a shaky breath, the weight of Zara's words sinking in. "You're right," she whispered. "But I'm scared, Zara. I'm scared of what I'll find if I push too hard. And I'm not the same when I'm around her. Something is happening to me. I feel like I'm losing myself. I did an awful thing. I feel so stupid."

"What happened?" Zara asked, leaning forward, her arms folding across her chest as she looked at Lila gravely.

"I took drugs. Cocaine." Lila said it quietly, her voice breaking with shame. "I don't know what came over me. She brought them into our house. The girls were there. It was only once..."

Zara, who had only ever seen Lila hungover at worst, looked shocked. "That was really stupid. Did Owen...?" Her words trailed off, leaving the question hanging again.

"I don't know. I passed out. And then she's standing there, in my house, in my husband's clothes, like butter wouldn't melt." Lila's voice trembled as she spoke, a lump swelling in her throat. "They've been working so hard on this deal. And it's fantastic. It's going to change our lives, but..."

Zara sat back and squeezed the bridge of her nose between her thumb and forefinger, exhaling slowly. "This has to stop. You're right—this isn't you. She's toxic." Zara paused, and Lila could see she wanted to say more, to push her further, but she held back.

"No matter what happens, I'm here. You're not going through this alone." Zara's eyes softened, and she squeezed Lila's hand gently.

Lila managed a small smile, though it was weak, and nodded. "Thanks, Zara. I don't know what I'd do without you."

"You won't have to find out," Zara said, her voice firm. "Now, we're going to figure this out together. You just need to be ready to face whatever comes next. And for God's sake, grow up. And toughen up. Don't let that poison back into your house. And I'm not just talking about the powder."

As Lila sat there, the weight of everything pressing down on her, she realised Zara was right. Something was happening—something she couldn't ignore any longer. She just wasn't sure if she was ready for the truth. But sooner or later, she'd have to face it, whether she liked it or not.

The office was quiet, the hum of computers and the soft tapping of keyboards the only sound filling the space. Owen leaned back in his chair, running his hands through his hair, reviewing the latest figures from the Kenneth Grahame account. Everything was on track, but his mind kept wandering. He glanced up at the clock, realising it was later than he thought. Cass sat across from him, flipping through her notes, the sharp click of her pen the only sign of her mounting agitation.

Owen was about to ask her a question when Cass's phone buzzed loudly on the desk. She glanced at the screen, her face tightening as she saw the name flashing across it.

"Shit," she muttered under her breath, clearly debating whether to answer. After a moment, she sighed and snatched up the phone, her hand gripping it tightly as she stood and walked towards the far corner of the office, her back to Owen.

"Yeah, what is it?" Her voice was sharp, the edge in her tone unmistakable. Owen raised an eyebrow, pretending to focus on his paperwork, but the tension in her voice pulled his attention fully.

There was a pause as she listened to whoever was on the

other end of the line. Her hand flew to her hip, her fingers drumming impatiently.

"I told you I'm working late. What do you expect me to do about it now?" she hissed, keeping her voice low but failing to hide the frustration.

Owen tried to keep his focus on the numbers in front of him, but the heated whispers from the other side of the room made it impossible. He couldn't help but feel like he was eavesdropping, but Cass's irritation was so palpable, it was hard to ignore.

"No, don't start with that again," Cass snapped, turning slightly so Owen could see her face, tight with barely restrained anger. "You've been doing this for weeks. I don't have time for your jealousy, Mark. I'm working, okay? It's not always about you."

There was another pause, and Cass's jaw clenched, her free hand balling into a fist at her side. "For God's sake, we've been over this. I can't just drop everything because you've got some insecurity about where I am. I'm here, at the office, with Owen, working. That's what this is about—work. You know, the thing that actually pays the bills?"

Owen shifted uncomfortably in his seat, sensing that the argument wasn't meant for his ears, but there was nowhere to go, no way to escape the tension building in the small office.

Cass's voice lowered, her tone turning cold. "Don't try to guilt-trip me, Mark. You're the one who checked out long before I did. This isn't about me. It's about you not being able to handle the fact that I have a life outside of your fucking temper tantrums." She paused again, listening to the response, her face growing harder with every passing second.

Owen could feel the weight of whatever was being said, though he couldn't hear it.

"No," Cass spat, her voice barely above a whisper now,

venom dripping from every word. "I'm not coming home tonight. In fact, maybe I shouldn't come home at all. Maybe that's what you want, isn't it? For me to just disappear so you can feel sorry for yourself."

Owen looked down at his hands, realising he was gripping his pen a little too tightly. Cass was pacing now, her anger radiating through the room like heat from a furnace.

"Fine. You know what? Do whatever the hell you want, Mark. I'm done with this conversation. I'll deal with you when I'm good and ready, not when you decide to throw another tantrum." She paused, then added, her voice icier than before, "No, you won't. I'm turning my phone off." With that, she jabbed at the screen and ended the call, tossing the phone onto her desk like it was a ticking time bomb. For a moment, she stood there, her chest rising and falling quickly, her lips pressed into a thin line as she tried to collect herself.

The silence that followed was heavy, almost oppressive. Owen didn't dare speak, but he could feel Cass's anger like static in the air. She exhaled slowly, closing her eyes for a second before turning to face him. The mask of control slid back into place, but not quickly enough to hide the raw emotion that had bubbled to the surface during the call. He could see not only was she angry but she was hurt. Cass did a good job of convincing people she was tough, but Owen knew better. He could see the person underneath the bravado. He could see the vulnerable, gentle woman, who cared deeply about others. He'd seen it himself with the way she was with him.

"Sorry about that," she said, her voice calmer now, though there was still an edge to it. "Mark's being a complete child. Again."

Owen nodded slowly, unsure of what to say. He felt a strange mix of sympathy and discomfort. "Everything okay?"

Cass gave a humourless laugh, shaking her head.

"Yeah. Just the usual. He can't stand it when I'm not at home, thinks I'm—" She stopped, catching herself, and then waved a hand dismissively. "It doesn't matter. He's being paranoid. He always is, when really he's the one who can't be trusted."

Owen felt a flicker of unease at her words but pushed it aside. "If you need to leave early, I can finish up here," he offered, though he knew she wouldn't take him up on it.

"No," she said, sitting back down at her desk, her hands trembling slightly as she straightened the papers in front of her. "I'm not going anywhere." Her eyes met his then, the intensity in them unmistakable. "I'm not letting him get to me anymore. We've got work to do, and that's all I care about right now."

Owen nodded, but something in her voice gave him pause. The way she said it, the way her focus seemed to lock onto him like he was the only solid thing in her life—he couldn't help but feel like he was caught in the middle of something far more complicated than just a marriage on the rocks.

Cass smiled then, a tight, determined smile, and leaned forward, her voice softening. "Let's finish this, okay? We've got bigger things to focus on."

Owen returned her smile, though uneasily. As they got back to work, the argument hung in the air between them, unspoken but heavy, like a shadow they couldn't shake.

SHE

The nursery is small but immaculate, a vision of soft whites and pastels. A golden light filters through sheer curtains, casting a gentle glow over every surface, every carefully chosen piece of furniture. The walls are painted a calming shade of cream, and the crib stands at the centre of the room, waiting. Above it, a mobile spins slowly, each delicate shape—clouds, stars, and moons—dancing in endless circles. Everything here is soft, comforting, serene.

But the sound. The piercing, relentless wail of the baby fills every inch of space, thrumming against the walls, echoing inside my skull. It's raw and visceral, as if the sound itself were scraping at the edges of my mind, clawing its way in and spreading, embedding itself in every nerve. It starts as a whine, a plaintive cry, but soon, it swells, growing louder and louder, until it feels like the walls are pulsing with it, until I'm certain the sound is ripping me apart from the inside.

I press my hands against my ears, but it doesn't help. The cry is everywhere. It fills the air, vibrating through my bones, seeping into my blood. My vision blurs, and the perfectly designed nursery—so clean, so flawless—starts to warp, edges wavering as the sound rises and rises, twisting the air around me.

I turn, desperate, looking for an escape, for anything to blot out the noise. But there's only the baby, lying in the white crib, tiny fists clenched, face red and twisted with rage. Its mouth opens in a wide, howling scream, the sound piercing, violent. The mobile above it keeps spinning, a cruel lullaby to a symphony of screams.

My heart pounds as I move closer, feeling a strange, visceral pull toward the crib. I should leave, but something holds me here, binds me to this room. I can't tear my gaze away from the baby, from its contorted, furious face, from the way it thrashes, tiny fists beating against the white sheet. The room is filled with the sterile smell of baby powder, clean linens, a faint hint of milk—scents meant to soothe, to comfort. But they're stifling, oppressive, trapping me in this room where the sound grows louder and louder, drowning out everything else.

I stand over the crib, staring down at the baby, my heartbeat merging with the shrill pitch of its screams. The sound is no longer just a noise—it's a feeling, a presence, clawing at me, tearing through me, tearing me apart. I press my hands harder against my ears, but nothing stops it. I feel the scream resonate in my chest, vibrating through my ribs, digging into the core of me.

My breaths come in short gasps as I hover over the crib, my vision narrowing, the room blurring into a hazy swirl of white and gold. The baby's face is all I can see, red and furious, its mouth stretched wide, emitting that unholy sound. And suddenly, I am no longer myself. I am something raw, something desperate, teetering on the edge of control, swaying between the urge to flee and the need to silence the sound forever.

And then, like a cold wave washing over me, a strange calm settles within me, creeping in slowly, pushing aside the panic, the desperation. I feel my heartbeat slow, my breathing even out. I am steady. I am calm. The sound is still there, filling the room, but it no longer bothers me. It feels distant, muted, as if the world around me has receded into silence.

I glance around the room, my eyes falling on a soft, white teddy bear perched on the shelf beside the crib. Its button eyes gaze out into the room, oblivious, innocent. I reach out, my palms brushing against its fur, so soft, so plush. It feels cool under my touch, a soothing contrast to the heat pulsing through my skin.

Without thinking, I lift the teddy bear, feeling its weight in my hands. It's light, almost weightless, soft and yielding. I turn back to the crib, my gaze settling on the baby's face, its tiny mouth still open, still screaming, though the sound has faded to a dull hum, like the distant roar of an approaching storm.

I stand there, holding the bear, feeling its softness, feeling the calm that has settled over me. I lean over the crib, looking down at the baby, watching its face contort, its eyes squeezed shut, its fists clenched tight. The sound is far away now, no longer a shriek, no longer unbearable. It is nothing more than a murmur, a whisper in the background.

Slowly, I lower the bear, my hand steady, my gaze fixed. The soft fur brushes against the baby's cheek as I press it down gently, feeling the muffled cries beneath the fabric, feeling the sound grow fainter, softer, until there is nothing but silence. The room is quiet, perfectly, exquisitely quiet, and I feel a strange, overwhelming peace settle within me.

I straighten, placing the bear back on the shelf, adjusting its small paws so it sits just right. The nursery is calm again, the light casting a soft glow over the crib, the mobile spinning lazily above. Everything is still, perfect, serene. The silence fills me, wraps around me, and I close my eyes, letting it wash over me, letting it seep into every corner of my mind, until there is nothing left but the silence.

The nursery is calm again. The bear watches silently, a

witness who will never speak, who will never tell. I take a moment to adjust its little paws, as though it's just another decoration in this pristine, quiet space.

The silence is thick now, so deep and consuming that it feels like a weight pressing down on the room, on me, filling every corner, every crevice. I breathe it in, letting it settle in my lungs, letting it become a part of me.

Turning back to the crib, I smooth the white blanket with deliberate care, tucking it gently around the baby's tiny form, covering its chest, its delicate fingers curled in sleep. Its face is peaceful now, a perfect stillness that seems almost angelic in the soft glow of the nursery. I pause, watching the way the light falls across the baby's features, casting a soft shadow over the curve of its cheek, the small button nose, the dark fringe of lashes lying perfectly still.

There's a tenderness in the act, a strange comfort in arranging the blanket as if it were simply time for sleep. I run my fingers along the edge of the crib, smoothing out every wrinkle, every crease, as if any imperfection might shatter the silence that has settled over us both.

The mobile above the crib continues to spin slowly, casting fleeting shadows on the walls. The stars and clouds move in their quiet, eternal dance, untouched, unchanged. I glance at them one last time, feeling the faint breeze from the gentle motion stir the air, a subtle lullaby in the hush of the room.

I step back, my hand lingering on the crib rail for just a moment, then let go. I turn toward the door, moving slowly, each step deliberate, careful. The silence follows me, clinging to my heels, to my skin, wrapping around me like a heavy shroud.

At the door, I look back one final time, taking in the nursery —the soft light, the clean white furniture, the gentle sway of the mobile. Everything is as it should be. Perfect. Peaceful.

I ease the door closed, the latch clicking softly, almost inaudibly. I press my hand against the smooth wood, feeling the faint warmth of the room behind it. And then, with a calm, steady breath, I walk away, leaving the silence undisturbed, as if nothing happened.

APRIL 2ND

The London Aquarium was bustling, the sounds of excited children echoing through the dimly lit corridors. Lila held Molly's hand, leading her towards the jellyfish tank where Ella was already pressed against the glass, mesmerised by the graceful creatures drifting inside.

Owen stood a few steps back, glancing at his phone. Lila noticed the familiar way his brow furrowed when he read something serious, but she ignored it, determined to enjoy their family day out without interruptions. They didn't get days like this often, and she wanted it to feel special.

Just as Lila was pointing out a particularly large jellyfish to Molly, Owen's hand landed on her shoulder, making her turn. His face was pale, his eyes darting anxiously between her and his phone.

"I need to go," he said, his voice barely above a whisper.

"What? Why?" Lila's brow knitted, instinctively holding Molly closer.

"Cass," he replied, glancing down at his phone. "She's... she's in hospital. They think it might be a heart attack."

Lila's eyes widened. "Oh, God..."

"She's alone. Mark's on a business trip. She messaged me. I need to get back to Cambridge. Someone has to be there for her."

Lila's stomach twisted. She looked around at their daughters, oblivious and absorbed in the glowing tanks, and felt a pang of resentment. They'd planned this day together, a chance to reconnect as a family. But Cass needed him now, and Lila couldn't argue against that. After all, what kind of friend would she be if she did?

"Really? This is meant to be our day," she said. "What will I tell the girls?"

"Come on, Li. This is serious. She's had a heart attack. She's our friend. Mark isn't there. She doesn't have anyone else. Would you want me to leave you alone in hospital to deal with something like this?"

"She should call her husband," Lila hissed.

"She did." Owen's eyes flashed with anger. "He said he was busy."

"Oh." All the fight in Lila evaporated as quickly as it had surfaced. "You'd better go then I suppose."

Owen looked at her, a mix of guilt and relief on his face. "Thank you, Lila. I'm sorry. I just... I have to be there. She might pretend she's a tough cookie, but we both know it's just a front."

Without another word, he squeezed her hand and hurried towards the exit, already pulling up train times on his phone. Lila watched him go, a hollow ache settling in her chest as he disappeared into the crowd.

The rest of the day passed in a blur. She did her best to keep the girls entertained, but her mind kept drifting back to Owen, to Cass, to the familiar feeling that she was coming in second to a relationship she didn't fully understand.

By the time they returned to Cambridge, Lila felt drained.

She tucked the girls into bed, then collapsed onto the sofa, her mind racing with unspoken worries and hurt. She pulled out her phone, needing someone to talk to. Zara's name appeared at the top of her contacts, and she hit 'call' without a second thought.

"Hey, you," Zara answered, her familiar warmth instantly comforting.

"He left us," Lila said, the words tumbling out before she could stop them. "Owen left us at the Aquarium... for Cass. She's in hospital, something with her heart."

There was a pause on the other end of the line before Zara spoke, her voice sharper than usual. "I'm sorry, Lila, but... he left you and the girls on a family day out to be with her? Seriously?"

Lila swallowed, feeling a mix of embarrassment and loyalty flare up. "I mean... she might be having a heart attack. And Mark's away. She's alone."

"Maybe," Zara replied, sounding unconvinced. "But if he's running to her side at the drop of a hat every time she needs something, where does that leave you?"

Lila felt a pang of defensiveness. "It's not like that. Cass... she's his colleague, his friend. And we don't know what's really happened. If she's seriously ill, he has to be there."

"Maybe," Zara said again, her voice softer now but still laced with scepticism. "But, Lila, you can't keep excusing this. Every time you turn around, she's there. I'm not saying she's pretending to be ill or anything, but... isn't it strange how she always seems to need him at just the wrong moments?"

Lila sighed, rubbing her temples. "I don't know. Maybe I'm overthinking it. I just... I feel like I can't compete."

"There shouldn't be a competition," Zara said firmly. "You're his wife, Lila. He should be putting you and the girls first. Cass has her own husband, her own life. She shouldn't be intruding on yours."

"Maybe," Lila murmured, though doubt lingered. "She's in hospital, Zara. I can't just... I can't be angry with her for that."

"I know, love," Zara replied, her tone softening. "But don't let this become a pattern. You deserve more than being an afterthought."

They chatted a little longer, but after hanging up, Lila couldn't shake Zara's words. She found herself staring at the empty side of the bed that Owen should have been occupying, wondering if he'd even come home tonight—or if Cass would need him for just a little longer.

As the hours crept by, sleep eluded her. All she could see was the image of Owen walking away, and the devastating realisation that she was beginning to feel like an outsider in her own marriage.

The front door opened just as she came downstairs, and Owen stepped inside, looking exhausted.

Lila crossed her arms, her voice cooler than she intended. "How's Cass?"

Owen let out a sigh, rubbing the back of his neck. "Fine, apparently. They discharged her by the time I arrived. She was waiting outside A&E when I got there."

Lila's eyebrows shot up. "Outside?"

"Yeah, she looked a bit shaken, but... I mean, she seemed fine. They ran some tests, but they didn't find anything conclusive. Just told her to take it easy for a few days." He shrugged, but his expression was tight, almost defensive.

"So... she wasn't admitted?" Lila asked, struggling to keep the doubt from her voice.

"No," he replied, glancing away. "They must've checked her over and decided it wasn't as serious as they thought."

The hollow ache in Lila's chest deepened. She wanted to believe him, to accept that Cass had genuinely needed him, but something didn't sit right. Why would she insist on Owen coming back to Cambridge if it hadn't been serious? And why had she waited outside, perfectly fine, instead of being kept in for observation?

"So why didn't you come back to London? What have you been doing all this time?"

She searched his face, hoping for some reassurance, but he seemed as uncertain as she was. He shrugged, moved past her towards the kitchen, and she followed, her unease festering.

"Owen," she started, choosing her words carefully, "do you really think... I mean, are you sure it was as serious as she said?"

He paused, hand on the kettle, and for a fleeting moment, she saw a flicker of doubt in his eyes. But then he shook his head, brushing it off. "Of course it was, Lila. She thought she was having a heart attack. You can't blame her for panicking."

"Right," she murmured, her stomach churning. "I suppose not." *But I can blame you for abandoning us,* she thought.

But the seeds of doubt had taken root. Lila knew Cass was a complex person, and there had always been something... calculated about her. She'd become indispensable to Owen, always there when he needed support with work, but now Lila couldn't help but wonder: was there more to Cass's call for help than met the eye?

They sat in silence, the sound of the kettle boiling filling the kitchen. Owen busied himself making tea, but his movements were tense, his shoulders hunched. She could tell he didn't want to discuss it any further, that he was already regretting the decision to rush to Cass's side.

Lila took a deep breath, glancing out the window at the garden beyond. She'd always trusted Owen, believed in his loyalty, his goodness. But as she watched him, a gnawing feeling took hold, one she couldn't ignore.

For the first time, she found herself questioning the boundaries between Owen and Cass, wondering if Cass had known exactly what she was doing—and if her supposed health scare was just another way to keep Owen close.

SHE

The room is pristine. The kind of neatness that feels unnatural, forced, uncreased, like no one has ever been here. A spotless glass surface is reflecting the warm glow of the overhead light. The air smells faintly of disinfectant, a scent meant to calm, but it feels cloying, suffocating. Everything here is in its place—a perfectly arranged bed and not a single speck of dust to mar the illusion of serenity.

But it's a lie. All of it.

My bare feet slap against the floor as I pace, the sound breaking the fragile stillness. The polished floor is smooth, cold, grounding in a way I can't decide if I hate or need. My hands hang at my sides, fingers twitching, curling and uncurling, desperate for something to do. Something to hold. My body feels electric, buzzing with restless energy, while the room around me remains still, indifferent, mocking me with its tranquillity.

My mind doesn't match this place. It's chaos. A storm of thoughts crashing into one another, no beginning, no end. The images come in rapid flashes, and I dig my nails into my palms until it stings. Do they think they're untouchable? Do they think they're safe?

I stop in front of the window, staring out into the darkness. The glass is so clean it barely distorts the reflection of the room behind me. For a moment, I see myself there—barefoot, wild-eyed, a figure of tension against the backdrop of carefully curated calm. I hate it. I hate them. And I hate myself for not being able to stop the hate.

The thoughts twist deeper, darker. It would be so simple. A single act to dismantle their perfect little world. To take what they have and leave them with nothing. They wouldn't even see it coming. My pulse quickens, and I clench my fists tighter, the knuckles cracking under the strain. The thought feels satisfying, almost soothing, but it doesn't last. The storm is never quiet for long.

I turn away from the window, pacing again, my feet making quick, sharp sounds against the floor. The air feels too still, too clean, and I want to shatter it, to ruin it. My chest tightens as memories creep in, unbidden. The sharp, biting words from my childhood that I still feel deep in my bones. The overwhelming helplessness.

I try to shove it all down, bury it beneath the weight of the present, but it claws its way back up, unstoppable. My breathing grows shallow as I keep moving, one end of the room to the other, back and forth, faster now. The perfect room feels smaller with every step, the order of it grating against the disorder inside me.

I stop abruptly, standing in the centre of the room, staring at the table and the perfect, gleaming surface. I imagine sweeping everything off it, hearing the crash, watching the glass shatter, sending shards scattering across the floor. The image is sharp, satisfying, but I don't move. I just stand there, trembling, frozen between what I want to do and what I'm afraid of becoming.

"I'm fine," I whisper, the words barely audible in the silence. "I'm fine. I'm fine."

The room stays calm. Perfect. And I remain broken.

APRIL 19TH

Owen and Lila decided the best way to enjoy their new-found wealth was to move to a house in the countryside, on the outskirts of Cambridge. The money was pouring into the business after the deal that had been closed and Lila had always wanted a house with a large garden. On the outside they looked happy. The perfect couple with the perfect marriage. Now they had the perfect house and being cash buyers meant they had been able to arrange the purchase quickly.

Granta Hall stood at the top of a gentle rise, its grand Georgian façade a picture of symmetry and elegance. Built from honey-coloured stone that seemed to glow under the soft April sunlight, it was every bit the dream home Lila had imagined for her family. Tall sash windows framed the front, their white-painted frames gleaming in the afternoon light. The front door, a rich shade of forest green, opened out onto a gravel drive that crunched underfoot, winding away from the house and towards the road that cut through the quiet countryside.

The land stretched for acres, surrounding them in a cocoon of green fields and gentle hills. Rolling lawns led down to a small lake, the water shimmering under the weak spring sun, and further beyond, a cluster of trees bordered the property, their branches just beginning to unfurl bright-green leaves. Here, on the outskirts of Cambridge, the world felt distant, the city's buzz a memory that Lila couldn't quite shake but also couldn't quite miss. Not yet anyway.

Daffodils lined the gravel path, their heads nodding gently in the breeze. The wisteria, beginning to bloom with pale-purple flowers, wound itself along the western wall, adding a sense of wildness to the otherwise stately structure. It was the sort of house people dreamt of. The kind of place that seemed to promise a slower, simpler life. A new chapter. A fresh start. They'd moved in only a week earlier, but it already felt like home.

Still, standing there, taking in the vastness of the grounds and the quiet, Lila couldn't quite shake the feeling that something wasn't right. The house was beautiful—there was no denying that—but it hadn't settled into her bones the way she had hoped. It felt like a house from someone else's life, not hers. There was a hollowness to it, an emptiness that the move had failed to fill. Maybe it was the strangeness of it all, this sudden shift from the city to the country, from their old, familiar life to something so new and alien.

She stood on the front steps, her hands wrapped around a cup of tea, looking out over the grounds. The air was cool, crisp, carrying the scent of damp earth and new growth, but even the promise of spring couldn't chase away the unease that had taken root inside her.

It was Easter weekend, a time for family, for celebration, for renewal. And yet, Lila couldn't help but feel like the move to the country was more of an escape than a new beginning. Owen had insisted that it would be good for them—good for the girls, for their relationship—but she wasn't so sure. The house was grand, and the countryside peaceful, but it felt like a temporary solution, like a plaster slapped over a deeper wound. A distraction rather than a cure.

APRIL 19TH

Lila placed the finishing touches on the table, adjusting the flowers in the vase and smoothing the linen tablecloth. It was a rare gathering for close friends and family—a quiet Easter lunch with the people she loved.

Her silent wish had been granted in an unexpected way. Just yesterday, Cass had called with the news: her mother had taken a terrible fall, slipping down the stairs and falling into a coma. She had sounded frantic, explaining that she'd be at her mother's bedside indefinitely, her voice tight with worry.

Lila had offered the expected condolences, voicing sympathy as sincerely as she could manage. But as soon as she hung up, she felt a weight lift from her shoulders. Cass wouldn't be coming. The tension that usually accompanied her wouldn't touch this gathering. For once, it would just be her, Owen, and a few friends, without that familiar thorn in her side.

As she poured the first glass of wine, she allowed herself a moment of peace. Today, she could breathe freely, laugh without self-consciousness, and simply enjoy the company around her. She knew she should feel more concern for Cass and her family, and part of her did. But as she heard Owen and the children's voices drifting in from the garden, she couldn't deny the relief that washed over her. For today, at least, things felt simpler, lighter, and she would savour that.

The dining room in their new home was filled with the rich, warm scent of roast lamb and rosemary. The table was set with white linen napkins and polished silverware glinting in the late-afternoon light. Lila had taken great care to make everything just right, even though the atmosphere around the table felt strained from the start.

Owen was at the head of the table, carving the lamb with steady hands. He seemed relaxed enough, but Lila knew him well enough to sense his distraction. The girls, Molly and Ella, sat to her left, whispering about their Easter egg hunt earlier in the day, their faces bright with anticipation for the meal ahead. Even Ella was still young enough to get caught up with the excitement.

At the other end of the table sat Margaret, Owen's mother. Her back was hunched, her lips pressed into a thin line as she watched Lila with those sharp, calculating eyes that never missed a thing. She wore her usual expression—disapproval disguised as politeness, a smile that never quite reached her eyes. There was no warmth in her presence, no softness in the way she carried herself. She had been brought to the house for lunch from her retirement home. The old woman was basically wheelchair bound these days but that never prevented her from ruining a family occasion. Owen wanted to show his mother their new home. He wanted her approval for all he'd achieved. He was never going to get it.

The tension between Lila and Margaret had always been there, simmering just beneath the surface. Margaret had never been openly hostile, but her disapproval was constant, ever-present in the small, pointed comments she dropped into conversation, each one like a jab in the ribs.

As Owen served the lamb, Margaret cleared her throat, her gaze shifting to Molly, who was fidgeting in her seat, her old hands clumsy as she tried to arrange her cutlery.

"Sit up straight, Molly," Margaret said, her voice clipped. "A lady doesn't slouch at the table."

Molly straightened immediately, casting a nervous glance at her grandmother. Lila shot Margaret a look, biting back the urge to defend her daughter. It was Easter, and she didn't want to start a row, not in front of the girls. But the way Margaret wielded her authority, always critiquing rather than encouraging, always so quick to point out a fault—it grated on Lila's nerves. All the while Margaret seemed oblivious to the fact none of her children loved her enough to look after her themselves and had packed her away in a retirement home.

Owen said nothing as usual. He passed Margaret a plate, smiling politely. "Here you go, Mum."

"Thank you," Margaret said with a shaky voice, her tone devoid of warmth. She took the plate, inspecting it for a moment. "Quite a generous portion, Owen. I won't finish all of this."

Lila's eyes flicked to Owen, who merely gave a small, resigned smile before passing plates to the girls. Margaret cut into her lamb with slow, deliberate movements, her lips pressing into that same thin line she always wore during family meals. It was like nothing ever quite met her standards, even something as simple as a Sunday roast.

"I'm surprised you didn't do the potatoes differently, Lila," Margaret remarked casually, her fork pushing the crispy roast potatoes around her plate. "Roasted with goose fat, perhaps.

That's the traditional way. It gives them more flavour, don't you think?"

Lila forced a smile, the tightness in her chest growing. "I thought olive oil would be healthier," she replied, trying to keep her tone light. "And the girls prefer it this way."

Margaret sniffed, taking a small bite of potato, chewing slowly. "Hmm. I suppose so. But tradition is tradition. Sometimes it's better to stick with what works. Was that how your mother did it?" Margaret's beady eyes fixed on Lila.

"You know I was in care, Margaret," Lila said through gritted teeth.

"But you reconnected with your mother." Margaret was not going to let it go.

"Yes, but only after years apart. I'd prefer not to discuss my childhood right now, if that's okay."

"You never have, dear." Margaret's false teeth bit into a piece of potato.

Owen, possibly sensing the tension but unwilling to engage, kept his focus on his own plate, cutting his meat with a little too much concentration. Lila could feel her frustration building. Margaret had this way of making everything sound like a well-meaning suggestion, but Lila knew better. It was just another criticism, another way to make her feel like she was never quite good enough.

Ella, ever the peacemaker, looked up from her plate and tried to change the subject. "Granny, did you see how many eggs Molly found in the garden?"

Margaret's eyes flickered to her youngest granddaughter, her expression softening just a fraction. "Yes, dear, I saw. Though I must say, I was surprised you didn't discover more. I certainly hid more eggs in my garden when Owen was your age."

Lila's jaw tightened. Even Ella's attempt at light

conversation wasn't safe from Margaret's subtle barbs. Molly was too young to understand the full weight of her grandmother's words, but Ella wasn't. Lila wondered if Ella could see the way Margaret's eyes never quite softened when she spoke to any of them, and how her compliments always came with a sting, a reminder of how things were supposedly better in the past, under her watch.

"Well, we had fun," Lila said, trying to steer the conversation away from the usual comparisons to Owen's childhood. "And that's what matters, right?"

Margaret didn't reply immediately, instead taking a sip of water before placing her glass down with a deliberate clink. "Of course," she said eventually, though the edge in her voice was unmistakable. "Though I do think a little more discipline wouldn't go amiss. Children thrive with proper structure, after all."

Lila felt her chest tighten. It wasn't just about the potatoes or the Easter egg hunt—it never was. It was always about something bigger, something unspoken. Margaret had never approved of her. From the moment Lila and Owen got together, Margaret had made it clear that she didn't think Lila was right for her son. She was too soft, too lenient, too... ordinary. Not what Margaret had envisioned for Owen, even though she never showed him an ounce of proper love herself. And to make matters worse, Margaret made it clear she thought Lila was a bad mother, even though both her girls were polite and well-behaved. So what if the girls were running around the garden searching for their eggs, barefoot. Children need freedom.

Owen, still oblivious, or perhaps just too tired to intervene, passed the gravy to his mother with a faint smile. "We'll make sure to have more structure next time, Mum," he said lightly, though Lila could hear the weariness in his voice. She was old and it was far too late for her to change her ways.

Margaret gave a curt nod, clearly satisfied with his response, and turned her attention back to her meal, her bony hands struggling to grip her cutlery.

Lila picked at her food, her appetite long gone, though she smiled and nodded whenever the girls spoke, doing her best to hide the growing resentment curling in her chest. Margaret's presence always cast a shadow over what should have been a peaceful, happy moment. Every meal with her felt like a battle Lila couldn't win, no matter how hard she tried to keep things civil.

"Do you remember the Easter lunches we used to have, Owen?" Margaret asked suddenly, her tone more wistful now. "The whole family gathered around, your father carving the roast... such wonderful memories."

Owen nodded, though his response was non-committal. "Yeah, Mum, I remember."

Lila bit back a sigh.

As the meal wound down, and the plates were cleared, Lila excused herself to the kitchen, grateful for a moment of solitude away from Margaret. She stood at the sink, washing the dishes, the sound of running water a welcome distraction from the tension still hanging in the air.

From the dining room, she could hear Owen and Margaret talking quietly, her voice still carrying that same air of superiority. And though Lila couldn't make out the words, she knew the tone well enough. It was the sound of Margaret asserting herself, making sure everyone knew that she was still in control, even if she wasn't.

Lila took a deep breath, staring out of the window at the rolling fields, her reflection faint in the glass. The house, the beautiful surroundings, the perfect Easter meal—it all felt like a façade, a carefully constructed illusion that did nothing to fix the deeper issues lurking beneath the surface.

Lila was still in the kitchen, drying her hands on a tea towel, when she heard the distinct sound of a car pulling up outside. She glanced out of the window and frowned. They weren't expecting anyone else—everyone invited was already here. But then, as she heard the unmistakable click of the front door opening, followed by the familiar sound of high heels on the hardwood floor, her stomach sank.

Cass.

APRIL 19TH

Lila moved to the doorway of the kitchen, as she saw Cass standing in the hall, her usual air of confidence wrapped around her like an armour. Dressed in a sleek black coat that fit her perfectly, she looked out of place among the soft, country surroundings. In her arms, she cradled two oversized chocolate eggs wrapped in bright foil, a bottle of expensive red wine, and a sad-looking bunch of wilting daffodils.

"Happy Easter!" Cass called, her voice ringing through the house as if she'd been expected all along.

Lila's smile faltered. Cass hadn't been invited. She'd deliberately left her out of the plans for this Easter lunch, hoping to avoid the tension that seemed to follow her everywhere she went. But now, here she was, as if she had every right to be.

Before Lila could say anything, Molly and Ella burst into the hallway, their eyes lighting up at the sight of the enormous chocolate eggs. Cass grinned at them, holding the eggs out like a gift.

"Look what I brought for you two!"

Lila forced herself to smile, even as a knot tightened in her stomach.

"Cass, this is... a surprise," Lila said, her voice strained. "We weren't expecting you."

Cass didn't falter for a second. "I had a bit of a bust-up with Mark." She handed the wine to Owen, who had appeared in the doorway. "Thought you'd like this. Something special for the occasion."

Owen's face brightened at the sight of the bottle, his previous discomfort seemingly melting away. "Cass, this is too much. You didn't have to bring anything."

Cass shrugged, her eyes twinkling with mischief. "Oh, please. It's nothing. Just wanted to spoil you all a little."

Lila's eyes dropped to the tired bouquet of daffodils in Cass's hand. Cass then extended the flowers towards her, their limp heads drooping. "And these are for you, Lila. A little something for the hostess."

Lila took the flowers, her fingers brushing against the wilted stems.

"Thank you," Lila said, forcing her smile wider. "That's very kind."

Cass flashed her another bright smile before turning her attention to Owen and Margaret, who had been watching the scene unfold with her usual sharp gaze.

Without missing a beat, Cass breezed past Lila and pulled up a chair between Owen and his mother at the dining table, as if she'd always been a part of the celebration. She gave Margaret a charming smile, setting down her coat and positioning herself comfortably. "Margaret, how lovely to meet you. I hope I'm not interrupting."

Margaret, who rarely showed warmth to anyone, let alone Lila, returned Cass's smile with a small nod.

Cass laughed, her eyes flashing as she glanced at Lila. "I'm full of surprises, as you know. I just couldn't resist dropping by."

Lila hovered in the background, clutching the wilted flowers as she watched Cass effortlessly charm her way into the conversation. Margaret, who was always so critical of Lila, seemed to soften under Cass's attention, as though her presence was a welcome addition to the day. The contrast was painful.

"Owen, you'll have to pour us a glass of that wine later," Cass continued, leaning slightly closer to him. "I picked it up from a little shop in London the other day—thought it would go perfectly with a roast."

Owen, clearly enjoying the attention, smiled and nodded. "Sounds great. We'll open it now."

As they continued to chat, Lila felt herself being edged further and further out of the conversation. Cass had a way of dominating the room, of drawing everyone's attention without seeming to try. And Margaret, of course, was eating it up, her sharp remarks momentarily softened by Cass's easy charm.

"So, Margaret," Cass said, turning her full attention to Owen's mother, "I've been meaning to ask—what's your secret? You don't look a day older than forty-five. What are you doing to stay so young?"

Margaret gave a small, pleased laugh, clearly flattered by the attention. "Oh, you're too kind, Cass. I'm afraid it's nothing more than good genes and a bit of discipline."

"I knew it," Cass replied smoothly. "You've got that sharpness about you, always keeping things in order."

Cass took a sip of her wine, her gaze turning distant for a moment, as if recalling some recent trauma. She placed her glass down with a sigh. "Speaking of keeping things in order, you won't believe the week I've had," she said, her voice carrying a hint of tragic heroism.

Lila glanced up, her curiosity piqued in spite of herself.

"My poor mother took a terrible fall down the stairs just a few days ago. She ended up in the hospital... in a coma, no less." Cass paused, clearly waiting for a reaction, her expression one of practiced sorrow.

"Oh dear, that sounds awful," Margaret said, her eyes wide. "Is she all right?"

Cass nodded, pressing a hand dramatically to her heart. "Well, miraculously, yes. She's just come out of the coma, thank God." She let out a shaky breath. "I was by her side day and night, barely slept a wink. I even made her favourite homemade soup—you know, the old family recipe she loves. And wouldn't you know it? The smell of that soup seemed to do the trick, as if it brought her back to us. The doctors said it was a miracle."

Lila resisted the urge to roll her eyes.

"Oh, that's wonderful," Owen said, his voice genuinely sympathetic. "I can't imagine how scary that must've been for you."

Cass looked at him gratefully, her eyes glistening. "Yes, well, I just couldn't leave her side until I was sure she was out of danger. But, once she woke up and recognised me—well, I knew she was going to be just fine. I finally felt it was safe to slip away and join you all." She flashed a brave smile, as if she were some sort of martyr.

Margaret's hand went to her chest. "You're a good daughter, Cass. Not everyone would drop everything to take care of their mother like that."

"Oh, it's just what family does, isn't it?" Cass replied, casting a sideways glance at Lila, her voice rich with self-satisfaction. "But thank you, Margaret. I just wanted to be there for her in her time of need."

Lila, still clutching the wilted daffodils, felt her forced smile slipping. It was so typical of Cass to turn even the gravest situation into a story where she emerged as the selfless, caring heroine. She'd bet anything that Cass's mother was likely as much a prop in this tale as those oversized Easter eggs were.

"Well, we're glad you're here, Cass," Owen said.

Cass beamed, tossing her hair over her shoulder with a confident, almost triumphant air. "And I'm so glad to be here, too. I thought, what better way to celebrate Easter than with dear friends?" She reached out, squeezing Margaret's hand. "And with such wonderful company."

Lila bit her lip, her frustration simmering under the surface. She felt the walls of her own home closing in on her, the once-warm atmosphere now stifling with Cass's presence. Lila stood in the doorway, watching the scene play out as if she were a stranger in her own home. Cass had slid into her place so effortlessly, so confidently, and now, here she was, sitting next to Owen, charming his mother, making everything look easy.

"I'll... just tidy up the kitchen," Lila said quietly, more to herself than to anyone else. But no one heard her anyway. No one noticed as she slipped back into the kitchen, the tired daffodils dangling limply in her hand, the sound of Cass's laughter ringing through the dining room. As she stood by the sink, Lila felt the same feeling she'd been trying to shake for months. The move hadn't fixed it. If anything, it had made the cracks in her life even clearer.

And as she stood there, listening to the voices in the dining room, Lila realised that no matter how beautiful the house was, no matter how perfect the meal, she couldn't escape the growing sense of loss.

Lila wiped her hands on the tea towel, her frustration simmering just beneath the surface. Cass's laughter echoing from the dining room was becoming unbearable. The once-welcoming warmth of the house now stifling, oppressive.

She needed someone on her side—someone who understood her, who could break the suffocating spell Cass seemed to have cast over the room. Without thinking twice, she grabbed her phone and dialled Zara's number.

"Zara, please tell me you're free," Lila said, her voice low but urgent.

"Of course I am," Zara's confident, unmistakable voice assured her. "What's up?"

"Just... I need you here. Now. It's a long story, but can you come by? Please?"

Zara didn't hesitate. "On my way. Give me twenty."

Lila breathed a small sigh of relief. Zara's loud, unapologetic presence was exactly what she needed right now. She could already imagine the shift in the atmosphere once Zara arrived—Cass wouldn't know what hit her.

In the dining room, the girls were getting restless, their chocolate stash from Cass sitting on the table, untouched. Margaret sat primly in her chair, casting glances at the clock every few minutes, as if she had somewhere far more important to be. Lila seized the moment.

"Molly, Ella, why don't you go upstairs and watch a movie?" she suggested, her voice overly bright.

As the tension in the room began to ebb with the winding down of lunch, Owen suddenly cleared his throat. He stood from the table, his usual awkwardness giving way to a rare moment of enthusiasm.

"There's one more surprise for you two," he said with a small smile, his eyes darting toward the hallway.

Molly and Ella perked up, their heads whipping around to look at their father in eager anticipation. Lila knew what was coming. She was in on the big surprise and couldn't wait to see the look on her daughter's faces.

Without another word, Owen disappeared into the hallway, leaving the girls bouncing with excitement in their seats. He returned moments later, holding something squirming in his arms—a small bundle of black-and-white fur, wide-eyed and floppy-eared.

"A puppy!" Ella shrieked, clapping her hands together, while Molly gasped, her eyes as wide as saucers.

"It's a Border collie," Owen said, grinning sheepishly. "Happy Easter."

Molly rushed forward, practically tripping over her chair in her haste to reach the puppy. "We love him!"

Ella was right behind her, both of them kneeling to pet the puppy as it wiggled in their father's arms, its tail wagging so furiously it could've powered a small windmill. Lila's heart swelled at the sight of their joy, the earlier tension with Margaret momentarily forgotten. The girls' laughter filled the room as the puppy licked their faces, clearly thrilled by all the attention.

Cass, however, remained seated, her expression less than enthusiastic. She pursed her lips slightly, her eyes narrowing at the squirming bundle of fur.

"I don't really like dogs," she said, her tone light but unmistakably disapproving. She leaned back in her chair, crossing her legs, which inadvertently dangled her expensive designer high heel a little too close to the puppy's level.

In the next instant, the Border collie, still learning about the world, spotted the dangling heel. And before anyone could react, it lunged playfully at it, sinking its tiny puppy teeth into the sleek leather.

"Hey!" Cass yelped, pulling her foot away, trying to shake off the puppy as it held on, determined to make a chew toy out of her shoe. "Not the heels!"

Lila bit her lip, struggling to stifle the grin that threatened to break free. It was almost too perfect—Cass, always so in control, now trying to fend off an eager puppy with a taste for designer leather.

Owen quickly jumped in to scoop up the puppy, laughing softly as he gently pried the shoe out of the pup's mouth. "All right, all right, no eating shoes, little guy."

Cass's expression was a mix of indignation and forced amusement as she inspected her shoe, which now bore the faintest imprint of puppy teeth. "I suppose that's what I get for sitting so close."

Lila couldn't help herself. "Puppies love shoes," she said, her voice a little too innocent. "They just can't resist."

Cass shot her a sidelong glance, catching the smirk playing on Lila's lips, but she said nothing. Instead, she took a large sip of her wine, clearly ready for the focus to shift elsewhere.

The girls, meanwhile, were oblivious to the exchange. They were too busy fawning over the puppy, their excitement boundless. "Can we take him upstairs?" Molly asked, practically vibrating with joy.

Lila smiled, nodding. "Go ahead but be careful with him. And no chocolate for the pup."

The girls grabbed their enormous Easter eggs from the table, carefully balancing them as they led the puppy toward the stairs. The little Border collie trotted along beside them, its tail wagging furiously, clearly happy to be part of the fun.

As the girls disappeared upstairs with the puppy, Owen turned back to the table, looking pleased with himself. "I thought they could use a little excitement," he said quietly, though his eyes flickered with uncertainty as if gauging Lila's reaction.

Lila gave him a small smile, the warmth returning to her chest. "You did good," she said softly, appreciating the gesture that had been his idea.

With the girls and the puppy out of sight, the house felt quieter, though Cass's earlier irritation still hung faintly in the air. But Lila didn't mind. The comic moment with the puppy had done its work—it had lightened the mood, and for the first time all afternoon, she felt a small sense of victory.

Margaret, always punctual, began gathering her things. "I should get going, too," she said, pushing back her wheelchair with a soft grunt. "The taxi should be here soon."

Owen smiled and stood up, helping his mother with her coat, while Cass remained in her seat, swirling her wine and watching the scene with a faint smirk on her lips.

"Thank you for lunch, Lila," Margaret said, her voice formal, though there was no warmth in the words. "The lamb was... well, different from what I'm used to."

Lila swallowed her irritation. "I'm glad you could join us, Margaret. The taxi will take you straight," she paused, "home."

With Margaret bundled into the taxi and the girls upstairs, Lila returned to the dining room, only to find Cass pouring herself another generous glass of wine. The tension in the room was palpable—Owen was trying to keep things light, but Lila could feel his unease. His body language was stiff, his smile too tight, the way it often was when he was caught between wanting to keep everyone happy and wanting the whole thing to just end.

Cass wasn't picking up on it, or if she was, she didn't care. She lounged in her chair, totally at ease, as if she belonged there. Owen caught Lila's eye for a split second, his brow furrowing slightly, but he said nothing. Lila couldn't tell if he wanted Cass to stay or if he simply didn't know how to ask her to leave without making it awkward.

Lila heard footsteps on the gravel, and her heart lifted. Zara.

"Don't get up," Lila said, realising no one was listening, rushing to answer the door, her voice deliberately bright. She opened the door to discover Zara standing there, dressed in a bold floral jacket, her wild purple hair slightly windblown, her grin wide as always.

"Hey!" Zara greeted her with her usual exuberance, pulling Lila into a tight hug before stepping inside. "What's going on? You sounded desperate."

Lila smiled, her tension easing slightly just from Zara's presence. "It's a long story, but... you'll see."

They walked past the dining room, and immediately Zara's eyes fell on Cass, who was reclining in her chair, swirling her wine like she owned the place. The energy in the room shifted as Zara took in the scene—the half-empty wine bottle, Cass's self-assured posture, Owen's tense smile. Zara raised an eyebrow, the glint in her eyes making it clear she wasn't impressed.

"Well, well, well," Zara said, her voice loud and breezy as she dropped her bag onto an empty chair in the kitchen. "Looks like the party's in full swing."

"Not at all," Lila said, her voice tight. "You're just in time."

Just then Cass called out, "I'm going to help Owen finish this bottle of wine." She cackled.

Zara tilted her head, eyes narrowing slightly as she sat down. "How thoughtful of her." She leaned back in her chair, her presence suddenly filling the room in a way that made Lila feel smaller, less certain.

Lila studied Zara, trying to read her expression. It felt odd being in one room with her friend while her husband sat at their dining table with another woman. Was he feeling uncomfortable because of Zara's obvious hostility?

Zara, ever bold, pressed on. "So, Lila," she said, her voice sweet but pointed, "how long has Cass been here?"

"Oh, she just popped by after visiting her mother at the hospital. She had a terrible fall."

Zara smiled, leaning forward slightly. "Oh. So she's not spending today with *her* husband?"

Lila suddenly couldn't remember why she'd invited Zara. She felt awkward and disliked the tension. "Do you want a drink, Zara?" she asked, the question coming out too quickly, her voice tinged with discomfort as she tried to steer the conversation away from Cass.

Zara grinned, clearly aware of the discomfort but unwilling to let Lila off the hook just yet. "Sure. You know I'm a gin girl myself. You wouldn't happen to have some in the cupboard, would you, Lila?"

Lila went into the dining room to fetch the gin, while Cass continued to sip her wine with a cool, unaffected air. But Lila could see the way her smile had become more rigid, the playful charm losing its edge. Maybe leaving them alone had been a good idea after all.

"Well," Cass said, glancing at the clock and setting her glass down, "I suppose I should be heading out. Don't want to monopolise the evening. I should probably go back to the hospital. I can't bear the thought of my mother being all alone."

"Oh, don't rush off on my account, love. But yes, it is getting late, isn't it?" Lila said, swinging the bottle of gin.

Owen exhaled quietly, a subtle relief passing across his face. He stood up, helping Cass with her coat, though there was something half-hearted about it, as though he wasn't sure if he was doing the right thing.

Cass turned to Lila, her smile still polite but noticeably strained. "Thanks for the hospitality, Lila. I'll see you soon, I'm sure," she said as she slipped out the door.

SHE

I didn't know this is how it would begin. I didn't realise that watching the old woman through a window would be my lightbulb moment. I didn't know what led me there. But something did. Life, it seems, had a sense of humour and for me to understand my own existence I had to witness something so tangibly sad, to understand.

Walking for what seemed like hours through the rain, my feet aching with each wet step that landed in each cold, still, puddle, my hair clinging to my face, like cobwebs do when you push your way through a dark, long-abandoned cellar, I just kept going. I had no destination, no end in sight. All I knew was that I needed to keep on moving. And maybe that is exactly why I ended up outside of the care home. Like the aging residents, I too was living like a zombie, putting one foot in front of another, with no purpose, trapped inside a body that felt alien, in a life I no longer recognised.

I always hated the smell in that place. I defy anyone to find comfort in that scent. Like old dusty books, cat food and urine. I couldn't understand why those people didn't take better care of themselves. Where was their pride?

As she tried to eat the sloppy food from a bowl with a shaking hand, I watched with disgust. When did she become such a burden?

The place made my skin crawl. I was just grateful that I didn't have to wash her or change her sheets. I don't think I could have done it. I don't know how anyone does.

But despite the resentment I felt bubbling beneath the surface, like a virus waiting to break free, I still couldn't make sense of what had led me there or why.

I didn't like her let alone love her. So why was I standing in the rain, my skin feeling like it was being burnt by each drop that splashed against it. It didn't make sense, but somehow, being near her brought me a strange kind of relief. The kind of relief a child feels when they curl up under an old moth-bitten blanket. It was familiar. It felt safe. But it was an illusion. Just as it had always been, except this time, I was on the outside looking in.

I'd tried so hard to please her. To fit in. To be what she wanted me to be. Now that idea was laughable. Here she was, hopeless and insignificant. I hoped, at last, she understood how that felt.

When you read about the stories in the news, of the abuse that goes on in care homes, if you take enough time watching the elderly slowly fade, you can start to imagine where the rage and frustration comes from, from those who are paid peanuts to pick up the pieces and those who watch our ancestors turn to dust.

Have you ever imagined yourself pushing an old person out of the way when they were blocking your path on the pavement, and you were in a hurry? Have you ever looked at your aging grandparent or parent and longed for the day you no longer had to watch them decay, taking up your precious time while they cling to life? If you don't recognise this feeling, you are lying. Or worse, you're not human.

We've all had the urge to push an old bitch or bastard

downstairs so we can get on with our day and do things that will make a difference to the people who really make the world go round.

What's worse, and what no one admits, is that they become so selfish with age. They are simply there to exist. Breathing in and out, their frail ribcages heaving with the effort, eating for the sake of it, getting no enjoyment from anything. They just do it because instinct tells them to. It's that simple. It's that pathetic. And for anyone stuck looking after someone who has nothing left to offer, but someone who sucks the life out of the living, you know that life would be better if they just gave up and died.

Watching her, through the open window of her downstairs care-home bedroom, I could hear the rattle coming from her chest, which gave me a strange kind of comfort. Surely, she wouldn't be on this earth for much longer. Something would kill her, and I hoped the day would come sooner rather than later.

I continued to watch with morbid fascination as her mouth opened and closed as she attempted to eat. She reminded me of a baby bird. Hopeless. Vulnerable. Pathetic.

The skin on her old, gnarled hands was nearly see-through now and bulbous blue veins protruded like throbbing rivers. As I focused more, I could see one pulsing and it made me smile. I could see life pushing its way around her body, forcing her to stay alive. Forcing her to live. Forcing the rest of us to suffer.

Everything else about her looked dead. She wasn't living. She was just surviving. In that moment the idea was born. Just like that.

As easily as a light can be switched on, it can be switched off.

It was time for her to go. Time for her to become nothing more than a pile of bones in the ground. Time for me to get some peace at last.

APRIL 26TH

Lila stood in front of the bedroom mirror, her reflection stared back, pale and hollow-eyed, as if the weight of the past few weeks had drained the colour from her skin.

She remembered she'd been looking for her earrings. They were a gift Owen had given her on their tenth wedding anniversary—the delicate sapphire studs that had matched the blue dress she wore that night. She'd worn them almost every day since, a small comfort in the midst of everything falling apart. But now... now they were gone.

She checked the nightstand drawer again, pulling it open with more force than necessary. Nothing. Her jewellery box sat there, as always, but the earrings weren't inside. They weren't in the bathroom either, where she sometimes took them off after a long day. Panic fluttered in her chest.

Her eyes darted to the vanity table. The perfume bottle looked out of place. The little hand mirror wasn't where she normally left it. The hairbrush, the stack of books—everything seemed slightly off. Had she moved them? She couldn't remember.

The more she looked, the more things seemed... wrong.

Subtle changes that gnawed at her. She was sure her things weren't where they'd been the day before.

Lila stood in the centre of the room, her pulse quickening, a knot forming in her stomach. Someone had been in here. Someone had touched her things.

"Owen?" she called, her voice tight as she stepped into the hallway.

She found him downstairs in the kitchen, leaning against the counter with a beer, his eyes scanning something on his phone. He looked up as she approached, his face drawn with the exhaustion that had become all too familiar lately.

"What's up?" he asked, his tone already carrying that edge of impatience.

"I can't find my earrings," she said, her voice coming out sharper than she intended. "The ones you gave me for our anniversary. They're gone, Owen."

He frowned, setting his phone down. "Gone? Are you sure you didn't put them somewhere else?"

"I've looked everywhere," Lila replied, her arms crossing over her chest. "And it's not just that. Other things... I think someone's been moving my stuff."

Owen sighed, rubbing his hand over his face. "Lila, no one's been moving your stuff. It's just you and the girls here."

"I know that," she snapped. "But things are out of place. I'm not imagining it."

Owen's expression shifted, growing tighter. "Maybe you just forgot where you put them. You've been... a bit scatter-brained lately."

Lila's breath hitched at the insinuation. She hadn't forgotten. She wasn't losing her mind. "I'm telling you, something's not right. I wouldn't lose those earrings."

"Okay, fine," Owen said, his tone clipped. "But they're just earrings, Lila. They'll show up. Why are you making this into such a big deal?"

Her frustration bubbled up, spilling into her words before she could stop herself. "Because it's not just the earrings! You've barely been home, Owen. You're always 'working late', and then Cass shows up uninvited on Easter. Everything is just—wrong."

Owen's face darkened. "Oh, here we go again."

"What's that supposed to mean?" Lila's heart pounded, her voice rising.

"I'm bored of this, Lila. The same argument, over and over. Cass, work. You're obsessing."

"I'm not obsessing! I just don't understand why she's always around, why you're always defending her. I mean, why was she even there?"

Owen stood up straighter, his hand gripping the edge of the counter. "You're making everything about Cass, and it's exhausting. I'm trying to do my job, keep things running, and you're acting like there's some conspiracy! We've finally made it. This house, the money. Can't you just be happy?"

Lila's anger flared. "I see the way she looks at you. The way you look at her."

Owen let out a bitter laugh. "You're losing the plot, Lila."

Her jaw clenched. "Don't talk to me like that."

"I'm serious," Owen said, his voice hardening. "You've been acting paranoid for weeks. The move, the girls, the house—you're spiralling. Maybe you should go see someone."

Lila froze, her heart pounding in her ears. "What did you just say?"

"You heard me," Owen snapped, his temper boiling over. "You need to talk to a doctor or something. I can't keep having this conversation. Every little thing becomes some massive drama with you."

Her breath came in shallow bursts. "So now you think I'm crazy?"

"I didn't say that," Owen shot back, his tone cooling slightly, but the damage was done. "I just think you need help."

Lila stared at him, disbelief washing over her. "Help? From what, exactly? From worrying about you? From worrying about us?"

Owen ran a hand through his hair, frustration etched into every line of his face. "No, Lila, from whatever's going on with you. You're so wrapped up in this. It's not healthy. I'm trying to keep this family together, to build something we can be proud of and all you do is pick fights."

The weight of his words hit her like a blow to the chest. She blinked, the room swimming around her. She didn't know whether to scream or cry. How had they ended up here, where every conversation felt like a battle?

"I'm not the one picking fights, Owen," she said, her voice quieter now, more wounded than she wanted it to be. "You're the one who's never here anymore."

Owen looked away, his jaw tight. "I'm providing for us."

Lila froze as she turned to leave, Owen's voice cutting through the air like a knife.

She stared at him, feeling the gap between them widen with every passing second. "That's what you keep saying."

"Lila, wait," he said, his tone softer, almost reluctant. A knot of tension was tightening in her chest as she turned back to face him.

"What is it?" she asked, her voice wary, bracing herself for another argument.

Owen sighed, rubbing the back of his neck. "Look... there's something I should tell you. It's about Cass."

Lila's pulse quickened. She didn't want to hear about Cass,

didn't want to know any more than she already did. But Owen's expression stopped her from brushing him off.

"She... found a lump in her breast," he said quietly, his eyes searching hers. "She's terrified, Lila. She thinks it might be cancer."

The words hung heavy in the air, casting a pall over the tension between them. Lila's irritation drained away, replaced by a sick, twisting sensation in her stomach. Despite everything, she felt a pang of guilt.

"I didn't know," she murmured, her voice barely a whisper. "She... she didn't say anything."

Owen shook his head. "She wouldn't. She's been trying to keep it together, but she's scared. I mean... imagine finding out something like that and having to go through it alone."

Lila swallowed, a lump forming in her throat. She imagined Cass, terrified and vulnerable, and it made her feel small and petty for the resentment she'd been carrying. The image of Cass, brave and defiant as always, crumbled under the weight of this revelation.

"Is she... all right?" Lila asked, her voice softer now, laced with genuine concern.

Owen nodded slowly. "She's waiting for test results. They'll know more soon. But... I just thought you should know."

Lila looked away, feeling a wave of shame wash over her. Here she was, obsessing over missing earrings and imaginary slights, while Cass was dealing with something so much bigger. She felt like she'd been stripped bare, her insecurities laid out for what they were—small, inconsequential things in the face of a real crisis.

"Thank you for telling me," she murmured, not quite able to meet his gaze.

Owen nodded as Lila caught a glimpse of something else in his eyes—an unspoken plea for understanding, a hint of the

Owen she'd once known, buried beneath the strain of recent months.

Lila went back upstairs and stared at her reflection in the mirror, the guilt and doubt swirling inside her. Cass had always seemed so untouchable, so strong. But maybe she was just as fragile, just as scared, beneath her polished veneer.

For the first time in a long time, Lila felt a flicker of empathy for Cass. And with it, an overwhelming sadness that they'd come to this—two women caught in the shadows of their own fears, each struggling to hold onto something that felt like it was slipping away.

But as she looked at herself in the mirror, that empathy didn't erase the gnawing sense of unease creeping through her. Cass's intrusion into her life, her home—it felt more unsettling than ever.

And as she thought this, Lila realised she was still holding the empty space on her earlobes where her earrings should have been.

She turned away, her hands shaking as she left the room, but it wasn't just the missing jewellery that haunted her now. It was everything—the unravelling of her life, her marriage, and the person she thought she was.

Until that moment she'd been unable to pluck up the courage for a heart-to-heart with Owen, the one that Zara had strongly advised. Afraid of making things worse, Lila had tiptoed around their situation and now, it had all come out wrong and she was left alone with a sense of dread.

Lila stood in front of a window staring at her reflection. The woman looking back at her seemed fragile, uncertain, as if the ground beneath her was crumbling. She pressed her hand against her chest, trying to steady her breathing, but nothing could calm the storm of doubt and fear brewing inside her.

She was losing control—of her home, her family, herself. And for the first time, she wondered if maybe Owen was right.

Maybe she really was losing the plot.

MAY 30TH

The sun was sinking low over the fields as Lila pulled up to the house, the golden hour casting everything in a warm, deceptive glow. The stone of the Georgian façade stood proud against the backdrop of the quiet countryside, the wisteria climbing up the walls, its delicate flowers swaying gently in the summer breeze. The large sash windows, now slightly ajar, let in the last of the evening air, but no sound came from within. The house looked peaceful, serene even, but the stillness of it felt wrong, as though it were holding its breath, waiting for something.

Lila paused for a moment before stepping out of the car, as she tried to shake off the unease that had settled in her chest. The time spent with her mother near Bath had left her emotionally drained. The care home had smelled of antiseptic and stale air, the kind of place where time seemed to stand still. Her mother had been confused again, calling her by the wrong name more than once. It had been a long couple of days, and all Lila had wanted was to return to her own home, her sanctuary.

But now, standing in the doorway with her luggage, she could sense something was wrong.

The house was unnaturally quiet. The kind of quiet that

didn't feel comforting, but suffocating. She dropped her keys onto the hallway table, their clatter echoing through the empty house.

She made her way to the kitchen, and the sight that greeted her stopped her in her tracks.

The room was a mess. Plates and cutlery were scattered across the counters, crusted with the remains of half-eaten meals. The faint scent of something sour lingered in the air, like wine left too long in a glass. Her eyes fell on the dining table, where two wine glasses sat side by side. One was tipped slightly, the dark-red stain of wine pooling on the wood beneath it. The bottle was almost empty, lying on its side as if abandoned mid-conversation.

Lila's stomach turned. Her heart began to race as the stale smell of food, mingling with the scent of the spilled wine, created an acrid undertone that made her throat tighten.

The two wine glasses—Owen hadn't been alone.

She could hear nothing but the low hum of the refrigerator and the faint ticking of the old clock on the wall. The kitchen, with its wide bay window overlooking the garden, felt claustrophobic now, as if the air had thickened in her absence. The once inviting space now felt tainted, the soft light filtering in through the window casting long shadows across the scene.

Lila's pulse quickened as she left the kitchen and ascended the stairs. Each step felt heavier than the last, the thick carpet muffling the sound of her feet. The house itself seemed to exhale, groaning slightly under the strain of old wood, the floorboards creaking beneath her weight. Just silence, oppressive and complete.

The soft scent of their bedroom's linen usually calmed her, but as she reached the top of the stairs and opened the door, the smell was different. Fainter. The smell of Owen's aftershave mixed with something subtler—a hint of perfume that didn't belong to her. The air was humid, like someone had been in the room too long with the windows closed, trapping their scent.

She stepped into the room, her eyes immediately drawn to the en-suite bathroom, where the sound of running water filled the silence. The bath was running. Steam curled out from the half-open bathroom door, the warm mist diffusing the faint smell of bath salts. Her bath salts.

Owen was lying in bed, the duvet pulled up to his waist, his chest bare. His face was soft in sleep, his dark hair falling messily across his forehead, his breathing slow and even. He looked peaceful, almost too peaceful for the chaos she had found downstairs. The soft glow from the bedside lamp cast a golden light over the room, but it did nothing to ease the tightness in Lila's chest.

She took a step closer, her heart pounding in her ears, her hand trembling as she gripped the strap of her bag.

And then, she heard it—movement behind her.

Lila turned slowly, her stomach lurching as she saw the door to the en suite bathroom creak open further. Cass stepped out, her bare feet barely making a sound on the hardwood floor, her black silk negligée clinging to her damp skin, glistening in the low light. Her hair, dark and wet, cascaded over her shoulders, droplets of water running down her collarbone, catching the soft glow of the bedside lamp.

Cass stopped when she saw Lila, her lips curving into a slow, almost lazy smile. Her eyes, sharp and unflinching, locked onto Lila's, and for a moment, the room seemed to shrink, the air between them crackling with electricity.

"Lila," Cass said softly, her voice smooth as silk, almost as if she were greeting an old friend. "I didn't expect you back so soon."

Lila's breath hitched, her throat tight as her gaze darted between Cass and Owen's sleeping form. The world seemed to tilt around her, her mind reeling, struggling to process what was in front of her. The wine glasses—the pieces fell into place with a sickening thud.

"What... what are you doing here?" Lila's voice cracked as she spoke, her body trembling. Her chest felt hollow, the room spinning slightly as she tried to force the words out.

Cass tilted her head, as if considering. She took a step closer, the soft fabric of her negligée catching the light, brushing against her skin like a second shadow. "Just having a bath," she said lightly, her smile widening. "Owen was tired, as you can see."

The smell of something heavy—something musky—filled the room, curling around Lila like a noose. She felt the warmth of the steam making her dizzy.

"I think... I think you should leave," Lila managed, her voice barely above a whisper, the tremor in it betraying the storm of emotions surging beneath her skin.

Cass didn't move. She stood there, her presence as thick and oppressive as the steam still billowing from the bathroom. "Do you?" she asked, her voice calm, measured, but there was an edge to it—something dark and cruel.

Lila's breath came in short, sharp bursts, her vision blurring with unshed tears. She couldn't bear to look at Owen, still sleeping so peacefully, so oblivious to the destruction he had wrought.

Without another word, Lila turned and fled the room, her feet barely touching the floor as she rushed down the stairs, her heart pounding in her chest, her mind spinning with the reality she had tried so hard to avoid. The house felt unfamiliar now, the thick carpet, the heavy drapes, the once welcoming scent of home all tainted by the presence of another woman.

In the kitchen, the wine glasses still sat on the table, cold, empty reminders of what she had lost.

Her knuckles were white, her breath coming in ragged gasps as the weight of everything crushed her.

She had lost him. And Cass had taken everything.

Lila walked out of the house in a haze, clutching her luggage like a lifeline, though her hands barely registered the weight of the bags. Each step felt distant, as if her feet were moving without her mind's permission. The light of early evening stretched long across the gravel driveway, casting the house in a soft, romantic glow. But the beauty of it was lost on her.

Her chest felt hollow, as if everything inside her had been scooped out, leaving only a fragile shell behind. She walked slowly, her body heavy with the weight of betrayal, every movement dragging her further from the place she had once called home. It wasn't home anymore. It hadn't been for a long time, she realised now.

She stopped at the edge of the driveway, her breath caught somewhere between her lungs and her throat. She turned and stared back at the house. The windows glimmered with the soft light of the setting sun, the wisteria that climbed the walls swayed gently in the breeze, its purple blossoms beautiful, serene. It all looked so peaceful, so perfect, so wrong.

For a moment, she stood there, staring at it—this beautiful place that had once symbolised a fresh start. And now, it was the place where it all crumbled. Where it had slowly rotted, piece by piece, until there was nothing left but lies, deceit, and Cass.

The world around her felt unreal, like she was standing in a dream she couldn't wake from. She wanted to scream, to yell, to throw something, but the silence was too thick, too impenetrable. It pressed in on her from all sides, suffocating her. The house, in all its stately elegance, stood there as if mocking her, witness to the betrayal.

Her fingers loosened on the handle of her bag, but she

forced herself to tighten her grip again. She needed to move, to walk, to escape. The longer she stayed, the more it felt like she might sink into the ground, disappear into the earth, swallowed whole by the weight of it all.

She turned away, her feet moving in slow, deliberate steps. The gravel crunched beneath her boots, each sound echoing in her head, louder than it should have been. Her body felt foreign to her, disconnected. The driveway stretched on before her, winding its way down toward the road, the fields on either side bathed in the soft glow of twilight.

She couldn't think clearly, couldn't form a single coherent thought beyond the echo of *Cass*. The image played over and over in her mind, torturing her. Owen's face as he slept, peaceful and unaware.

When she reached the road, she stopped again, her legs trembling, her body weak with exhaustion she didn't remember feeling until now. The wind brushed against her skin, cool and indifferent. She stood there, staring down the road, her vision blurring as tears welled up in her eyes. Her mind was blank. Empty. She had no idea where she was going, no plan, no destination. Just the certainty that she couldn't—*wouldn't*—go back.

She sank to the ground, her knees hitting the gravel with a dull thud. Her hands clawed at the earth, trying to find something solid to hold on to, but there was nothing. The cool, damp ground pressed against her skin, grounding her in a way nothing else could. Her body trembled violently, but her mind felt strangely numb, the shock of everything slowing her thoughts, making everything feel distant and unreal.

A car passed by, but she didn't look up. The sound of its engine fading in the distance, leaving her alone again. Another car passed, and still, no one stopped. No one cared. The world kept moving, indifferent to the storm she realised was raging inside her.

Her phone buzzed in her pocket, a small lifeline in the silence. She fumbled for it, her hands shaking so badly she nearly dropped it before she managed to swipe the screen and find Jen's number. Owen's sister. She needed to hear Molly and Ella. She needed to hear their voices, to remind herself that they were still out there, still safe, still untouched by the nightmare at home.

The phone rang in her ear, the sound slow, distorted, like everything else around her. When Jen's voice finally came through, it felt like a distant echo, as if she were speaking from another world.

"Lila! Hi! Everything okay?"

Lila swallowed hard, the lump in her throat nearly choking her. She couldn't tell Jen. She couldn't say the words, couldn't bear the weight of them on her tongue. So she lied.

"Hi, Jen," she whispered, her voice barely audible. "I just... I wanted to check in. How are the girls?"

Her throat burned as she spoke, the words catching on the edge of her grief, but she forced them out.

Jen's voice softened. "The girls? They're having a blast! They've been swimming all day, playing with their cousins. You know how it is. Do you want to talk to them?"

"Yes," Lila said quickly, her voice breaking. "Please."

There was a shuffle of movement, distant laughter in the background, and then the sweet sound of Molly's voice came through the phone, clear and bright.

"Mummy?"

Lila's breath caught in her throat, the sound of her daughter's voice like a dagger to her heart. Tears spilled down her cheeks, but she forced herself to smile through the pain, even though Molly couldn't see it.

"Hi, sweetheart," Lila whispered, her voice trembling. "Are you having fun?"

"Yes!" Molly's excitement was infectious, a brief balm for Lila's wounds. "We went swimming today, and there's this really big pool, Mummy! It's amazing. And Ella made a new friend!"

Lila's chest tightened as she listened, every word cutting deeper. She should have been there. She should have been with them, but instead, her world had fallen apart in the quiet shadows of her own home. "That sounds wonderful, baby," she whispered, her voice shaking. "I miss you so much."

"I miss you too, Mummy," Molly said, her voice softening. "Are you okay? You sound sad."

Lila's breath hitched, and she pressed her hand to her mouth, trying to keep the sobs from breaking through. "I'm okay, love," she lied. "I just miss you and Ella."

Another tear slipped down her cheek as she asked to speak to Ella, who came on the line and only made Lila's heart ache more.

"Hi, Mum!" Ella's voice rang with happiness, and Lila's chest felt like it might shatter into a thousand pieces.

"Hello, girlie," Lila whispered, barely able to get the words out. "I love you so much."

After the call ended and the silence returned, Lila sat there on the side of the road, clutching her phone to her chest, her tears falling unchecked. The world around her seemed to fade away, the soft rustle of the wind in the trees, the distant hum of passing cars, all of it moving too fast, too far away from her.

She had no idea what to do next. But she knew the marriage was over.

SHE

The air in the room was thick, clinging to my skin like damp wool. It smelled of bleach and decay, the stench of time passing slowly, of forgotten things. The old woman lay there, propped up against her pillows, her grey hair thin and brittle, her chest rising and falling in shallow, rattling breaths.

She didn't stir when the door creaked open, not at first. Her skin was paper-thin, almost translucent, stretched tightly over her fragile bones. Her eyelids fluttered briefly, but she was too far gone to do much more than that. The TV flickered in the corner, casting odd shadows across the walls, but the sound was muted, leaving only the faint buzzing of the fluorescent lights overhead.

The room felt too still, too quiet, like everything had paused for this moment.

I watched her for a while. Watched the way her lips parted slightly with each breath, the way her chest struggled to move under the weight of all those years. She had lived too long. Her body was betraying her, bit by bit, and there was something obscene about it, this slow unravelling of life. She wasn't meant to keep going, and yet, here she was, tethered to this world by nothing more than the air she dragged painfully into her lungs.

Her eyes fluttered again, this time opening fully. Cloudy, grey-blue, and glazed with confusion, they darted around the room before landing on me—or maybe on the space around me. It was hard to tell if she really saw me or just the vague shape of something unfamiliar.

Her lips moved, dry and cracked, and a sound like a soft moan escaped her. I could hear the desperation in it, the weakness. But there was no strength left for words. Just a sound, a ghost of a plea that never came.

I stepped closer, and the floor creaked under the weight. Her eyes widened slightly, but there was no fight in her. No panic. Just the dawning realisation that something wasn't right. Her breathing became more laboured. The rhythm, already strained, faltered. The soft wheeze in her throat grew louder, raspier. Her body knew before her mind did—knew what was coming.

I reached out, my hand brushing the coarse fabric of the pillow beside her head. The moment stretched out, time-warping, bending around us. The TV flickered again, the fluorescent lights above buzzing angrily, like they too sensed the wrongness of what was about to happen.

Her eyes locked on mine—no, past mine. Searching for something, for anyone. But there was no one here. No one but us.

Slowly, deliberately, I pulled the pillow from behind her, watching her face carefully, waiting for the recognition to dawn. Her lips parted wider, another sound escaping—this time more frantic, more urgent. A dry, pitiful gasp.

I lowered the pillow toward her face.

Her hands twitched, the frail fingers curling into the sheets, trying to find purchase, trying to lift themselves. But it was no use. Her arms barely moved an inch before falling limp again, useless.

The pillow hovered over her face for just a second, suspended in the stale air between us. Her eyes, wide now, frantic, pleaded silently, the only fight left in her coming from her stare.

And then, I pressed it down.

The sound she made—a muffled, wet gurgle—wasn't loud. It was pathetic. The kind of sound you'd expect from someone who had long since run out of strength to protest. Her legs jerked beneath the blankets, kicking once, twice, before falling still. Her chest heaved, trying to draw in air that was no longer there.

Her hands reached up, weakly clawing at the pillow. I could feel her desperation through it, the tremor of her fingers brushing against my arm, but the pressure was steady, unrelenting. Her body bucked again, a final, involuntary reflex, but she was fading quickly now. Her heart—a frail, overworked thing—was losing the battle.

The room filled with the sound of her dying. Wet, gasping, struggling for air. The pillow absorbed most of it, but the sound still escaped, faint and awful, like a trapped animal whimpering in the dark.

Her legs twitched once more, and then nothing.

The quiet that followed was deeper than the silence that had come before. It felt final, absolute. I held the pillow there, even though I knew she was gone. The body underneath it was still. Lifeless.

I stepped back slowly, lifting the pillow from her face. Her eyes were still open, frozen in that last look of terror and helplessness. Her mouth hung slightly open, her lips a deep, unnatural blue, like she had tried to scream but never got the chance.

The room felt cold now, colder than it had before. The air stagnant, unmoving, as though death itself had settled into the space, filling it with its presence. The TV continued to flicker in the corner, indifferent to what had just happened.

I turned away from the bed, the dim light casting long shadows against the wall. There was no sound except the buzzing of the lights and the faint hum of the heater in the hallway outside.

No one would discover her until the morning. By then, she would be just another body to wheel away.

JUNE 27TH

Owen stood in the expansive living room of Granta Hall, a glass of whisky dangling from his fingertips as he gazed out over the grounds. The house felt different now—empty, haunted almost. Lila and the girls had gone, leaving an eerie stillness behind. It was as if the echoes of their lives had been packed up and carted away, leaving only the husk of a once vibrant home.

Footsteps echoed in the hallway, light and brisk, and soon Cass appeared in the doorway. She wore a fitted cream dress, her heels clicking purposefully on the polished floor. Her gaze swept over the room with a proprietorial air, as if she were already mentally redecorating it.

She crossed over to Owen, slipping an arm around his waist with a bright, slightly too-wide smile. "Contemplating our new empire?" she teased, her voice lilting with excitement.

"Our empire," he murmured, though the words felt hollow. He took a sip of his whisky, his gaze distant. There was something unsettling about Cass's confidence, her ease in this space that was meant to be a family home. Now, with her here, it felt strangely foreign.

Cass didn't seem to notice his lack of enthusiasm. She was

too busy taking in the details of the room, her eyes lingering on the dated furniture, the muted walls. She leaned back, sighing with exaggerated contentment. "I've been dreaming about this day for ages, you know. Granta Hall... all ours. Just think of the potential."

"It's definitely a new beginning," he said, though there was a weight to his words, an unspoken hesitation.

Cass turned to face him, a glint in her eyes. "Oh, and speaking of new beginnings," she said, her tone light, almost blasé, "I had my last test results today. Completely in the clear. No cancer." She fiddled with a sapphire earring that glinted from her earlobe.

"That's... that's wonderful, Cass," he said, noticing the earrings which looked very familiar. He remembered the tears, the anxious phone calls, her dramatic confessions of fear. Now, all of that seemed to have evaporated, dismissed with a casual wave of her hand.

"Yes, isn't it?" she replied, waving her hand dismissively. "I told you it would probably turn out to be nothing. These things usually do." She shrugged, as if the past few weeks of worry and whispered concerns had been nothing more than a minor inconvenience.

"Yes. It's wonderful news. Cass," he wondered if it was right to mention it, "where did you get those earrings?"

"Oh these," she twisted one round in her ear casually, "I found them in the bathroom."

"They belong to Lila."

"Finders keepers." She waved a hand in his direction. "She won't miss them, I'm sure."

Owen nodded slowly, a strange sensation creeping over him. He didn't recognise the woman standing in front of him. He remembered the nights she'd called him, her voice low and trembling, the way she'd clung to him, her eyes full of unshed tears. But now, looking at her, he wondered if any of it had been real, or if it had simply been a means to an end—a way to cement her place in his life.

Cass, oblivious to his thoughts, gave a little laugh. "All that fuss, and it turns out I'm perfectly fine. Really, the doctors have no idea how much they worry people with their endless tests and scans."

"I'm just glad you're all right," he said, though the words felt heavy. There was something about her flippant attitude that unsettled him, a nagging sense that he'd been drawn into something he didn't fully understand. Owen forced a smile, his gaze drifting back to the window.

"Me too," Cass said breezily, squeezing his hand. "Now that we can put all that behind us, we can focus on what really matters." She gestured around the room, her eyes lighting up as she took in the high ceilings, the expansive windows, the antique furniture. "I have so many ideas for this place. It could be... spectacular."

He looked around, taking in the familiar details—the worn leather armchair his father had loved, the hand-carved bookshelves lined with decades of family history, the muted, earth-toned walls that seemed to blend seamlessly with the countryside beyond. To him, Granta Hall had been more than just a house; it was a link to his past, a legacy he'd hoped to preserve.

But Cass's gaze was different. To her, it was a canvas, a project, something to mould and reshape in her own image. She walked across the room, her fingers trailing over the back of an armchair as she began to speak, her voice rich with anticipation.

"I've been thinking," she said, almost to herself. "We'll need to open up this space, bring in more light. Maybe floor-to-ceiling windows there," she pointed to the far wall, "and we'll need to update the furniture. Something modern, sleek. This old stuff... it doesn't really fit our style, does it?"

Owen shifted, discomfort prickling at him. "Our style?" he echoed, a faint edge to his voice.

Cass rolled her eyes, smiling indulgently as if he were a child clinging to an old toy. "Oh, Owen, don't be sentimental. We'll be creating something new here. We don't need to live in a museum." She laughed, a light, tinkling sound that somehow grated on his nerves.

"There's a lot of history here. I don't want to just... erase it."

Cass waved her hand dismissively. "We're not erasing it, darling. We're enhancing it. Updating it. Besides, a house like this should be alive, vibrant, a reflection of who we are now." Her gaze swept over the room, a glint of determination in her eyes. "Trust me, once it's done, you'll wonder how you ever lived with all this... colour."

Owen forced a chuckle, but his smile was strained. The thought of replacing the well-worn furniture with sleek, modern pieces—it felt like a betrayal, as though he were casting aside his own family in favour of something that didn't quite fit.

Cass seemed oblivious to his hesitation. She was already moving around the room, gesturing as she described her vision— a marble-topped table here, bold artwork on the walls to replace the faded watercolours Lila had chosen.

"We'll need to get rid of that dreadful old armchair," she said, pointing to his favourite seat by the fireplace. "It's practically falling apart, and it doesn't match anything."

Owen bristled, his hand tightening around his glass. "That was my father's chair."

Cass paused, glancing at him with a faintly exasperated smile. "I know, darling, but we should replace it with something that better reflects us."

Her words hung in the air, heavy with implication. Owen

stared at the armchair, remembering his father's laughter. It was as if she were asking him to sever the last ties he had.

But Cass didn't see it that way. She saw only an opportunity —a blank canvas onto which she could project her own desires, her own ambitions. And as she continued to talk, her voice bright with excitement, Owen felt a chill settle over him.

He forced himself to focus on her words, nodding along as she described her plans, but his mind was elsewhere, caught in a whirl of memories and doubts. He thought of Lila, of the life they'd shared, the warmth she'd brought to this house. Cass's laughter filled the room, a sound that felt hollow, discordant, as though it didn't quite belong here.

And then his phone buzzed, breaking through his reverie. He glanced down at the screen, his heart sinking as he saw the name of the retirement home flash up. He answered, his voice tense, a cold knot forming in his stomach.

The voice on the other end was gentle, compassionate, but he barely heard the words. His mother had passed in the night, they told him. She'd gone peacefully, they said. But the words didn't register. All he could feel was a hollow ache, a yawning emptiness that seemed to stretch out in front of him. He was losing everyone he loved, one by one.

When he lowered the phone, Cass was watching him, her face a mask of polite sympathy, though he could see the impatience in her eyes, the flicker of annoyance at the interruption.

"It's... my mother," he said, his voice barely a whisper. "She's gone."

Cass's expression softened, her hand reaching out to rest on his arm. "Oh, Owen, I'm so sorry," she murmured, but there was a detachment in her voice, a sense that her sympathy was more for formality than true feeling.

He nodded, his throat tight, and for a moment, he felt an

overwhelming urge to walk away, to retreat somewhere Cass couldn't follow. But he stood there, rooted to the spot, his mind swirling with memories and regrets.

"We'll get through this together," she said softly, her voice low and comforting, but there was something hollow in her tone.

JUNE 27TH

The smaller house felt foreign to Lila, though she'd lived here once, before everything had collapsed. The familiar creak of the front door, the faint scent of the worn wooden floors that had once made the place feel like home now felt like the roof was falling in. She hadn't planned on coming back here—had never imagined she would—but now, here they were, boxes stacked haphazardly in the hallway, the girls silent as they stood, looking around, as though they weren't sure what to do in this new version of their life. Even the dog was missing. Owen had insisted that Bongo stay with him, in the vain hope it would entice the girls to want to visit.

Molly and Ella were quiet, more so than usual. They hadn't said much on the drive over from Granta Hall, just watched the passing fields and buildings with blank expressions, their faces pale and unreadable. Lila wanted to ask them if they were all right, but the words kept catching in her throat.

The house was smaller, simpler—nothing like the sprawling, grand space they had grown used to in the countryside. Here, the walls were closer, the rooms fewer.

No one mentioned Owen.

He had stayed behind at Granta Hall. Lila couldn't stay in that place. She decided to move herself and the girls back into their old home on Humberstone Road. The plan had been to rent it out, and enjoy the income. Lila was now extremely grateful.

The front room felt smaller than it ever had. The sunlight streamed in through the bay window, casting a glow over the old armchair they had left behind. Lila's eyes drifted to the empty walls. It was nothing like the life they had before, but it was theirs now. And that had to be enough. Her heart was beating erratically, trying to catch up with everything that had crumbled around them.

Ella wandered over to the window, while Molly stood by the door, clutching her favourite stuffed rabbit tightly against her chest, her eyes wide and uncertain.

Lila took a deep breath, her chest tight. She knelt beside Molly, trying to summon a smile that didn't feel forced. "Do you like it, sweetheart? It's a little different from before, isn't it?"

Molly nodded but said nothing, her grip on the rabbit tightening.

Ella turned from the window, her expression distant. "Is this where we're going to live now?"

Lila hesitated, her throat constricting. "For a while, yes," she said softly. "It'll be nice. We can make it feel like home again."

But it didn't feel like home. It felt temporary, like everything else in their lives had become—uncertain, fragile. The rooms quieter than they had been before and the emptiness around them seemed to seep into everything, lingering in the air between them, unspoken.

Lila ran a hand through her hair, trying to shake off the heaviness that seemed to settle deeper with every passing moment. She looked around the room again, trying to picture how she could make this space warm, comforting, a place where they could rebuild. But it was hard to imagine anything resembling happiness in this house, the place they had once been a family.

The kitchen still smelled faintly of the fresh lick of paint that had been applied to make the place suitable to let. Lila moved through the space, her hand brushing over the cool surface of the counter as she mentally made a list of what needed to be done, what repairs she could make, how she could make it liveable for them.

The girls didn't follow her. They stayed in the front room, quiet and still, as if they weren't sure how to move through this new life yet. Lila listened to the soft sound of their feet shuffling on the floor, their whispers to each other too faint to hear. The weight of their silence pressed on her more than anything.

They hadn't asked about Owen, not once. And she hadn't offered any explanations. What could she say? That he had betrayed them? That everything had fallen apart? That the future was now uncertain?

Her phone buzzed in her pocket, but she ignored it. She didn't need to check to know it wasn't Owen. He hadn't called. He hadn't texted. They had exchanged almost no words when she'd left, and whatever remained between them now was broken.

Lila leaned against the counter, her hands gripping the edges as she stared at the chipped tiles on the floor. She could hear the faint murmur of Molly and Ella talking softly still.

The truth sat heavy on her chest, unspoken but unavoidable. She didn't know how to make this house a home for them. She didn't know how to make any of it okay.

Outside, the street was quiet, the sound of distant traffic a low hum in the background. The old neighbourhood was a far cry from the vast countryside they had grown used to, with its rolling hills and sprawling green fields.

Lila sighed, walking back to the front room where the girls were still standing by the window.

"How about we unpack a bit? Maybe put your things in your rooms, and then we can order some dinner? What do you think?"

Ella shrugged, her fingers tracing patterns on the glass. Molly nodded quietly but didn't move.

Lila's heart sank. The girls were waiting, just like her. Waiting for something to change, for something to make sense again. But all she could offer them was this—this small house, this quiet room, and the distant hope that maybe, just maybe, they could find a way forward.

JUNE 27TH

That evening, the smell of the Chinese takeaway filled the small living room, the faint scent of soy sauce and ginger mingling with the musty air of a house that had been sitting unused for a few months. Packing boxes were stacked haphazardly against the walls, the remnants of their half-hearted attempt at unpacking scattered across the floor. Lila sat on the floor with Molly and Ella, the three of them surrounding the plastic containers of food, but no one seemed particularly interested in eating.

Molly was quiet, her fork pushing the noodles around her plate in slow, absent motions, her gaze distant as she stared at the uneven floorboards. Ella, however, was more restless, shifting in place, her frustration barely contained. Lila could feel the tension building between them, the unspoken questions hanging in the air like thick fog, suffocating in its heaviness.

Lila took a small bite of her rice, her stomach too knotted to hold much more, and glanced at the boxes in the corner of the room. They had unpacked the essentials but the house still felt as though it belonged to someone else. The walls were bare, the smell of dust still clinging to the furniture. It wasn't home—not anymore, and not yet again.

Ella set her container down with a clatter, her voice sharp and cutting through the silence. "Why did we have to move back here? Why are *we* the ones who left the big house?"

The question hung in the air like a knife, and for a moment, Lila didn't respond. She had known this conversation was coming—had known the girls would ask—but she still hadn't prepared herself for it. She couldn't muster the energy to answer in a way that wouldn't feel like another blow.

"We planned to rent this out when we moved to the countryside," Lila said softly, her voice steady despite the weight pressing down on her chest. "And now... we've moved back. It's where we lived before."

Ella huffed, crossing her arms over her chest, her anger simmering just beneath the surface. "But why are *we* the ones who had to move? Why couldn't we stay in the country house?"

Lila glanced at Molly, who remained silent, still picking at her food, her face impassive. The tension between the two sisters was palpable, but Molly said nothing, letting Ella's frustration speak for them both.

"We had to come back here," Lila said, her voice tight with exhaustion. She hadn't slept well in weeks, not since everything had unravelled. The move back—all of it had drained her completely. "The tenants who were renting this place needed to leave so we could return."

"But why did *we* have to leave the big house?" Ella asked again, her voice louder this time. "Why did Dad stay there?"

Lila felt a sharp pain in her chest at the mention of Owen, but she swallowed it down. The girls hadn't mentioned him much since they'd returned to the Cambridge house, but his absence was a constant, heavy shadow over them all. They hadn't asked why he had stayed behind, why they had moved without him, but it was clear Ella had questions—questions Lila wasn't sure how to answer.

"There's a lot you don't understand," Lila said, her voice barely above a whisper. "But I don't want to get into it right now."

Ella's eyes flashed with frustration. "That's always your answer. Why won't you just explain what's going on?"

Lila felt the fatigue wash over her, pulling at her limbs, at her very will to engage. She didn't have the energy for this, not tonight. She wanted to explain, to give Ella the answers she was demanding, but how could she explain the truth when she was still struggling to make sense of it herself?

She caught Ella's gaze, her voice soft but firm. "Ella, you'll be going off to university soon. You've got your whole life ahead of you. You don't need to worry about all this."

Ella's face reddened, her hands curling into fists in her lap. "That's not the point, Mum! You can't just keep pretending like this doesn't matter, like everything's okay. Why did we have to move back to this tiny house? Why did *he* get to stay?"

The silence that followed was suffocating, the weight of everything unsaid pressing down on Lila like a lead blanket. She didn't want to tell Ella that she had seen it—*them*—in the flesh, that it wasn't just whispers or suspicions. She didn't want to say the words aloud and break her daughter's heart any more than it already had been.

"I know you're angry," Lila said, her voice breaking slightly. "But right now, we just need to focus on settling in."

Ella's phone buzzed suddenly, breaking the quiet, and she glanced at the screen. Her face hardened as she saw the name flashing, but after a moment's hesitation, she answered, her voice cautious. "Dad?"

Lila's heart sank, her grip tightening on her plate. She hadn't expected Owen to call. She looked over at Ella, trying to gauge the conversation from her daughter's expression.

"Yeah... okay." Ella's voice wavered slightly, her bravado slipping. "When did it happen?" She listened for a few moments, then swallowed, nodding as if he could see her. "All right. Yeah, I understand. Bye."

Ella lowered the phone slowly, her face pale, her hands clenched tightly around the device. For a moment, she just stared down at her lap, her expression a mix of confusion and sadness.

"Ella?" Lila's voice was soft, but filled with concern. "What's happened?"

Ella looked up, her eyes shining with unshed tears. "It's Grandma Margaret... she's gone. Dad said she passed away last night."

The room fell silent, the air thick with the weight of the news. Lila felt a pang of grief, a loss that was unexpected but sharp all the same. Margaret had never been warm or loving toward her, but she was still family. She was the girls' grandmother, a constant figure in their lives. And now, she was gone.

But beneath the sadness, there was something else—a bitter twist of hurt. Owen had called Ella directly, bypassing her entirely. He hadn't thought to tell Lila first, to break the news together as parents. Instead, he'd gone straight to Ella, burdening their daughter with something that was too heavy for her young shoulders.

"Are you all right?" Lila asked gently, reaching out to place a comforting hand on Ella's knee.

Ella nodded, but her eyes were distant. "I don't know. It just feels... weird. Like, I should be sad, but I don't know if I really am."

Lila nodded, understanding the conflicted feelings that

came with Margaret's passing. Margaret had been a difficult woman, and her relationship with Ella and Molly had always been complicated, marked more by formality than genuine affection.

Molly looked up, her face crumpling in confusion. "Grandma Margaret is... gone?"

Ella nodded, her voice quieter now. "Yeah. Dad said it was peaceful."

The silence stretched, and Lila struggled to find the right words, the ones that would soothe her daughters even as she grappled with her own feelings. She wanted to be strong for them, to shield them from the raw pain she felt at the way Owen had handled things. But she couldn't deny the ache in her chest, the feeling of being left out, of being shut out of something that should have been shared between them.

"It's okay to feel confused, or even not to feel anything at all," Lila said gently, brushing a strand of hair behind Ella's ear. "Grief is... complicated. And Grandma Margaret... well, she was complicated too."

Ella gave a small, sad smile, nodding in agreement. "She was always a bit... hard to get close to. But still, it's weird to think of her not being there."

Molly shifted closer, leaning against Lila's shoulder. "Are we going to have to go to the funeral?" she asked, her voice small.

Lila hesitated, not wanting to make promises she couldn't keep. "I'm not sure yet, love. We'll... we'll talk about it."

She looked down at her daughters, her heart aching for them, wishing she could protect them from the harsh realities of loss and fractured families. But she knew, deep down, that she couldn't shield them forever. All she could do was be there for them, as much as they would let her.

Ella shifted, placing her phone aside, a frown creasing her forehead. "Why didn't he tell you first, Mum?"

Lila swallowed, feeling the sting of Ella's question hit harder than she'd expected. "I... I don't know, Ella," she admitted, her voice barely above a whisper. "Maybe he thought you'd want to hear it from him."

But even as she spoke, she felt the bitterness rise, an anger she hadn't wanted to feel. Owen had once been her partner, her confidant, and yet he'd chosen to bypass her completely, as if she no longer had any role in their family, as if she were no longer worthy of sharing in these moments.

"I wish he'd called you first," Ella muttered, a trace of resentment in her voice.

Lila forced a smile, brushing her hand gently over Ella's arm. "It's all right, love. We'll get through this together, okay?"

Ella nodded, but the tension lingered, an unspoken weight pressing down on them all. Lila knew that this wasn't just about Margaret's passing; it was about everything they had lost, the fracture that had split their lives apart and left them struggling to find a way forward.

They finished their meal in silence, each lost in their own thoughts, the Chinese takeaway growing cold as the weight of grief and betrayal settled over them.

As much as she wanted to be strong, to hold everything together for her daughters, she couldn't ignore the hurt that Owen's actions had caused. He was no longer her partner, no longer her confidant. She was on the outside now, left to pick up the pieces of a life that had once been whole.

And as she sat there, staring at the cold remains of their meal, she realised that this was her new reality—a life defined by loss and the slow, painful process of rebuilding. She had her daughters, her home, and the fragile hope that somehow, they would find their way through the darkness together.

But deep down, she knew that some scars would never heal, and some wounds would always linger, a reminder of the life they had lost and the family they had once been.

"Are we going to be okay, Mum?" Molly said, her voice small and tentative.

Lila opened her eyes and looked at her youngest daughter, her heart breaking all over again at the uncertainty in Molly's voice. Molly, who had always been quieter, more introspective, was now looking to her for reassurance she wasn't sure she could give. Lila wanted to promise that things would get better, that they would find a way to rebuild, but she didn't have the strength to make that promise. Not yet.

"We'll figure it out," Lila said softly, brushing a strand of Molly's hair behind her ear. "One step at a time."

Molly nodded, but Lila could see the uncertainty still lingering in her eyes. There was no magic fix for this, no way to patch up the hurt that had been caused, and no way to make this new, smaller life feel whole.

Lila leaned forward, resting her elbows on her knees, staring down at the half-eaten boxes of food, the mess of their lives scattered around them. She was too tired to face it all, too worn down to think about what came next. All she could do was sit there, waiting for the pieces to fall wherever they would.

Ella's mouth set in a hard line, but she said nothing as she crossed the room to grab her phone so she could message her friends and continue to ignore her mother.

The tension in the room thickened as Lila sat, her legs drawn up under her, staring at the half-eaten takeaway containers scattered around them. Ella hadn't left the room after all. She stood by the window now, arms folded, her back rigid as she stared out into the darkening evening. Molly sat beside Lila, her hands fiddling with her fork, the noodles on her plate untouched.

Lila sighed, knowing there was no way to avoid the conversation any longer. She shifted her weight slightly, her exhaustion dragging at her every movement, but the reality of their new life was already beginning to weigh more heavily than she had anticipated.

"I need to talk to you both about something," Lila started quietly, glancing between her daughters. "With everything that's happened… I'll need to go back to work now that I'm no longer working with your dad."

The words felt heavier than she expected, sinking into the quiet room like stones dropping into water. She hadn't worked properly since moving to the countryside, and the thought of returning to the grind filled her with a sense of failure, though she tried not to let it show.

Ella turned from the window, her expression unreadable, but there was a hardness in her eyes. "And what job is that going to be?" she asked, her voice sharper than necessary.

Lila bit her lip, willing herself not to rise to the provocation. "I don't know yet. I'm going to start looking as soon as I can."

Ella's gaze was unwavering, her voice laced with something bitter. "You've only ever worked for Dad in the last few years. Are you going to be a receptionist again?"

The words stung. Lila felt the bite of them deep in her chest. It was true—she had worked for Owen, managing his office, organising his appointments, taking calls for his marketing business. But she had done it to support their life together, to help the family. And now it felt like a weakness, something Ella could throw back at her as a reminder of how much had changed, of how dependent she had been on Owen.

Lila tried to steady herself, but the exhaustion in her bones made it hard to fight back. "I don't know what I'll do yet," she said softly, her voice faltering just a little. "But I'll find something. I'll make it work."

Molly, sensing the tension between them, piped up in her small voice, "Mum, I can take myself to school now. I'm old enough."

Lila's heart sank as she looked at her nine-year-old. Of course, Molly would want to be independent, to take control of something when so much of their life had spiralled out of control. But the thought of Molly navigating the school run on her own made Lila's chest tighten. She wasn't ready to let go of that part of their routine—not yet.

"We'll see, Molly," Lila said softly, trying to sound reasonable. "It's just... a lot's changing right now. And I'll need Ella's help."

Ella let out a frustrated sigh, crossing her arms tighter over her chest. "So, what? I'm supposed to be Molly's babysitter now? Just because you need to go back to work?"

Lila flinched at the edge in Ella's voice, the thinly veiled accusation that Lila was failing them, even in this. "I'm asking for your help, Ella," Lila said quietly, her voice pleading. "Just until we figure things out. It's not permanent."

Ella shook her head, her expression hardening. "It's always 'figure things out', Mum. But we wouldn't have to if you hadn't—"

She stopped abruptly, biting her tongue, but the unsaid words hung in the air between them. They both knew what she had been about to say. If Lila hadn't caught Owen and *her*, if everything hadn't fallen apart. If they hadn't been forced to leave the big house and come back to this small, cramped place.

Molly shifted uncomfortably beside her, sensing the tension she didn't fully understand. "I don't mind if Ella doesn't take me to school," she mumbled, her eyes downcast. "I can go by myself."

Lila closed her eyes for a moment, feeling the weight of it all crashing down on her—her daughters' silent disappointment;

Ella's anger, Molly's quiet attempts to grow up too fast. She felt like she was failing them, like every decision she made pushed them further into the chaos that had become their life.

"I know this isn't what any of us wanted," Lila said, her voice barely above a whisper. "But we'll get through it. We'll figure it out. I just need you both to help me right now."

Ella didn't respond. She turned back towards the window, her shoulders tense, her arms still folded across her chest. Molly stayed silent, picking at her food, her movements slow and distracted.

Lila sat there, staring at the takeaway containers, the boxes, the remnants of the life they had tried to build now scattered in disarray around them. The exhaustion was pulling her down, deeper, into a sense of failure she couldn't shake.

She had lost Owen, lost the life they had built together, and now, she was losing her grip on her daughters. Everything was slipping away, piece by piece.

Lila leaned back, closing her eyes, trying to hold back the tears threatening to spill over. She didn't have the energy to fight this. Not tonight.

SHE

The air was thick with humidity, pressing against my skin like a cold, heavy hand. I stood in the shadows at the edge of the churchyard, hidden behind the gnarled branches of an old yew tree, its twisted limbs reaching out like skeletal fingers. The ground beneath my feet was sodden, sucking at my boots with every slight shift of weight, but I didn't move. I wanted to watch.

A thin veil of mist clung to the ground, swirling around the gravestones, making the few mourners gathered by the open grave look like fading figures from another world. They stood huddled together in their dark coats, shivering against the cold, their heads bowed under the weight of both the weather and their silence. It was such a pitiful sight—a handful of sad, shrunken shapes in the mist. The sort of funeral no one would remember, for a person no one had cared for.

A slow smile crept across my face.

The priest mumbled something, his voice low and lost in the sticky air, barely more than a murmur. His words fell flat, like they, too, didn't want to be here. I could just make out the movement of his lips, but the words themselves didn't matter. No prayer or blessing could undo a lifetime of poison. The coffin, slick with rain, was slowly lowered into the gaping mouth of the earth, swallowed whole by the grave. A dull, hollow thud sounded as it hit the bottom, and I watched the mourners flinch, their shivering intensifying, as if the weight of finality was too much to bear.

A crow swooped low from the ominous sky, its wings a sharp, jagged silhouette against the mist. It cawed once, a harsh, mocking sound that echoed through the churchyard. I watched it land on a nearby gravestone, tilting its head as it stared at the pitiful gathering, black eyes gleaming like polished stones. It was as if the bird knew. It was as if it, too, had come to witness this end and was just as satisfied as I was.

There were fewer than a dozen people by the grave. I counted them, one by one. They shifted uncomfortably, casting quick glances around, as if they wished to be anywhere but here. They wore their sadness like a mask, but I could see through it. I could sense the relief in the way their shoulders sagged, the way they avoided looking at the coffin. None of them would mourn for long, if they ever mourned at all.

Good.

The mist curled around me, cold and heavy, but I stayed rooted to the spot, watching. My breath came in slow, measured puffs, blending into the mist as I stood in silence. The grave, now partially filled with dirt, looked like a wound in the earth—a wound that would soon be covered over, forgotten, as though it had never been there at all. The mourners lingered, but only out of some sense of obligation, their hands thrust deep into their coat pockets, their faces pale and drawn.

They wouldn't stay long. They couldn't wait to leave.

The crow cawed again, louder this time, and it made a few of the mourners shift uneasily, their eyes flicking towards the dark shape perched on the gravestone. The sky above was a blanket of grey, heavy and oppressive, the kind of sky that crushed you *beneath its weight. Another crow joined the first, then a third. They circled the air, black feathers cutting through the mist like blades.*

I felt a chill run through me, but it wasn't from the cold. It was from the satisfaction, the finality of it all. I watched the mourners turn their backs on the grave, shuffling away slowly, almost reluctantly, as if they feared they'd be judged for leaving too soon. But they were ready to go. I could see it in the way they moved, eager to escape the cold, the damp, and the memory of the person they had come to bury.

The priest stayed a little longer, muttering something over the grave before he, too, retreated, his black robes sweeping through the mist like a shadow. The crows cawed in unison as he passed, their calls harsh and unforgiving, like the judgement that hung in the air.

And then it was just the grave, sinking into the earth, the coffin now hidden beneath a thin layer of dirt. The mist thickened, swallowing the scene, erasing the figures from view as if they had never been there. As if this whole, pathetic display had never taken place.

I didn't feel sorrow. I didn't feel loss. I felt something darker. Something more satisfying.

The wind picked up slightly, rustling the wet leaves of the yew tree above me, and I turned, my back to the grave, my heart cold and steady in my chest. The sound of the crows followed me as I walked, their calls merging with the wind, the mist closing in around me like a shroud.

No one would remember this day. No one would remember them.

And that was exactly how it should be.

JULY 11TH

Owen stood in the doorway of what had once been Ella's bedroom, now unrecognisable. The room smelled of fresh paint—something crisp and cool, like the faint scent of a new beginning—and Cass had replaced the soft turquoise walls with a stark, modern grey. The space, which had once been cluttered with books, stuffed animals, and the personal chaos of a teenager's life, was now a sleek, minimal home gym. The treadmill gleamed under the low light, the mirrored walls reflecting the pristine order Cass had imposed on the house.

He shifted uncomfortably, the feel of the new carpet beneath his feet unfamiliar, too plush, too soft. Nothing about this room resembled his house anymore. It didn't smell like home; it smelled like change and something too sharp to place. The house had become Cass's project, and though Owen had agreed to most of the changes, he couldn't shake the feeling that the place was slowly erasing the memories of the life he used to have.

Cass appeared at the door, smiling as she crossed the threshold into her new gym, her eyes scanning the room with a satisfied glint. "It's coming together, isn't it?" she said, her voice bright, as if she hadn't noticed his discomfort. "I've ordered some weights and a yoga mat. It's going to be perfect."

Owen nodded absently, though he couldn't help but feel the hollow emptiness of the space. He stared at the treadmill, wondering what Ella would say if she ever saw this room. Not that she ever would—Ella had stopped speaking to him altogether. She hadn't returned his texts, hadn't answered his calls. After everything had come out, she had shut him down completely. The last time he had seen her, she had walked past him, her eyes cold and distant, as if he were nothing more than a stranger.

Molly... well, that was thankfully different. She'd still see him sometimes. She didn't like to stay at the house and preferred to meet him for lunch or a walk in the park, somewhere neutral, somewhere far away from Cass. Every time he brought up the possibility of her staying over, Molly would shake her head, her quiet but firm refusal a painful reminder that nothing was as it had been.

Cass didn't seem to notice the strain. If she did, she never let on. She had moved in with an energy that didn't waver, redecorating the house like it was hers to transform. It was hers now, in a way. The rooms that had once held his daughters' laughter and the warmth of family now felt cold, sharp, each corner curated by Cass's aesthetic—minimal, sleek, utterly removed from what Lila had built.

"I thought we could put bunk beds in one of the spare rooms," Cass continued, breezing past him as she gestured down the hallway. "You know, in case the girls ever decide to stay. It makes more sense than keeping two rooms just for them. They're not here often enough to need that much space."

Owen winced at her words but said nothing. Cass didn't understand. She couldn't. The girls *had* needed those rooms.

Once, this had been their home. And now? Now it was just a house that didn't belong to any of them.

The spare room Cass was referring to had once been Molly's—a bright bedroom with warm yellow walls that Molly had insisted on painting herself. Now it was stripped bare, waiting for the bunk beds Cass had chosen, as if the children who had once filled the space were nothing more than occasional visitors.

The warm, inviting space of the dining room that had once been filled with family photos and worn furniture now felt clinical, as if he had walked into the pages of a design magazine. Cass's influence was everywhere—sleek black furniture, minimalistic art, and harsh metallic accents that seemed to absorb any warmth the house had left.

Gone were the photos of Ella and Molly. The cluttered shelves that used to house the girls' books and belongings were now stripped bare, replaced by expensive sculptures and statement pieces that looked beautiful but felt lifeless. Even the walls had been painted a stark white, erasing any trace of the muted colours that had once made the house feel lived in, welcoming.

He felt like an intruder in his own home, a guest in a showpiece that bore no resemblance to the life he'd built here with Lila and the girls. Cass swept past him, her heels clicking on the marble floors, carrying a box filled with yet another piece of décor. She barely acknowledged him as she placed a glass vase on the mantel, adjusting it to catch the exact right angle of light.

"What do you think?" she asked, finally turning to him, her eyes gleaming with pride. "Isn't it stunning?"

Owen forced a smile, trying to ignore the hollow feeling gnawing at his insides. "It's... different," he managed, his voice sounding strange in his own ears.

Cass laughed, brushing a hand over his arm. "Different is exactly what we need, Owen. We're building a new life here. Out with the old, in with the new." She moved over to the sofa, adjusting the cushions with a meticulousness that bordered on obsession. "I know change can be hard, but just wait until it's all done. You'll love it."

He nodded, but as he looked around, he couldn't shake the sense of loss, the feeling that he was slowly being pushed out of his own life. Cass was so determined to leave her mark on everything, to erase every trace of the family that had once lived here, and it left him feeling unmoored, adrift in a sea of cold, impersonal surfaces.

After a moment, he cleared his throat, grasping for something to ground him. "How's your mum doing, by the way?" he asked, trying to sound casual. He realised, with a pang of discomfort, that he'd never even met the woman. For all the talk Cass had made of her, she was more of a ghost than a real person in his life.

Cass glanced over, her expression brightening. "Oh, she's fantastic now. Completely recovered. She's moved in with my brother in Scotland, actually. A fresh start, just like us."

"Your brother?" Owen repeated, surprised. "I didn't know you had family in Scotland."

"Oh, you know, we're not exactly close," Cass replied with a casual shrug, waving a hand dismissively. "He's a bit of a recluse. But Mum's thrilled to be with him, and it takes the pressure off me, you know? I was thinking I'd have to be the one to look after her, but she's settled, and it's all worked out perfectly."

Owen nodded, feeling an odd sense of detachment from the conversation. He hadn't met her mother, hadn't even spoken to her. Everything Cass had told him about her family felt vague, as though they were characters in a story she'd crafted rather than real people with lives and personalities of their own.

Cass moved on, barely giving him time to process what she'd said. "Oh, and I've filed for divorce from Mark," she announced breezily, her tone as light as if she were discussing the weather. "It was long overdue, to be honest. I should have done it years ago."

Owen felt a jolt at the mention of her husband. He realised, with a creeping sense of unease, that he'd never met Mark either. Cass had spoken about him in passing, always framing him as some distant, irrelevant figure from her past, but there was an almost surreal quality to it now. Cass's life before him seemed like a series of half-finished sketches, details that never quite came into focus.

"Well... I hope that goes smoothly," he said slowly, feeling unsure of what else to say. He found himself wondering, for the first time, why he had never questioned her more, why he had taken everything she'd said at face value without looking deeper.

Cass smiled, unfazed, and stepped back to admire the living room. "It's a relief, really. A fresh start is exactly what I need."

Owen swallowed, looking around at the 'fresh start' she'd imposed on his home. The sleek furniture, the colourless walls, the absence of anything that held meaning or memory—it felt like a shell, beautiful on the surface but hollow underneath.

He forced himself to focus on her, searching for some hint of the woman he'd fallen for, but all he could see was a stranger, someone who had taken over his life with a determination that left no room for the past.

For a moment, he wanted to ask her if she remembered Ella and Molly, if she understood the pain he felt at seeing their lives wiped away, their photos and mementos relegated to boxes in the attic. But he knew the answer before he'd even spoken. Cass didn't care about what had come before. To her, everything was disposable, replaceable, part of a life she was determined to leave behind.

And as he looked at her, he felt an uncomfortable truth settling over him—a realisation that chilled him to the core. Cass wasn't just transforming his home; she was transforming him, reshaping him into someone he didn't recognise, someone who had willingly let go of everything he'd once held dear.

A fresh start. That's what she kept calling it.

But for Owen, it felt like the beginning of something far darker—a life stripped of warmth, of family, of everything that had once made him whole.

Everything looked perfect, just the way Cass wanted it—stylish, coordinated, devoid of the mismatched charm Lila had once created.

SHE

I stand in front of the mirror, staring at the reflection that barely looks like me anymore. My hair is wild, a tangled mess, falling around my face in knotted clumps. Strands stick out in every direction, some glued to my skin from the heat of sweat and fury. Clothes—what's left of them—hang in shreds, torn apart by my own hands in a fit of something I can't even describe. Rage? No, it's more than that. It's power.

The room around me is a battlefield. The glass from the picture frames lies shattered on the floor, glittering shards scattered across the cream-coloured carpet, which is now stained with the red wine I took so much pleasure in pouring slowly onto it. It seeps into the thick pile, spreading like blood from an open wound. The bottles sit on their sides, emptied in some wild moment that I can't quite recall, but the aftermath is beautiful in its chaos.

The mirror in front of me is cracked, long jagged lines cutting across the surface, distorting the reflection. I can't even tell what's real anymore—the fragments of me that I can still see or the broken, twisted pieces that are reflected back. But it doesn't matter. In the brokenness, there's a kind of freedom. The cracks make sense. They make more sense than the smooth, perfect glass that was here before.

Red lipstick is smeared across the mirror in uneven, angry strokes. The lipstick is thick, bright, a violent shade that cuts through the reflection like a scream. The words—if there were words—are smeared now, unreadable. It doesn't matter what they were. I understand their meaning. Chaos. Ruin. Liberation.

I step back, surveying the destruction I've created. Shoes are scattered everywhere—high heels flung in every direction. Some lie tipped over, others are propped up against walls and furniture like they were thrown with force, with intention. Once so pristine, so polished, now discarded in the wreckage.

The wine, the lipstick, the torn clothes—it all feels so... right. Like I've finally let go of something that's been holding me in place for too long. I've broken out of the cage. I've let the mess spill out of me and into this room. There's no need to hide it anymore, no need to pretend. This is the truth of who I am, and I'm not ashamed.

I look back at the mirror, at the twisted reflection staring back at me through the cracks. Her smile is wicked, sharp, full of something dark and triumphant. I smile back. It's me. More me than I've ever felt before. The version of me that I've kept buried, hidden beneath layers of pretence, is standing here, in the open.

I smooth down my clothes, adjusting them as though it matters, as though I'm about to step out onto a stage for the world to see. And in a way, I am. It's a new act now. A new performance. One where I must keep up appearances.

Carefully, I step over the broken glass, feeling it crunch beneath my feet, careful not to cut myself. It feels good, being careful in the chaos. Being in control amidst the ruin.

I glide across the room, my bare feet barely making a sound on the wine-soaked carpet. It's almost peaceful now, this destruction. The room looks beautiful in its brokenness, like it was always meant to be this way. All the mess, the ruin—it's a reflection of what was always inside me, hidden away, waiting for its moment.

With one last look at the shattered room, I reach for the door. The handle feels cool and smooth against my hand. I turn it slowly, savouring the moment. Then I step through, into the hallway, and close the door gently behind me.

It's done.

And I smile.

AUGUST 18TH

After an intruder had broken into the house and ransacked the place, Cass had insisted on redecorating everything. She moved around the house with a certain satisfaction.

"This house is made for a Christmas drinks party," Cass said, turning to Owen with a bright smile. "You know, something really nice. Champagne, hors d'oeuvres, maybe even hire a pianist. It'll be the perfect way to show off the house. What do you think?"

Owen nodded absent-mindedly, though the idea of a party felt strange. He hadn't seen the girls for more than a few hours here and there, and the thought of celebrating anything felt hollow. But Cass was already deep into her plans, talking excitedly about guests, caterers, and invitations, as if Christmas was just another rung on the social ladder.

Cass crossed the room and kissed him on the cheek, her eyes sparkling. "I was also thinking we could talk about presents," she said, her tone teasing but serious.

Owen glanced at her, feeling something shift in the air. "Presents?" he repeated, trying to keep his tone light, though something in her expression made him uneasy.

Cass sat down beside him, leaning in closer, her hand resting on his knee. "Yes," she said, her voice softer now. "I know what I want this Christmas."

Owen raised an eyebrow, trying to smile, but the tension in his chest grew. "What's that?"

Her hand tightened on his knee, her voice dropping to a whisper. "I want a baby."

The words landed like a punch to the gut. Owen's body tensed, and his throat felt raw. He pulled back slightly, the air between them growing thick and uncomfortable. He forced a smile, but his mind raced, panic rising in his chest. "A baby? Cass, I... I'm already a father."

Cass's eyes darkened, her expression then softening but with a strange kind of determination. "I know you're already a father, Owen. But this would be different. This would be *our* baby. I want a family with you."

Owen sat in silence, the weight of Cass's words pressing down on him like a lead blanket. She hadn't looked at him since she'd said it—*I want a baby*—and the room, which had felt too cold and too unfamiliar with its fresh paint and new decorations, now felt suffocating. He could see the summer sunshine beaming through the window, but even its warmth wouldn't reach him.

Cass stood by the window, her back to him. She was quiet for a moment, and Owen felt the tension in the air shift as she took a deep breath.

"There's more you don't know," she said, her voice barely above a whisper. "Something I've never talked about... not with anyone. Not even you."

Owen felt his chest tighten as he turned toward her. Cass had always seemed so composed, so controlled, like someone who could bulldoze through life without looking back. But now, she was unravelling, her vulnerability laid bare in a way that made Owen realise just how little he really knew about her.

Cass turned to face him, and her eyes—usually so bright, so sharp—were now filled with something darker, something sadder. She didn't meet his gaze at first, her hands twisting nervously in the fabric of her sweater. Then she spoke, and the words hung heavy between them.

"My father," she began, her voice trembling slightly, "he... he killed himself when I was young."

The air in the room shifted again, colder now, the fire's crackle distant and faint. Owen's heart lurched in his chest. He hadn't expected this.

Cass wrapped her arms around herself, as if trying to hold herself together. "I was nine years old," she continued, her voice small and hollow. "He was a drunk. Violent when he wanted to be. But then there were days when he was... charming, even. Days when I thought maybe things would be different. But those days never lasted. One night, I heard him shouting with my mum. They were always fighting, and she was always trying to protect me from him, even though she couldn't protect herself."

Cass's voice wavered, and she looked down at the floor, blinking back tears. "That night, I heard a gunshot. I ran downstairs, and... there he was. Lying on the floor in the kitchen, blood everywhere. My mum was just standing there, screaming. I didn't understand what had happened at first, but I knew—I *knew* he was gone."

Owen's breath hitched. He hadn't known any of this. The strong, confident woman he knew had been shaped by something so dark, so devastating, that he could hardly reconcile it with the Cass he had met.

Cass swallowed hard, blinking quickly as if trying to hold back the tears that threatened to spill over. "My mum... she fell apart after that. I had to grow up fast. There was no one to look after me, not really. I had to look after *her*. And after a while, she stopped even pretending to care. She blamed me. I think she needed someone to blame, and I was the easiest target. So, I ran away when I turned eighteen. I never looked back."

Owen didn't know what to say. His throat tightened as he watched Cass struggle with the memories she had clearly buried for years, memories she had built her entire life around forgetting. And here she was, sharing them with him, her voice raw and broken in a way he had never heard before.

She wiped at her eyes quickly, her vulnerability like a fragile thread she was trying to keep from snapping. "I thought I'd left it all behind," she whispered. "But it never really goes away. The fear, the anger, the feeling that no one could ever love me for who I was. I've spent my entire life trying to control everything, to make sure no one else could ever hurt me again."

Cass took another deep breath, her voice steadying, but still soft, still fragile. "Then I met Mark. And at first, I thought he was the answer to everything I was running from. But he wasn't. He was a bully, controlling me in every way. He didn't want children because he didn't want me to have anything that could take my attention away from him. And when I got sick... he didn't care if I could have kids or not. He didn't even care if I survived."

Owen's heart twisted painfully. He hadn't known the depth of what Cass had been through. He'd seen glimpses of her pain, of the walls she had built around herself, but this was different. This was everything—the foundation of her life, her fears, her need to be loved in a way she had never experienced.

"I had ovarian cancer, Owen," she said quietly, her voice breaking slightly. "It was early stages, and I was lucky. But when I had the surgery... it was always there in the back of my mind, the thought that I might never have children. And now,

I'm getting older. I'm almost forty. This might be my last chance to be a mother."

Owen's hands felt heavy as they rested on his knees. He had never seen Cass like this—so open, so vulnerable. She wasn't the sharp, confident woman who had moved into his house and changed everything. She was fragile, haunted by a past that had nearly destroyed her, and now all she wanted was something that would help her heal. Something she could love and protect, the way no one had loved and protected her.

"I'm sorry, Cass," Owen whispered, his voice strained with the weight of everything she had shared. "I didn't know."

Cass shook her head, wiping her eyes again. "No one knows. I've spent my whole life keeping it buried. But... I want something real now, Owen. I want to be a mother. I want a family of my own."

Owen's heart pounded in his chest. He understood her pain now, the desperation behind her desire for a child. But he was already a father. He already had two daughters who barely spoke to him. The idea of bringing another child into this fractured world felt overwhelming, terrifying.

"I don't know if I can do this," he said quietly, the words falling heavy between them.

Cass's eyes met his, the raw vulnerability still there, but mixed with something else—hope. "Just... think about it," she whispered. "Please."

The room felt suffocating, the fresh paint on the walls reminding Owen of how much had changed, how much had been lost. Cass had laid everything bare, and yet, he still wasn't sure he could give her what she wanted.

He nodded slowly, not trusting himself to speak, not sure what else to say.

Cass turned back to the window, wiping at her face one last time.

Owen wasn't sure if he could do this, wasn't sure if he could start over. But for the first time, he understood why Cass needed it so badly. And that made it harder to say no.

Owen sat at the edge of the sofa, his hands clasped tightly between his knees. His face was expressionless, eyes fixed somewhere in the middle distance, as if he were watching something no one else could see. Across from him, Cass perched delicately on an armchair, her legs crossed and fingers absently tracing the edge of her sleeve. She had chosen her words carefully so far, but silence had stretched between them for too long.

"Owen," she started softly, voice almost hesitant, "I know she wasn't... the easiest person. But this is still a loss. You can let yourself feel it."

He didn't look at her. "I don't know what I'm supposed to feel," he muttered, the words flat and devoid of weight. "She's gone, Cass. Just... gone."

Cass shifted slightly, leaning forward. "You don't have to pretend with me. I know you were never that close, but she was still your mother. She raised you; she was there. That matters." Her voice softened. "I'm sure there's some part of you that feels something."

He let out a sharp, humourless laugh, though his face barely registered it. "Raised me? She was a shadow in my life, Cass. She was always around but never really there. Just watching from the sidelines, judging, criticising..."

Cass reached out and touched his knee, her fingers light but insistent. "I know. But now... now it's over. And maybe that means something too."

He closed his eyes, the weight of her words sinking in. There was relief, an unexpected lightness in her absence, and he wasn't sure what to make of it. The memories of her cold, assessing gaze, her passive-aggressive barbs, all seemed to drift away, as if they had lost their hold over him. And yet, an emptiness remained, like a room he didn't know what to do with.

"She didn't like me," he said finally, voice almost a whisper.

Cass nodded, her face a mask of sympathy, though he noticed the subtle glint of something else in her eyes — maybe satisfaction. She, too, had felt Margaret's coldness, and for once, Cass looked almost... triumphant, as if Margaret's passing had removed a shadow that had hung over both their lives.

"What matters is that she can't hurt you anymore," Cass murmured, her voice low and comforting. "And you can finally be free of it, free of her."

He nodded, absorbing her words as he studied her face. There was an urgency in her tone he hadn't heard before, as if Margaret's death had opened a door she had been waiting a long time to step through.

But Cass wasn't finished. "We can start fresh, Owen. You and me—we can make a family that doesn't carry all that... weight."

He turned his gaze away, letting her hand fall from his knee. The room felt too quiet, too still, as if a storm had passed but left the air thick with something unresolved.

Cass offered a small, encouraging smile, but there was a spark in her eyes that made him uneasy. He couldn't shake the sense that, even in death, his mother had managed to gift Cass with exactly what she'd wanted all along.

SHE

The moonlight barely touched the earth tonight, a thin veil of clouds swallowing most of it, casting everything in shades of grey. I moved silently, as I always did, through the trees that lined the estate. The house loomed in the distance, grand and imposing. A monument to everything I hated.

I waited in the shadows, my breath steady, my mind sharp. The hate simmered just beneath the surface, coiled tight in my chest, but I kept it leashed. Tonight wasn't about rage. It was about patience. Control.

The dog with soft black-and-white fur, padded out into the garden as if it had been waiting for me. I crouched lower, letting it see me slowly, so it wouldn't spook. It was a good dog—trusting, sweet.

"Hey, boy," I called softly, my voice carrying just enough kindness to make it come closer. My hand slipped into my pocket, feeling the treats I'd brought, crumbling slightly between my fingers. I tossed one onto the ground, and the dog sniffed the air, curious.

It trotted toward me, eyes bright, tail wagging. Foolish thing.

"That's it," I whispered, holding out another treat, letting it nibble from my palm. "Good boy."

I scratched behind its ears, my touch gentle. Tender, even. The dog leaned into it, trusting, as if I'd always been the one to show it affection. I could feel the warmth of its body as I knelt beside it, giving it more treats, talking to it in low murmurs. "Such a good boy... They don't deserve you, you know that." The dog's tail wagged harder, happy, oblivious. I stroked its fur, soft as silk beneath my palms. It was almost a shame, really. But not quite. Not enough to stop me. I stood, slipping the leash out of my coat pocket, looping it easily through the dog's collar. It didn't resist, just looked up at me with those trusting eyes.

"Come on, let's go for a walk, okay?"

I led it down the path, away from the house, away from where prying eyes might notice. The field stretched out ahead of us, and the trees rustled in the faint breeze, their branches seeming to whisper secrets only I could hear. We walked far enough, far enough that the house was a mere shape in the distance, barely a memory.

Under the old oak tree, I stopped. The dog looked up at me expectantly, still waiting for another treat. I knelt again, scratching behind its ears. Its head leaned into my hand, its eyes closing slightly. "There we go," I whispered, my voice soft, almost cooing, like I was speaking to a baby. I was its friend now. I was giving it attention, treats, love—things it never got enough of.

I gave it one more treat, the special one. The one I had prepared. It took it eagerly, trusting me as it chewed, tail still wagging. For a few moments, nothing changed. It sat there, looking up at me, happy. Then its movements slowed. Its tail dropped. The muscles in its legs trembled, and it lowered itself to the ground, curling up as if it were just going to sleep.

My hand stroked its fur as I watched. I stayed with it,

whispering soft, soothing words as its breathing grew shallow, its eyes drooping.

"That's it, just sleep now," I murmured, my voice a hollow, tender lullaby. "Good boy. You've been such a good boy."

The dog's breaths grew weaker, each one shallower than the last. I watched its chest rise and fall, each movement slower, more laboured. My fingers brushed gently against its fur, tracing the contours of its small body as it lay there, so peaceful, so trusting.

I didn't look away. Not once. I wanted to see it. I needed to see it. The moment when life slipped away. The exact instant when the light in its eyes flickered out, when its little body fell still.

The dog gave a final, tiny twitch, then nothing. Its chest no longer rose. Its eyes were open, but vacant, staring into a world that no longer existed for it.

I stayed there for a while, just watching it. The silence was complete now, the night wrapped around me like a shroud. The hate inside me was quieter now, soothed by the stillness. This was right. This was what they deserved.

When I was ready, I stood, removed the leash and collar, and slipped them into my pocket before I lifted the dog into my arms. It was lighter than I expected, soft and limp against me. I carried it back toward the house, stepping carefully through the shadows.

I laid it down on the edge of the garden, close enough to be found in the morning. They would see it. They would wonder. They would feel it—just a piece of the pain I had felt for so long.

I stepped back, watching the lifeless shape of the dog against the dark grass, and for a moment, I felt a twisted sense of satisfaction. I had taken something from them. Something pure. Something they didn't deserve.

The night swallowed me as I slipped away, disappearing into the trees, leaving only silence in my wake.

AUGUST 28TH

The coffee tasted a little bitter, but Lila didn't mind. She needed the jolt. Sitting at the small kitchen table, she stared at her laptop screen, scanning job listings with a kind of detachment she hadn't expected. The house was eerily quiet, with Ella out with friends and Molly at school. Normally, she would welcome the silence, but today it felt wrong, almost oppressive. Even with Zara sitting across from her, filling the space with her usual confident energy, the house still felt... off. Maybe it had something to do with the fact she'd been told about Margaret passing.

Zara stirred her coffee, her eyes wandering around the kitchen. "This place feels so different without Owen," she said, her voice casual but carrying an undertone of observation. "There's an emptiness here, like the soul of the house is somehow with him."

"It's okay," she muttered, though the words felt hollow. She hated how true Zara's comment was. The house used to be full of colour—pictures on the walls, flowers on the table, a lived-in warmth that made it feel like a home. Now, it felt more like a waiting room. Neutral. Lifeless.

Zara tilted her head, watching Lila closely. "You used to have so much colour in your life, Lila. This place... it doesn't feel like you. Not anymore."

Lila shrugged, her eyes flicking back to the laptop screen, though she wasn't really seeing the words. "I guess I'm just focusing on practical things right now. No time for decorating or... whatever."

Zara leaned forward, her voice softening. "And how are the girls handling everything? I mean, are they seeing Owen at all?"

Lila's shoulders stiffened, her fingers tapping anxiously against the edge of the table. "Not really. I mean, he says he wants to, but it's complicated with work, or so he says."

Zara nodded slowly, her gaze steady. "That's tough. And you?"

"What about me?"

Zara raised an eyebrow. "Are you seeing him?"

Lila's lips pressed into a thin line. "No. And I don't want to. It's over, Zara. We're just not—" She hesitated, swallowing hard. "We're not right for each other anymore. He made his choice. I am not it."

Zara studied her for a long moment before speaking. "Do you think divorce is on the cards?"

Lila flinched at the word. *Divorce*. It hung in the air like a cold draft, creeping under her skin. She hadn't said it out loud, not yet. Even thinking it felt like an admission of failure.

"I don't know," Lila said, her voice tight. "Maybe. Probably. But the girls... I don't want to put them through that. It's already hard enough."

Zara leaned back in her chair, her eyes softening. "Lila, I get it. I do. But dragging it out isn't going to make it any easier for them. If anything, they need stability. And you... you need to be happy. You can do this. You can start fresh, make a new life for yourself and the girls. You don't need Owen. You never have."

Lila felt a knot tighten in her chest. Zara made it sound so simple, like it was just a matter of making a decision and moving on. But nothing about this felt simple.

"I'm trying," Lila said, her voice barely above a whisper. "I really am."

Zara smiled gently, leaning forward and tucking a stray strand of hair behind her ear.

Lila's head felt light, the room seeming to shift around her as a strange, creeping unease slithered through her thoughts.

"Lila?" Zara's voice snapped her back to the present. "You okay?"

Lila swallowed hard, her throat dry. "Yeah," she lied, forcing a smile that didn't reach her eyes.

Zara smiled, completely unaware of the storm brewing in Lila's mind.

Lila nodded absently, the fake smile still plastered on her face. But inside, her thoughts were a tangled mess. A hundred questions swirled in her mind, but none of them made sense. Nothing had since that day she came home to find her husband with a woman who she thought was her friend.

"I'm really glad you came over," Lila said, her voice strained, trying to shift her focus away from the sapphire earrings which were still missing. "It's just been… a lot, you know?"

Zara gave her a sympathetic look, leaning forward. "That's why I'm here. You've been through hell. But listen, you're strong. You can handle this. And you're going to be okay."

Lila forced another nod, but her mind was elsewhere. The things out of place in the house. Her growing sense that something wasn't right. She didn't feel okay. She felt like she was standing on the edge of something dark and dizzying, and she had no idea how to stop herself from falling.

Zara stood up, moving toward the door. "I've got to run, but we'll talk soon, okay? Call me if you need anything."

Lila followed her to the door, her heart still pounding, her thoughts in a frantic whirl. "Yeah, I will. Thanks, Zara."

As the door closed behind her friend, Lila slumped against the wall.

The house, already feeling too empty, too cold, seemed to press in on her, suffocating in its silence. And for the first time since all of this had begun, Lila felt truly afraid.

Later, Lila sat on the edge of the bed, her phone clutched tightly in her trembling hands. The room seemed to close in on her, the walls pressing inward, suffocating. She had been putting it off for days, pretending she could handle it, that everything would just settle on its own. But the weight on her chest had become unbearable. Owen's words echoed in her head, twisting tighter with each passing hour—*you need help.*

Her finger slid over the screen as she dialled the GP's number, her breath coming in shallow bursts. The phone rang once, then twice, before a crisp voice answered.

"Good afternoon, East Cambridge Medical Centre. How can I help you?"

Lila swallowed, her voice cracking as she spoke. "Hi, I... I need to make an appointment. It's—it's urgent."

The receptionist asked for her details, routine questions that Lila could barely focus on. The words felt distant, like they were coming from somewhere else, not her own mouth.

"What is this concerning?" the receptionist asked.

Lila hesitated, her throat tightening. How could she explain? That everything was falling apart? That she was spiralling and couldn't stop herself? "I'm not... I'm not okay," she stammered. "I just—I don't feel right. I can't sleep. I feel like I'm losing control."

The receptionist's voice was sympathetic but professional, asking a few more questions before offering an appointment time. "We can see you tomorrow at 9.30am."

"Yes," Lila whispered, her voice barely audible. "Thank you."

She hung up, her hand shaking as she set the phone down on the bedside table. She closed her eyes, trying to breathe, trying to convince herself that this was the right thing to do. Maybe it would help. Maybe the doctor could fix whatever was broken inside her. But all she felt was fear. Fear of what they might say, fear of admitting that she couldn't keep it together anymore.

"You're pathetic."

The voice was cold, dripping with disgust. Lila's eyes snapped open, her heart lurching in her chest. Ella stood in the doorway, her arms crossed tightly over her chest, her expression twisted in contempt.

"Ella," Lila breathed, stunned. "I didn't—how long have you been standing there?"

"Long enough," Ella spat, stepping into the room, her eyes flashing with anger. "I can't believe you. You're falling apart, and for what? *Dad* should be the one falling apart, not you! You're the one who's supposed to hold it together!"

Lila stood, reaching out towards her daughter, but Ella recoiled as if her mother's touch would burn her. "Ella, I'm just—"

"You're weak, Mum!" Ella screamed, cutting her off. "God, you're so weak! No wonder Dad can't stand being around you anymore. Look at you! You're behaving like you're some kind of victim, and it's disgusting!"

Lila's breath hitched, her heart pounding in her chest. "I'm trying, Ella. I'm trying to hold everything together for you and Molly, but it's—"

Ella's bitter laugh cut through the air like a slap. "Hold it together? You're not holding *anything* together. I can't stand being in this house anymore, listening to you whine and fall apart like everything is the end of the world. You know what? I can't wait to leave. I can't wait to get away from you and this pathetic place."

Lila stared at her, stunned into silence, her hand trembling as she lowered it. "Ella, please…"

Ella's eyes burned with fury. "And you know what? I feel so sorry for Molly. Poor Molly, left behind with two useless, weak parents who can't even get through a day without collapsing. She's going to be stuck here with you, with all of this, and it's just pathetic."

The words hit Lila like a blow to the chest. She felt her knees wobble, her whole body trembling. "Don't say that," she whispered, her voice cracking. "Please, don't say that."

But Ella wasn't done. She shook her head, her lips curling into a sneer. "I don't care anymore, Mum. I don't care about you or this house or Cambridge. I'm leaving as soon as I can, and I'll never look back. You and Dad can keep drowning in your own misery, but I won't be a part of it."

With that, she stormed out of the room, slamming the door behind her so hard it rattled the walls.

Lila stood frozen, the silence in the room deafening. She couldn't move, couldn't breathe but she was shaking and something was stirring in her. Something long buried, long forgotten.

The words echoed in her mind, each one like a shard of glass cutting deeper into her. *Pathetic. Weak. Disgusting.*

Tears blurred her vision, and she sank to the floor, her hands clutching at her chest as if she could somehow hold herself together. But it was no use. The cracks were already there, and with Ella's words still ringing in her ears, they had begun to break open, wider and wider, until there was nothing left to hold onto.

She was falling apart. And this time, she didn't know how to stop it.

The morning was eerily quiet as Owen made his way outside, his breath misting in the crisp autumnal air. The garden had always been Bongo's domain, a place of joyful chaos where the Border collie would chase squirrels, roll in leaves, and run circles around anyone who dared to wander in. But today, there was a strange, unnatural stillness hanging over the grounds.

"Bongo!" Owen called, his voice breaking the silence. He hadn't seen his dog since the night before, and a prickle of unease had taken root as he realised that he hadn't heard the usual morning bark from the kitchen where he slept, or the familiar scratch at the door.

He walked across the lawn, scanning the garden for any sign of movement. The trees stood bare, their leaves scattered like a carpet of red and gold across the ground. Owen's gaze drifted to the far side of the garden, near the hedgerow, where a dark shape lay, unmoving.

His heart lurched, and he quickened his pace, a sick feeling twisting in his stomach. "Bongo?" he called again, his voice smaller now, hesitant, as if he feared the answer. The shape on the ground grew clearer as he approached, the black-and-white fur unmistakable, splayed across the damp grass in an unnatural, lifeless sprawl.

"No..." Owen whispered, falling to his knees beside his dog, his hands trembling as he reached out to touch Bongo's still, cold body. He felt the roughness of the fur beneath his fingers, the once bright eyes now dull and vacant, fixed on some far-off place. His heart shattered as he cradled Bongo's head, willing the dog to wake up, to give him just one last wag of the tail, one last bark of recognition.

But there was only silence.

"Oh, Bongo..." he choked out, the grief crashing over him like a tidal wave. Bongo had been with him through everything—the move to Granta Hall, the strained family dinners, the cold nights when he'd felt like a stranger in his own home. The dog had been his one constant, a loyal companion who'd never left his side, even when everything else in his life had fallen apart.

Owen felt tears prick his eyes, and he made no effort to hold them back. He buried his face in Bongo's fur, inhaling the faint, familiar scent that lingered, a reminder of better days, of happier memories. His shoulders shook as he wept, the pain raw and unfiltered, filling the empty spaces within him that he hadn't even realised were there.

He didn't know how long he knelt there, clutching Bongo's lifeless body, his heart breaking with every passing second. The world around him seemed to fade, the edges blurring as he became consumed by his grief, by the unbearable weight of loss.

Finally, he pulled back, wiping his eyes with the back of his hand. His fingers lingered on Bongo's collar, the small silver tag engraved with the dog's name. A wave of bitterness rose within him as he realised that, once again, something precious had been taken from him, ripped away with no warning, no chance to say goodbye.

As he stood, a flash of movement caught his eye from the direction of the house. Cass stood by the kitchen window, watching him with an expression he couldn't quite decipher. There was no sympathy in her gaze, only a faint look of curiosity, as if she were observing a stranger's grief rather than her partner's.

She opened the door, stepping outside with an air of mild

irritation. "What's going on?" she asked, her tone impatient, as if his pain were an inconvenience.

Owen turned to her, his eyes red-rimmed and raw, his hands shaking with grief and anger. "It's Bongo," he managed, his voice hoarse. "He's... gone."

Cass's face remained impassive, her gaze flicking briefly to the dog's body before she shrugged. "I'm sorry," she said, her voice devoid of warmth, of empathy.

The coldness of her words struck Owen like a physical blow, and he felt his anger rise, mingling with his sorrow. Bongo had been his friend, his companion, a beloved presence in his life that Cass would never understand, could never understand. She hadn't known the late-night walks, the games of fetch, the quiet moments of companionship that had meant more to him than words could express.

"He was so young," Owen said, his voice thick with emotion. "The girls will be devastated."

Cass pursed her lips, glancing back toward the house. "I know he meant a lot to you," she said, her tone patronising, dismissive. "But it's just a dog, Owen. Life moves on."

With that, she turned and walked back inside, leaving him standing alone in the garden, clutching the last remains of a helpless being who had given him unconditional love.

As Owen looked down at Bongo's still form, he felt an overwhelming sense of isolation. The house had changed, his family was gone, and now, so was Bongo. He was truly alone in a life that no longer felt like his own.

Kneeling down, he gently stroked Bongo's fur one last time, whispering a quiet goodbye before he forced himself to let go. He would bury his beloved friend beneath the oak tree, in the place where they'd spent countless afternoons together, where he would always remember him.

And as he dug, he felt the weight of his loss settle deep within him, the realisation that his life, his home, and even his heart, had been transformed into something unrecognisable, something he no longer knew how to reclaim.

AUGUST 29TH

She stood in the hallway, staring at the boxes and packing cases with a hollow feeling that had been gnawing at her for days. The house was quiet—too quiet—but the weight of last night's argument still lingered in the air like a storm that hadn't fully passed. The words, sharp and cutting, replayed in her mind, and she couldn't shake the sense of loss that had settled deep inside her.

Ella's words had hurt more than she expected. *Pathetic. Weak. Disgusting.* She never thought she would hear such contempt from her daughter—someone she believed understood her. And yet, there it was. Laid bare in the heat of Ella's anger. Now, it was all she could think about.

As she looked down the hallway, her gaze fell on the kitchen where Ella stood, texting someone, her posture rigid, her face unreadable. There was a chasm between them now, a gulf that Lila didn't know how to cross. Ella had screamed at her last night, blaming her for everything. *You're falling apart, and for what?* Dad *should be the one falling apart...* The accusation was still raw. Ella's words about Molly too, how she felt sorry for her sister being stuck with parents too weak to hold themselves together.

Those words echoed, hollow and cruel, in Lila's mind, and she felt lost. She had always believed that she and Ella had a bond that couldn't be broken, something special between them. Now, that certainty was shattered.

She tried to keep her composure. Today was Ella's day—her chance to go to university and start her own life. Lila wanted to be strong, the mother Ella had once believed in, but after last night, she wasn't sure she knew how to be that person anymore.

Ella was bustling around, checking her list one last time, making sure she hadn't forgotten anything crucial. Her anticipation was infectious; Lila couldn't help but smile, even as she felt the sting of her daughter's impending departure. A piece of her heart was leaving with Ella, and she wondered if she'd ever feel whole again.

Her phone buzzed in her pocket, pulling her from her thoughts. She glanced down at the screen, expecting to see a message from Zara or perhaps a last-minute reminder from Ella's university. But instead, her heart sank as she saw Owen's name.

With a sense of dread, she opened the message.

> Bongo's dead. I thought you should know.

The simple words hit her like a punch to the gut, and she had to steady herself, closing her eyes for a moment. Her beloved Bongo, the gentle Border collie who had been part of their family, was gone. She felt a sharp, unexpected pain, as if she'd lost a piece of her past, a reminder of happier times. The thought of him alone, without them, without her, was almost unbearable.

Lila glanced at Ella, who was obliviously organising her

things, excited for her new adventure. She knew, in that moment, that she couldn't bear to ruin this day for her daughter. Ella deserved to step into this new chapter without the weight of grief, without the sadness that Bongo's death would inevitably bring.

But the anger simmered beneath her sorrow—anger at Owen, for putting this on her, for making her the one who would have to break the news to the girls. She hated him, in that instant, for his thoughtlessness, for his ability to disrupt their lives even from a distance. He hadn't bothered to call, to soften the blow. Just a text, as if he were informing her of something trivial.

Lila swallowed hard, pushing down her anger and the rising tears. She wouldn't let this overshadow Ella's big day. Bongo had been part of their lives and his passing deserved its own moment of grief, but today wasn't that moment. Today was about Ella.

"Everything all right, Mum?" Ella asked, glancing up and catching the strained look on Lila's face.

Lila forced a smile, tucking her phone away. "Yes, love. Just a message from a friend."

Ella seemed satisfied with that, her attention returning to her packing. Lila watched her daughter, feeling the weight of the secret she was now carrying.

As they continued packing, Lila's mind wandered to Molly. Her youngest, who was so attuned to the world around her, who would surely notice Bongo's absence immediately. Lila knew she'd have to tell her after Ella had left, break the news gently and find a way to comfort her. They may not have known the dog for long, but the girls loved him.

And beneath the heartbreak of Ella leaving, there was something else pressing down on her—a weight that had grown heavier with each passing day. The responsibility. She still hadn't found a job, and the thought gnawed at her constantly. How was she going to manage everything on her own? How could she take care of Molly, make sure she was okay, without a stable income? Owen's help had been inconsistent at best, and she couldn't rely on him. The silence of the house, once a sanctuary, only made the worries louder, more overwhelming. She needed to find work. She needed to keep it together. She couldn't afford to fall apart. Not now.

From the hallway, she could see Ella, now leaning against the fridge, her face illuminated by the light of her phone screen. She looked so grown up, so composed—nothing like the little girl who used to crawl into bed, afraid of the dark. Lila wanted to say something, to reach out before Ella left, but the words wouldn't come. They stuck in her throat, heavy and unspoken.

She walked into the kitchen, her voice small as she offered, "Fancy a hot chocolate before you go?"

Ella didn't look up from her phone. "Mum, I'm not ten." The eye-roll that followed was automatic, dismissive, and it stung more than Lila expected.

"Right. Sorry," Lila muttered, turning off the kettle, feeling deflated. Every interaction felt like a failure now, as though she were trying too hard and still coming up short. "Have you seen my watch? I could have sworn I left it by the sink in my bathroom, but it's vanished."

Ella glanced up, her expression softening just slightly. "No, haven't seen it." She sighed, walking over to her mother. "It's going to be fine, Mum. I'll be okay. We'll talk all the time, you know that." Her tone was an attempt at reassurance, but the emptiness in her words made Lila's sadness feel deeper, more profound.

Lila swallowed the lump in her throat, forcing a small smile. "I know. But I'm allowed to miss you, aren't I?"

Ella wrapped one skinny arm around her mother's

shoulders, pulling her into a quick, reluctant hug. "I know, but you should really find something to do, Mum. A hobby or something. Maybe an art class?"

Lila tried to laugh, but it came out strained. "That's exactly what I've been thinking."

"Good," Ella said, sounding surprised but pleased.

"I'll be okay," Lila said, trying to convince herself as much as Ella. "I'm a tough old bird, remember?"

Ella cringed playfully, nudging her. "Less of the 'old', please, Mum. You know that makes me cringe."

Lila forced another smile, though her heart ached. She wanted to drive Ella to university herself, to be there for every moment, but she knew Ella didn't want that. Not after last night. Not after everything.

"Mum, it just makes sense for Robbo to drive me," Ella said, as if reading her thoughts. "No point in you driving all that way, then turning around to come back. Plus, I don't need you getting upset at Halls when I arrive. Not a very cool way to start my first year."

Ella was right, of course, but that didn't make it easier. Lila wanted to be the one to help her settle in, to cling to these last moments together, even though she knew she couldn't. Robbo and Ella had been friends for years, and Lila was glad they had chosen to go to the same university.

"Your father would be proud of you," Lila said, wrapping her arms around Ella again, trying to find some comfort in the embrace. "You know that, don't you?"

Ella stiffened slightly, her voice flat. "Pity he's not around to show it."

Lila let go, the weight of Ella's words hanging heavily between them. Owen's absence was a wound that refused to heal. Lila wanted to say something, to make it better, but she knew there was nothing that could fix it.

Before she could think of a response, the doorbell rang, echoing through the house. Robbo had arrived. The moment Lila had been dreading was finally here.

Ella grabbed her rucksack, her face brightening as she headed for the door. She was ready. More than ready.

Lila followed her into the hallway, watching as Ella loaded her things into Robbo's car. He was already behind the wheel, puffing on a vape, his sunglasses pushed up onto his head. "You all set, El?"

"Yup," Ella said, giving her mother one last look. For a moment, Lila thought she saw a flicker of nerves cross her daughter's face, but it was gone in an instant.

"You take care of my girl," Lila said to Robbo, trying to sound strong, trying to hold herself together, even though her mind was racing with questions—how would she balance everything? How could she take care of Molly, keep the house running, and still get a job?

"Yes, ma'am," Robbo said with a smile, but the loud music from his car drowned out most of the words.

Ella threw her last box into the car and turned to Lila, her eyes bright. "I'll message you tonight, okay?"

Lila nodded, unable to speak. Her throat felt too tight. Instead, she handed Ella a hundred pounds, a little extra for whatever she might need. "Just... in case," she said softly.

Ella took the money, folding it into her bag. "Thanks, Mum."

"Don't spend it all on sex, drugs, and rock 'n' roll," Lila joked, trying to hide the heartbreak in her voice.

Ella laughed, her eyes twinkling with that mischievous smile. "Promise I won't spend it on sex."

Lila forced a laugh, even as her heart cracked a little more. "Deal."

Ella slid into the car, and Lila stepped back, waving as they pulled away. Just before the car disappeared down the street, Ella put her hand against the window in a final goodbye.

And then she was gone.

Lila stood there for a long time, watching the empty street, the silence of the house pressing in around her. She closed the door gently and walked back into the hallway, where the last traces of Ella's presence still lingered. But they were already fading, replaced by the crushing emptiness of knowing that her daughter was gone.

She still needed to get a job, still needed to keep things going for Molly. There was no time to break down, no time to fall apart. But for now, the grief felt overwhelming, the responsibilities suffocating. And she let the tears spill, knowing that, for just a little while, she couldn't pretend to hold it all together.

But deep down, Lila knew she had to take control of her life. It was time to stop being the victim, no matter what it took.

DECEMBER 9TH

The house was alive with a kind of joy that Lila hadn't felt in so long, it was almost foreign to her. Laughter echoed through the halls, feet pounded against the wooden floors, and bright, colourful balloons floated from every corner, adding bursts of life to the rooms. The scent of freshly baked party food filled the air—homemade sausage rolls, mini-sandwiches, and cupcakes Lila had stayed up late preparing the night before. It had been worth it. Every second of effort had been worth it to see Molly's face light up with pure, unfiltered excitement. It had been a long time since she'd seen Molly smile.

"Mum, is the magician here yet?" Molly bounded down the stairs, her dark hair bouncing as she darted into the kitchen, her wide eyes gleaming with anticipation. She was practically vibrating with energy, wearing a rainbow-striped dress Lila had bought just for the occasion.

"Not yet, love," Lila said with a smile, her heart lighter than it had been in months. "But he'll be here soon. Why don't you help me put the last few sandwiches on the table?"

Molly huffed but grabbed the plate of sandwiches, carefully placing them next to the other party treats. "I hope he's really magic," she said, her voice full of wonder. "Like, real magic."

Lila chuckled. "He'll be magical, don't you worry."

She glanced at the front door, waiting for Jen to arrive with the cake she'd promised. It had been a long time since their house felt this full, this warm. Since it felt like home again. Parents mingled in the living room, chatting casually while keeping one eye on their children as they raced through the house, squealing with laughter. The cheerful chaos filled Lila with a sense of peace she hadn't realised she'd been missing.

The doorbell rang just as Lila was straightening the decorations on the cake table. Molly's head snapped up, her face brightening. "The magician!"

Lila smiled, though she knew it was more likely to be Jen, her aunt, with the cake. "Go check, sweetheart."

Molly dashed to the door, flinging it open with all the enthusiasm of a girl on her tenth birthday. "Jen!"

There she stood, larger than life as always, holding an enormous cake box. Jen grinned, stepping inside with her famous exuberance. "Happy birthday, Molly!" she said, leaning down to give her a kiss on the cheek. "Look what I brought!"

Molly's eyes widened as she tried to peek into the box. "Is that my cake?"

"Only the best for my favourite birthday girl," Jen said, winking at Lila as she carried the box into the kitchen.

Lila followed, laughing. "I knew you'd outdo yourself."

Jen set the box down on the table, carefully lifting the lid to reveal the masterpiece beneath—a three-tiered cake covered in swirls of pastel buttercream, dotted with edible glitter and topped with a sugar-crafted unicorn. It was perfect.

"Jen, it's beautiful," Lila breathed. "You really outdid yourself."

"Anything for Molly," Jen said with a smile. She glanced

around the room, taking in the balloons, the decorations, the lively chatter of parents and children alike. "This place looks amazing, Lila. It's been a while since I've seen it this... alive."

Lila nodded, her heart swelling. "It feels good, doesn't it?"

Jen shot her a knowing look. "It's been a long time coming." She paused. "Look, Li... Owen — I'm, I'm so sorry..." Her cheeks flushed as her eyes pricked with tears.

Just then, the front door opened again, but this time, the figure stepping through wasn't the magician either. It was Cass, her entrance as grand and uninvited as if she owned the place, with Owen trailing reluctantly behind her. Lila's smile faltered, the warmth of the day receding as she took in the sight of Cass striding confidently into her home, a forced, saccharine smile on her face.

"Oh, isn't this cosy?" Cass remarked, glancing around with thinly veiled amusement, as if the party was some quaint spectacle beneath her notice. Her gaze landed on Molly, her face twisting into a performative smile. "Happy birthday, Molly! Look what I brought!"

Lila stiffened as she watched Cass saunter into the kitchen, her arms loaded with brightly wrapped gifts that seemed as much for show as for Molly. She reached out to greet Lila, her eyes glinting with something just shy of malice.

And that's when Lila noticed it—the earrings Cass was wearing. Her breath caught, her heart pounding with sudden recognition. They were her earrings, the ones she'd been searching for, convinced she'd misplaced them in the chaos of the move. But there they were, gleaming on Cass's ears like a trophy, as though they belonged to her.

An icy rage surged through Lila, bubbling up from a place she hadn't known existed. She stepped forward, her voice low and trembling with barely contained fury. "Cass," she said, her gaze fixed on the earrings, "where did you get them?"

Cass glanced at her coldly, her hand reaching up to touch one of the earrings, her expression smug as she twisted it in her fingers. "Oh, these?" she said lightly, with a casual smile. "Aren't they lovely? I found them the other day. Thought I'd give them a little wear."

"You *found* them?" Lila's voice was low but sharp, each word dripping with accusation. Her anger was spiralling, taking on a life of its own, fuelled by months of tension and betrayal. "Those are mine. You stole them."

Cass raised an eyebrow, her lips curving into a mocking smile. "Don't be ridiculous, Lila. It's just some earrings. If you'd kept better track of your things..."

The insinuation sent Lila over the edge. The anger that had been simmering beneath the surface exploded, and before she knew what she was doing, she took a step towards Cass, her fists clenched. "You've been taking my things, haven't you? Moving them, making me feel like I'm losing my mind. You've been gaslighting me!"

Cass let out a laugh, tilting her head as though she found Lila's fury amusing. "Oh, come on, Lila. Don't make a scene in front of all these people. It's not a good look."

But Lila was beyond control. All the hurt, all the manipulation, all the times Cass had undermined her and stolen pieces of her life—she couldn't hold it in any longer. She lunged, grabbing at Cass's wrist, yanking her arm with a force that made Cass stumble back, her smug expression slipping as she fell backwards onto the floor.

"You are a thief, Cass," Lila spat, her voice trembling with rage. "And you've been trying to drive me mad."

Cass's eyes narrowed, her face twisting with anger and embarrassment as she rolled into a ball.

"Let go of me, Lila!" she hissed, pulling her arm back, but Lila wouldn't relent.

The room had fallen silent, all eyes turned towards the scene unfolding before them. Parents clutched their children's hands, some casting uncertain glances, others whispering in shock. Zara stood by the wall, watching it all, frozen in horror. Owen stood motionless, watching the fight, unable to move as Cass staggered to her feet.

"Get out of my house!" Lila's voice rose, shaking with the force of her fury. She shoved Cass backward, her anger blinding her to the horrified looks around her, to the gasps of the remaining parents. She didn't care. She'd had enough—enough of Cass, enough of her lies, enough of the invasion of her life.

Cass stumbled, catching herself with a snarl. "You've lost it, Lila. You're a madwoman."

Lila stepped forward, her hands still trembling, her breathing ragged. "You're the one who's poisoned everything. You, with your games, your thefts, your lies."

Zara, who been standing quietly in the corner nursing a cup of tea, watched in silence, still unable to help. She knew it wasn't her place to interfere.

The silence that followed was thick, suffocating. Parents gathered their children, murmuring hurried goodbyes as they edged toward the door, their faces pale and wary. Molly stood by the staircase, her face a mask of shock and fear, her wide eyes brimming with confusion as she looked at her mother.

"Mum..." Molly's voice was barely a whisper, breaking through the haze of Lila's anger. "Why did you... what are you doing?"

Lila's fury ebbed slightly, the reality of what had just happened beginning to sink in. She looked at her daughter, at the stunned faces of the few remaining guests.

Cass, her face flushed with humiliation, shot Lila a scathing look before turning on her heel, storming out of the house without another word, with Owen trailing behind her, his face pale, his gaze averted.

The door closed behind them, and the silence that remained was crushing. Lila looked down at the watch in her hand, feeling a wave of shame wash over her. She had wanted today to be perfect, a day of joy for Molly—a chance for them to feel whole again.

Lila looked at her daughter, her breath catching in her throat. The truth of what she had just done hit her like a crashing wave, and she had no idea how to explain it. How to explain any of it. She had wanted so badly for today to be perfect. For Molly to have the birthday she deserved. But instead, she had ruined it.

SHE

I stand just outside the window, hidden in the shadow of the large oak tree, watching them. The glass is fogged slightly from the warmth inside, but I can still see everything. The lit candles, casting a soft, orange glow over the room. Fairy lights twinkle on the Christmas tree, each one reflecting off the carefully placed ornaments that hang from the branches like glittering jewels. Everything is perfect. Sickeningly perfect.

They sit together on the couch, side by side, her head resting on his shoulder as they laugh softly, wrapped up in their own little world. Their faces are bathed in the soft, golden light of the room, their smiles radiant, content. She looks so happy. Her face glows with the warmth of the fire, her laughter ringing out like she's got everything she could ever want. The perfect woman with the perfect life.

I want to tear it all apart. I want to watch it burn.

They don't know I'm here. They never do. I've been watching them for weeks now, slipping in and out of the shadows, always just out of sight. They think they're safe in their cosy little world, surrounded by their pretty things, their love, their happiness. But they're not. No one is safe from me.

I've been waiting for this moment—this moment—when everything is just right, just perfect, and I can feel it building inside me, the hate, the bile rising in my throat like poison. They've made it so easy, haven't they? Flaunting their happiness like it's theirs by right. As if they've done anything to deserve it.

Her hand rests gently on his leg, and I can see the way he looks at her, with that softness in his eyes, like she's the only thing that matters. His hand comes up to stroke her hair, fingers twining through her perfect, glossy locks. It makes me sick. The way he touches her, the way she leans into him like she belongs there, like it's natural.

I'll rip it all away.

She doesn't know yet. She has no idea what's coming. But she'll learn. She'll learn what it's like to lose everything, to feel the ground crumble beneath her feet, to watch the world she's built come crashing down. I'll make sure of it. I'll watch her break, piece by piece, until there's nothing left of that smug little smile, nothing left of that happiness she clings to so desperately.

She stands up, walking toward the Christmas tree, reaching out to adjust one of the ornaments. It's a small thing, delicate, glass, catching the light in a way that makes it sparkle. I wonder if it's something meaningful, something they've shared. A memory, perhaps. Something they've collected together, tied to their perfect life, their perfect love.

I want to smash it.

I can already see it—her face when it all falls apart. The look in her eyes when she realises she's lost everything. The fear. The desperation. The tears that will streak down her perfect, glowing face. She'll beg. They always beg. But it won't matter. Not to me.

She doesn't deserve him. She doesn't deserve any of it. The house, the love, the warmth that fills this room. I'll take it all from her, piece by piece, until there's nothing left but ash. I'll tear her down, rip away every little thing she holds dear, and then I'll watch as she crumbles, as the light in her eyes goes out.

I'll be patient. I've waited this long, haven't I? What's a little more time? It will make the moment even sweeter, watching her fall when she least expects it. Watching the life she's built disintegrate in front of her, and knowing that it was me who did it. Me.

She'll never see it coming.

I clench my fists at my sides, the sharp bite of my nails digging into my palms, grounding me in the intensity of it all. The anticipation. It's almost intoxicating, the way it builds and builds until I can hardly breathe, until the only thing that matters is the thought of her suffering.

I imagine her in that moment, when she realises everything is slipping away. Her face, twisted in fear, in pain. Her perfect life collapsing around her. It will be beautiful.

The fire crackles louder, and she turns, looking back at him with that smile, that fucking smile, as if nothing in the world could touch her. As if she's untouchable. As if she's won.

But no one's untouchable. Not her. Not anyone.

I'll make sure of that.

I step back, melting into the shadows, watching her laugh again, her voice soft and sweet, as if the world is hers. For now. Let her enjoy it. Let her live in this pretty little dream she's built for herself. Because soon, very soon, I'll be the one who destroys it all.

DECEMBER 25TH

Granta Hall was eerily quiet for Christmas morning. No sounds of children tearing into presents, no shrieks of excitement echoing off the walls. Instead, the soft clink of teacups filled the silence, as Cass and Owen sat in the kitchen, sipping their morning tea in the warm glow of the fireplace. Outside, the garden was covered in a thin blanket of frost, the air crisp and still, but inside, everything felt tense. Forced. As if the cheer of the day was something they had to perform, rather than feel.

Owen glanced at Cass, giving her a small, strained smile, but she could see the lines of worry etched into his face. He hadn't mentioned Lila once, and Cass didn't need him to. The absence of Ella, the way Molly had been withdrawn since she arrived—it all pointed back to the same thing. No one wanted to talk about it, least of all him.

Molly padded into the room in her flannel pyjamas, her hair messy from sleep, her expression distant. She was always the one who woke up early on Christmas, eager to tear into her presents, but this year she looked sad. She shuffled over to the table, sitting down between Owen and Cass, her face pale and drawn.

"Morning, sweetheart," Owen said softly, putting his arm around her, trying to summon some of the festive spirit that was so elusive. "Merry Christmas."

Molly managed a small, weak smile but didn't respond. She wrapped her arms around herself, her eyes scanning the room, but avoiding the Christmas tree that stood in the corner, sparkling with lights and surrounded by neatly wrapped presents.

Cass, who had been watching the interaction closely, smiled as brightly as she could manage. "Merry Christmas, Molly. Do you want to open a present before breakfast?"

Molly shrugged. "I guess."

There was a long pause, the silence growing heavier, until Molly spoke again, her voice small.

"Why did Bongo die? I miss him. He always sat next to me. Where has he gone?" Molly looked up, her eyes wide and brimming with a sadness that made Owen's heart ache.

Cass and Owen exchanged a glance.

Cass set her teacup down, her hands fidgeting slightly. "Maybe... maybe it's better we don't talk about that right now?"

Molly sighed, looking down at her lap. "And where's Ella? Why isn't she here?" Her voice cracked on her sister's name, and the room grew even colder. "She always makes Christmas fun."

Owen's jaw tightened. The truth was too bitter to speak aloud, and he hated how tangled everything had become. Ella had refused to come this year. She couldn't stand being under the same roof as Cass, and though Owen had tried to reason with her, Ella had made it clear. She was spending Christmas with friends, far away from this house, from the tension, and far away from Cass.

"She wanted to be here," Owen lied softly. "But she's staying with her friends this Christmas. She misses mum, like we all do. But mummy is in the best place. The doctors are taking care of her. El's sent you a present, though. It's under the tree."

Molly's face fell further, but she nodded, her hands twisting together in her lap. "I wish she was here. It doesn't feel the same without her."

Owen squeezed her shoulder, glancing at the tree. "How about you open her gift now? I know she'd want you to."

Molly hesitated, then stood slowly, walking over to the tree and searching through the neatly wrapped gifts until she found the one with Ella's familiar handwriting on the tag. She unwrapped it carefully, her hands moving slower than usual. When the paper fell away, she stared at the present for a long moment, her lip trembling.

It was a silver picture frame. Inside was a photo of Molly, Ella, and their mother—Lila—taken in the summer of last year, back when things were normal. The three of them smiled brightly in the photo, their arms wrapped around each other, happy and carefree.

Molly's face crumpled, tears welling in her eyes. "I miss them," she whispered, clutching the frame to her chest. "I miss Mum and Ella."

Owen's throat tightened, guilt flooding his chest as he watched his youngest daughter crumble. He reached out to her, but before he could comfort her, Cass interjected.

"Molly," Cass said quickly, her voice smooth, her eyes narrowing slightly as she glanced between Owen and the photo. "How about we open another present? You'll feel better once you see what else Santa brought you."

But Molly wasn't listening. She was already slipping away, retreating into herself as she clutched the frame tighter, her tears falling silently onto her pyjamas.

Cass felt a hot surge of jealousy flare in her chest. This was supposed to be *their* Christmas, *their* chance to move on, and yet everything always circled back to Lila. Even Ella, who wasn't here, managed to pull the focus away from them. And now Owen was watching Molly, his face etched with concern, his attention fully consumed by someone else once again.

Cass spoke quietly, her usual air of confidence diminished. She watched Owen for a moment, her eyes wary, as if gauging his mood before speaking.

"Owen," she began softly, her voice tinged with frustration and hurt. "I need you to know that I didn't mean to upset Lila."

Owen glanced at her, his expression a mixture of exhaustion and scepticism. "Then why did you wear them, Cass? Because from where I'm standing, it looks bad—really bad."

Cass took a deep breath, her hands fidgeting in her lap. "I wasn't thinking." She looked at him, her eyes wide, pleading for understanding. "I'd never be so cruel on purpose."

Owen's brow furrowed as he absorbed her words.

Cass nodded, her expression earnest. "It was just a mistake. A stupid mistake. If I'd known she was going to react like that..."

Cass's face flushed, her eyes hardening slightly. "You know I didn't steal them. I found them here. In this house. In our house."

Owen rubbed his temples, feeling a pounding headache forming. "I don't know what to think right now, Cass. You must understand how it seemed to her."

Cass's expression shifted, a flicker of indignation crossing her face. "This is ridiculous. I didn't steal anything. They were there, in our bathroom, like I told you."

Owen sighed, the tension between them thickening. He looked at her, searching her face for any sign of deception, but all he saw was frustration and hurt. "Maybe... I don't know, but Lila thinks you did it on purpose."

Cass's eyes narrowed slightly, her tone becoming defensive.

"Lila has been spiralling for months, Owen. You know that. I've done nothing to push her over the edge—she's doing that all on her own. I'm here, trying to build a life with you, and she's determined to paint me as the villain in some story she's made up in her head."

Owen held up a hand, trying to calm her. "Cass, I just... I need to understand this. Because right now, it's hard for me to know what to believe."

Cass took a deep breath, forcing herself to calm down. She leaned forward, her voice softening. "Owen, you have to trust me. I swear to you, I didn't steal them. I'm not some common criminal. I'd never do something like that. I'm not the enemy here."

Owen stared at her, his mind a storm of conflicting emotions. He wanted to believe her, to trust the woman he'd chosen to share his life with. But the events of the day had shaken him, casting a shadow over everything he thought he knew.

Finally, he nodded, though his voice remained hesitant. "All right, Cass. I'll believe you. But we must find a way to resolve this with Lila. We can't keep having these... these confrontations. It's not fair on anyone, especially not Molly."

Cass looked away, a flicker of annoyance passing over her face before she composed herself. "Of course. I want things to be civil too. But that's going to require Lila letting go of her suspicions and accepting that I'm here, and I'm not going anywhere."

Owen nodded, but his heart was heavy. He wondered if peace was even possible, or if the tensions between Cass and Lila would continue to tear their lives apart, piece by painful piece.

Cass needed to change the direction of the day—quickly.

She reached into her pocket, her fingers closing around the

small velvet box she had been keeping hidden since that morning. "Owen," she said, her voice soft, but firm. "I have something for you too."

He blinked, still focused on Molly, but Cass's words seemed to pull him back. He turned toward her, forcing a smile. "Oh?"

Cass smiled sweetly, placing the small box into his hands. "Go on. Open it."

Owen glanced down at the box, his brow furrowing slightly, but he did as she asked, lifting the lid. Inside was a small white stick—the unmistakable symbol of two faint lines staring back at him. A positive pregnancy test.

His breath caught, his eyes flicking back to Cass in shock. "Is this…?"

Cass nodded, her smile widening, her eyes bright. "Yes. I'm pregnant!"

For a moment, the world seemed to freeze. Owen looked down at the test, then back at Cass. He opened his mouth to speak, but the words didn't come. He was still processing the news, the weight of it settling in his chest.

Molly, oblivious to the exchange, was still holding the frame close to her chest, her tears quiet, but steady.

Owen's heart was torn, caught between the past and the future—between the family he had lost, and the life he was supposed to be building. He wanted to be happy, he knew he should be. But as he looked at Cass's glowing face, all he could feel was the ghost of the life he had left behind, and the cold realisation that it would never fully leave him.

DECEMBER 26TH

Owen sat slumped in his home office chair, staring blankly at the phone in his hand. The holiday season was supposed to bring warmth, peace, and family, but this Boxing Day was drenched in bitterness and tension. He could feel the weight of it pressing down on him, heavy and suffocating. The conversation with Ella still echoed in his mind, every word she had thrown at him like a dagger, each one cutting deeper than the last.

The house, usually filled with the sounds of laughter, of Molly and Ella bickering over Christmas gifts, was unnervingly quiet now. It wasn't just the physical silence that disturbed him—it was the emotional void that seemed to have seeped into every corner of their lives. He rubbed his hands over his face, trying to shake the sense of dread that had settled in his chest, but it was useless. Nothing about this Christmas had been right.

The festivities had been awkward from the start. With Lila gone, sectioned after her breakdown, and the anonymous call to the police about her being a danger to herself and others, there had been no traditional Christmas morning at home, no stockings hung with care, no smell of her homemade fig pudding wafting through the house. Instead, Owen had gone through the motions with Cass, desperately trying to pretend everything was normal for Molly.

He pushed away the bitter memory of Christmas morning. Molly had woken up early, her excitement dulled, her face pale and drawn as if she already knew the day was going to be a failure. They had opened gifts in near silence, Molly sitting on the floor by the tree, carefully unwrapping presents that Owen had picked out half-heartedly, not knowing what would really make her smile this year. She had thanked him, but her voice had been flat, her eyes distant. She wasn't there with him—just like Lila wasn't there anymore either.

Cass had tried. She really had. She'd bought Molly expensive gifts—huge, gleaming chocolate boxes, a new phone, clothes Owen never would have chosen—but none of it had been quite right. Molly had thanked her, too, but the distance between them was palpable, unspoken and vast. Cass had smiled through it, pretending not to notice, but Owen had seen the flicker of hurt in her eyes. She wanted to make it work, to step into this role, but the space between her and Molly was impossible to ignore. It had been a miserable day for everyone.

Owen's mind drifted back to the phone call with Ella. She had been furious when she heard about Cass's pregnancy, but her anger was about more than that. It was about the crumbling foundation of their family, the pieces that no one could ever put back together. Ella's words—"You'll regret this, Dad"—had hit him hard. Maybe she was right. Maybe he was making a mistake by trying to hold everything together, by trying to protect everyone and failing miserably.

A soft knock at the office door pulled him from his thoughts. He turned just as Cass stepped inside, her eyes filled with a kind of hesitant concern. She stood in the doorway for a moment, her hand resting protectively over her stomach, before she spoke.

"Owen, is everything okay?" Her voice was gentle, but there was a tremor of anxiety underneath. "I heard you talking to Ella."

He looked at her, and for a moment, he didn't know how to respond. Cass had been through so much already—far more than she had let on when they first met. She'd told him about her abusive marriage, about her father's suicide when she was just a child, about how she had never imagined she'd have a chance at happiness again. And now, after everything she had been through, she was finally pregnant, finally looking toward a future that wasn't wrapped in trauma and pain.

But even with all that knowledge, Owen couldn't ignore the deep unease that gnawed at him. Could he really protect her? Could he really keep her and their unborn child safe, with the chaos that had consumed them both?

Cass took a tentative step forward, her hand still resting on her belly. "Ella's upset, isn't she? About the baby?"

Owen nodded, feeling the weight of the conversation settling on his shoulders.

"She's furious," he admitted quietly. "She's angry about everything. She blames me, Cass. She thinks I'm abandoning their mother."

"Owen, I know this is hard. I know they're struggling to understand. But you're doing the right thing. You're trying to protect Molly, to give her a stable home. And now, with the baby on the way, you have even more reason to make sure this works. We have everything we need." Cass's face softened, her brow furrowing with concern.

Owen closed his eyes for a moment, feeling the exhaustion pulling at him. Cass was right, but that didn't make it any easier. Molly had spent Christmas with him and Cass, but she wasn't really there. Her silence, her distance—it had been almost unbearable. He had tried to distract her, to make her smile, but her mind was elsewhere.

"I'm going to fight for custody of Molly," Owen said, his voice heavy with resolve. "I've already spoken to a lawyer. After everything that's happened, I can't leave Molly in her care. Not after the breakdown."

Cass's eyes flickered with something Owen couldn't quite place, but she nodded, stepping closer to him. "Molly needs you now more than ever. We both do."

He stared down at his hands, his mind drifting back to the day he had found his dog dead in the garden. He could still see it—the cold, lifeless body. He hadn't understood it then, hadn't been able to make sense of the violence, the suddenness of it. But when Cass had told him she'd seen Lila sneaking around that night, everything had shifted.

Cass's face softened as she reached out, placing a hand on Owen's shoulder, as if reading his mind. "Lila's not well, Owen. You know that. She needs help. But you can't be the one to save her."

Owen nodded slowly, knowing that Cass was right, but feeling the crushing guilt that came with accepting it.

And now Cass was pregnant. The stakes were even higher. He had to protect her, protect their child. He couldn't let this spiral any further.

"The break-in," he said after a moment, his voice dropping lower. "After everything with Lila, I didn't want to say anything, but... Cass, it shook me. It shook *you*. That's why we have to keep Molly here, with us. I can't let her go back to Lila—not when things are this unstable."

Cass nodded again, her hand tightening slightly on his shoulder. "I know. We need to focus on keeping this house safe, on keeping our family safe. Molly needs us while her mother is in that place." Her voice softened, and she looked down at her stomach, despite there being no sign of a baby bump yet. "Do you really think Lila was responsible for breaking into our house?"

Owen swallowed hard, the weight of everything pressing down on him like a suffocating blanket. The dead dog, the outburst at the party—it all pointed to something darker, something Lila had become that he didn't recognise. And now, with a child on the way, he had to fight. He had to take custody of Molly, had to make sure this house was safe.

"I don't recognise her anymore, Cass. I don't know what she's capable of. It scares me." He buried his face in his hands.

As the dusk outside the window settled into the bones of the house, Owen felt the cold creep in. Christmas had been nothing but a hollow shell of what it used to be. The laughter, the warmth, the family—all of it was gone.

Cass stood by him, strong and resilient, but even she couldn't mask the fear that lurked behind her eyes.

JANUARY 4TH

Fulbourn Hospital, a mental health facility, was on the outskirts of the village, five kilometres from the centre of Cambridge. Owen approached it, feeling the weight of its unwelcoming exterior long before he stepped through its doors. That twinned with the guilt that he was keeping this visit a secret from Cass, made the pressure bear down on him even more.

The large, impersonal brick buildings loomed under a slate-grey sky, their worn façades a testament to years of quiet suffering within. Tall fencing wrapped around the hospital grounds, punctuated by strict, sterile signage that seemed to forbid more than it welcomed. Any hint of greenery was sparse, the occasional patch of grass or struggling shrub doing little to soften the institution's severe presence.

The architecture was stark and utilitarian, its sharp lines and lack of warmth echoing the building's long history as a former Victorian asylum. Owen shivered, feeling a chill unrelated to the weather, as if the very walls of the hospital were holding onto shadows of its past. Each step towards the entrance felt heavier, as though the landscape itself was designed to discourage visitors from lingering too long, to remind them that they were stepping into a place of confinement rather than comfort.

Owen sat stiffly on the cold metal chair opposite Lila, the harsh fluorescent lights casting a pale, unforgiving glow over the small, sterile room. The walls were a bland shade of beige, bare except for a clock that ticked steadily, slicing through the heavy silence. The whole room felt oppressive, as if it were designed to squeeze out any shred of comfort or warmth.

Lila sat across from him, her once vibrant eyes dull and ringed with exhaustion. Her hair was unkempt, falling around her face in tangled strands, and her hands fidgeted constantly, her fingers twisting together in restless, frantic motions. She looked at him, but there was no recognition, no softness. Her gaze was sharp, darting around the room as if expecting someone to leap out of the shadows.

"They've all turned against me, Owen," she whispered, her voice a tense, brittle thread. "Cass, Zara… even the girls. They're all part of it. Don't you see?"

Owen's chest tightened as he listened to her, a mix of pity and despair weighing down on him. "Lila, that's not true. Molly and Ella—they love you. They're just… they're confused, that's all."

Lila let out a sharp, mirthless laugh, her eyes narrowing. "Confused? They're not confused, Owen. They've been poisoned. Poisoned by her." Her voice dropped to a harsh whisper, as though speaking too loudly might summon the very person she despised. "Cass. She's been trying to ruin my life from the start. Zara knows it. Everyone can see it. Everyone except you."

"Zara?" Owen glanced around uncomfortably, feeling the walls closing in on him. The starkness of the room, the distant sounds of doors clanging and footsteps echoing in the corridors, amplified his own sense of helplessness. He was here, alone, trapped between his guilt for hiding this visit from Cass and the overwhelming sadness of seeing Lila like this—a shadow of the woman she'd once been.

"Lila," he began softly, his voice catching in his throat. "No one's trying to ruin your life. We all just... we all want you to get better."

Lila's face twisted with a bitterness that cut him to the core. "Get better? You think I'm mad, don't you?" She leaned forward, her voice rising in desperation. "They've set me up, Owen. Can't you see it? The earrings, the things going missing, everyone was part of it. They wanted me to snap, to make me look crazy."

Owen swallowed, struggling to keep his composure. The Lila he remembered was slipping away, replaced by this frantic, broken version who saw enemies in every shadow. "Lila, please... listen to yourself. You're not making any sense"

Lila's eyes flashed. "You don't understand. None of you do." She looked around the room, her gaze wild and unfocused, her voice dropping to a conspiratorial whisper. "They're all in on it, Owen. Even the doctors here... they're trying to keep me here, to silence me."

Owen felt a shiver run down his spine, the oppressive atmosphere of the hospital pressing in on him like a weight he couldn't shake. The institutional harshness of the place—the sterile smell, the clinical walls, the heavy security—made him feel trapped, as though he were the one confined, as though he too were being suffocated by something he couldn't name.

"Lila," he whispered, leaning forward, his voice trembling. "Please, you have to trust the doctors. They're here to help you."

Lila's face twisted in anger, her hands balling into fists. "Help me? They're helping *her*, Owen! Helping Cass get exactly what she wants. Don't you see? She's taken everything from me—our home, our life... even our girls." Her voice broke, and for a moment, he glimpsed the anguish beneath her paranoia, the raw pain that fuelled her fractured mind.

"I miss them," she murmured, her voice barely a whisper. "Molly, Ella... they don't even know the truth. They think I'm the villain. But they are wrong. I haven't done this. None of this is me."

Owen reached out, hesitating before he took her hand in his, feeling the tension thrumming beneath her skin. "They don't think that, Lila. They're just... they're scared, confused. They need their mum to get better."

Lila snatched her hand away, her gaze hardening once more. "So I'm the one who's broken, is that it?" She spat the words with a venom that sent a chill down his spine. "You're on her side too. All of you are."

Owen felt his resolve crumbling, the guilt gnawing at him as he realised how powerless he was, how helpless he felt in the face of her illness. This woman before him, the woman he had once loved so fiercely, was lost to him, trapped in a world of shadows and betrayals.

He took a deep breath, his voice barely a whisper. "I just want you to be okay, Lila. That's all I want."

She scoffed, leaning back in her chair, a bitter smile tugging at the corners of her mouth. "Okay? You want me to be okay?" She shook her head, her gaze distant. "You left me, Owen. You left me for her."

The weight of her words settled over him, filling him with a hollow ache that echoed in the empty room. He could feel the walls closing in, the oppressive atmosphere pressing down on him, the overwhelming sense that he was losing her completely.

As the silence stretched, Lila's eyes grew distant, her fingers tracing circles on the cold metal table between them. She seemed to retreat further into herself, her expression hollow and lost, as though she were slipping away even as she sat before him.

Owen wanted to reach out, to hold her, to reassure her that things would somehow be okay. But the truth was, he didn't know if they would be. He didn't know if she would ever come back from this dark place, or if the Lila he knew was already gone.

The distant sound of a door opening broke the silence, and a nurse entered, giving Owen a gentle nod. "Visiting time is over, Mr Wellington."

Owen's heart sank, the finality of the moment hitting him like a blow. He stood slowly, glancing at Lila one last time, hoping for some sign of recognition, some glimpse of the woman he'd once known.

But she didn't look at him. Her gaze was fixed on some unseen point beyond the room, her expression vacant and unreachable.

With a heavy heart, Owen turned to leave, the sterile, impersonal walls closing in around him as he walked away. The weight of his guilt and despair followed him, a constant reminder of the life he'd left behind and the woman he'd lost, perhaps forever.

SHE

I remember being a teenage girl, sitting on the torn sofa in our living room, listening to my parents scream at each other. My little brother had been found dead in his cot a few years earlier. After that everything started to fall apart.

The house was always a mess, the air thick with the smell of stale cigarettes and the sour reek of spilled beer. Dishes piled up in the sink, crusted with old food. Dust clung to every surface, coating the mismatched furniture that was tired and worn out. The carpet, once beige, was now stained and grimy, with a path worn thin down the middle from years of footsteps. It seemed like everything in that house was broken or on the verge of it.

My father was sprawled in his chair, beer in hand, his clothes wrinkled and stained, with a faint odour of sweat that never seemed to leave him. He barely noticed me, and if he did, it was usually to shout some complaint or order. My mother, thin and worn down, moved through the house with the same dull, glazed expression, her own way of retreating from the world around her. She didn't care much for me either, her attention mostly focused on herself, absorbed in the endless grind of resentment that kept her tethered to my father.

Love was something I saw on TV or read about in books. It didn't exist in our house. My mother's rare words to me were sharp, dismissive, or else tinged with a bitterness that seemed to poison everything around her. My father's voice was always loud, always rough, either in anger or disdain. I was invisible to them, a nuisance at best, someone to ignore and avoid. Any affection I craved was met with cold indifference or outright irritation.

And then there was the fighting. My parents fought like animals, loud and vicious, tearing into each other with words that cut like knives. I would sit there, pretending to be invisible, watching them spit accusations, their voices rising higher and higher. Tonight was no different.

"You're useless, can't even clean up after yourself!" my mother snapped, her voice a sharp hiss as she flung a dirty dish across the room. It shattered against the wall, fragments raining down onto the floor where it joined a pile of other broken things.

My father barely flinched; his face twisted into a sneer as he took another swig from his can. "Look who's talking. All you do is complain. Can't even look after your own kid, let alone this place!"

They kept going, louder and louder, their voices clawing at each other, each word meant to hurt. The words weren't even about me, but each one felt like a slap, a reminder of my place in this house—an unwanted bystander, caught in the middle of their hate.

The fight escalated, their voices rising to a pitch that filled every corner of the house. I was still on the sofa, watching my mother's face harden with every insult thrown. Her eyes, dull and exhausted, flickered with a rare determination I hadn't seen in years. She left the room abruptly, disappearing into the back bedroom, the shouts from my father fading into a low murmur as he muttered to himself, cursing the empty space she'd left.

After a few minutes, she reappeared, clutching an old, beaten-up duffel bag. Her movements were fast, almost frantic, as she shoved clothes and other items into it without a second glance. She didn't look at me, didn't even acknowledge I was there, sitting on the edge of the sofa, my hands gripping my knees. I wanted to speak, to ask her what she was doing, but the words stayed lodged in my throat, a mix of fear and anger bubbling up inside me.

"Are you... leaving?" *I managed, my voice a hoarse whisper, as if afraid that saying it out loud would make it true.*

She froze for a moment, her hand still on the zipper of the bag. She looked at me briefly, but there was no softness, no regret in her eyes. Just that same hardened, hollow look she always wore. "I can't do this anymore," *she muttered, more to herself than to me.* "I need to get out of here."

Her words cut through me, as cold and unfeeling as the house itself. I didn't move, didn't say anything, just watched as she slung the bag over her shoulder.

As she walked to the door, I wanted to scream, to reach out, to ask her to stay, but stubborn pride held me back, a voice in my head that told me it wouldn't make a difference. I stayed rooted to the spot, watching her turn the doorknob, her movements slow but deliberate. She didn't look back, not once. The door shut behind her, the sound echoing through the silence, final and unforgiving.

And just like that, she was gone, leaving nothing behind but the stale smell of cigarettes, the grime on the walls, and the emptiness that filled every room. I sat alone, the quiet settling over me, realising that for all the years she had stayed, she had left long ago.

I didn't cry. I'd learned long ago that crying only drew attention, and attention meant anger. Instead, I sat there, staring at the damp walls, the peeling paint, the chaos around me. The house felt like a cage, every room echoing with years of anger and neglect. The only thing I ever felt in that house was the certainty that someday, I'd escape it. Someday, I'd be anywhere else, someone else.

FEBRUARY 6TH

Outside, the February weather had settled in a bone-chilling dampness that seeped through the walls of Granta Hall, lingering in every room despite the hum of the central heating. The darkness had come early, thick and oppressive, casting an eerie gloom over the expansive grounds. Thin branches of bare trees scratched against the windows in the wind, and the skies hung low, heavy with clouds that had blocked out the weak, pale sun all day.

Inside, Cass had arranged the dining room meticulously, a pristine but soulless display that felt as formal as it was stifling. The room itself was an exercise in monochrome: white walls, black leather chairs, and a glass-topped dining table that looked as if it belonged in a magazine more than in a family home. The furnishings were all sharp edges and gleaming surfaces, the sort that repelled warmth. A vase of artfully arranged white lilies sat at the centre of the table, their sterile beauty doing little to soften the room's cold atmosphere. Around the walls, a few minimalist black-and-white photographs hung in silver frames, each perfectly placed, each adding to the overall effect of precision rather than comfort.

Cass had gone all out with the meal, preparing a whole fish and an array of sides that looked like something straight from a high-end restaurant. Steam rose from the serving dishes, but despite the careful presentation, the food remained untouched, cooling slowly under the dim recessed lights that cast a stark glow over the scene.

Molly sat across from Cass, staring down at her plate, her fork listlessly pushing around her food. Her face was pale, her eyes tired, and the usual sparkle in them had been replaced by a dullness that seemed to reflect the lifeless décor around her. She had barely spoken a word since they'd sat down, and her shoulders were hunched, as if she were trying to make herself invisible.

Owen sat beside her, equally silent, his mind elsewhere, barely registering the food in front of him, the lines of his face tense, deepened by the sharp shadows cast by the overhead lights. His thoughts had drifted into a heavy fog, his mind circling anxiously around Lila, around the unsettling events that had led them here, to this cold, unfamiliar house that somehow felt emptier every day. His attention only snapped back to the present when he realised Cass was speaking, her voice too bright, almost brittle, breaking the silence.

"So," Cass said, her tone cheerful but forced. "How was your day?" Her eyes moved between Owen and Molly; her smile fixed as she waited for one of them to respond.

There was a pause, the silence stretching on longer than was comfortable. Molly glanced up briefly, before quickly looking back down at her plate. She shrugged, barely moving, her voice a mumble. "Fine."

Cass's smile didn't falter, though a faint irritation flickered in her eyes. She turned to Owen, her tone still light, but with a subtle undercurrent of impatience. "And you, Owen? Busy day at work?"

Owen looked up, blinking as if waking from a daze. "Uh... yes, busy," he muttered, picking up his fork and cutting into his food, though he barely tasted it.

"Good, good. I'm glad you both had a good day."

The words felt hollow, her tone forced. She was trying to play hostess, the perfect wife, her demeanour polished and polite, but there was a stiffness to her movements, a practiced quality that felt all wrong. The smile never quite reached her eyes, and the brightness in her tone felt like it was covering something darker, something colder.

Molly shifted in her seat, casting a quick glance at Owen before returning to pushing her food around her plate. She'd barely eaten anything, and the dark shadows under her eyes betrayed her weariness. She seemed to wilt under the harsh lighting, her small frame swallowed up by the oversized velvet dining chair.

Outside, the wind picked up, rattling the windows slightly, and Cass's forced smile wavered as she looked around the table, the tension in her posture more obvious with each second that passed. She took a sip from her water glass, her eyes darting between Owen and Molly, as if hoping one of them might suddenly engage, might suddenly fill the silence that had settled over the table like a heavy fog.

"So, Molly," Cass said, her tone softening slightly as she looked at the girl. "Do you have any fun plans for school this week?"

Molly shrugged again, her voice barely audible. "Not really." Then, after a moment, she glanced up, her voice slightly stronger, tinged with sadness. "I miss Ella."

The words hung in the air, striking something raw in Owen who shifted uncomfortably, guilt washing over him. He hadn't spoken to Ella in days, her distance from him widening since Lila had spiralled out of control. But hearing Molly's quiet admission made the absence of her sister feel painfully present.

Cass's forced smile tightened, her expression hardening almost imperceptibly. She set her glass down a bit too hard, the clink of glass against glass filling the silence. "Well, I'm sure Ella is enjoying herself wherever she is," she said, her tone dismissive, as though brushing the mention of Ella away like an unwelcome intruder.

Molly frowned, her hands clutching her fork. "She's with her friends, but it's not the same," she mumbled. "She... she would've come home if things weren't so... different."

Cass's mouth thinned, the practiced warmth in her eyes cooling into something sharper. She opened her mouth as if to say something, but Owen quickly cut in, sensing the undercurrent of resentment building.

"Molly," he said gently, touching her hand. "We'll see Ella soon. I'll make sure of it." But even as he spoke, he felt the hollowness in his own words, the doubt that he could fix what had fractured between him and his older daughter.

Molly sighed, nodding, though the sadness remained in her eyes. She glanced back down at her plate again, her appetite gone.

Cass watched them both, her face an unreadable mask, before she forced another smile, her tone brightening again, though the bitterness was hard to miss. "Well, we're here together now," she said, her voice brittle, "and we're very lucky to have each other."

The words fell flat against the silence that settled over the table once more. Owen knew, as did Molly, that this wasn't what 'together' was supposed to feel like.

Outside, the wind howled, a lonely sound that echoed through the empty halls of the house, screaming like a soul trapped in purgatory.

SHE

It's close to midnight. The house is quiet, thick with the kind of silence that settles after too much noise. Everything here has that sticky feel, that stale smell of yesterday's sweat, smoke, and beer, like the whole place is coated in a film I can never scrub away. Outside, the rain taps softly against the glass, a gentle, steady whisper, coaxing my father to sleep as I sit and wait.

He's in his room now, sprawled on his bed. I've watched him like this before, in that same lifeless slump, one arm flung out, legs parted like he just dropped dead. He probably won't wake for hours, at least not until the first light worms through the blinds and burns through his closed eyelids. Not even then sometimes. I learned a long time ago to slip past him quietly, step around the creaky boards in the hallway, hold my breath until I can't feel his presence clawing at me from behind the walls.

I listen for that heavy, laboured breathing that confirms he's out cold, the same rhythm I've grown used to as a backdrop for nights spent huddled in my room, wishing for the locks on my door that never came. Tonight, though, I'm the one prowling, moving soundlessly towards his room instead of away from it.

In the shadows, I slide open the wardrobe, slipping my fingers between the worn slats until I find it. The wood is smooth, polished in places by his grip alone. A man who once had enough strength to swing it in a game but now keeps it close for different reasons. The weight of it rests heavily in my hands, grounding me, whispering my intentions back at me in a voice that sounds nothing like my own.

He told me he kept it for protection. Protection—as if he ever protected me. As if either of them did. When she walked out the door, that silent, final slam of goodbye without so much as a glance back. She didn't leave him; she left me. She abandoned me. Because of him.

I grip the bat tighter and step toward him. His face is slack, mouth open like a gaping wound in the dark. He mumbles, a low sound, caught somewhere between a grunt and a groan, and then goes still again. Just a limp, sleeping heap.

I take another step, bringing me to the edge of his bed. There's something sharp and hot clawing up my spine, setting every nerve on fire until I can barely feel the bat in my hands. My heartbeat fills my ears, loud and demanding, a pulse that drowns out every other thought until I'm left with one singular image— one that's burned into my mind. Her silhouette, backlit by the setting sun, that brief pause before she walked out, leaving me with this stranger in his wrecked kingdom of dust and dirt and shadows.

I raise the bat over my shoulder, the muscles in my arms trembling as I steady it, my eyes locked on his chest rising and falling, that unfazed slumber that only he seems capable of finding in this hellhole. There's a part of me that wants him to wake up, to see what he's made of me. To look at me one last time and realise he's the one who put this in my hands.

I hesitate, gripping the bat so tightly my knuckles go white. Because if he wakes, he might understand—or maybe he'll just give me that lazy, half-lidded look he always does, the one that

THE OTHER WOMAN

does not care. That's his specialty, after all: the lack of anything real, the emptiness he surrounds himself with like a shield. Maybe that's what I hate the most. Not him, exactly, but the ghost of him. The way his silence became my life's soundtrack, filling every corner, every moment, until I couldn't hear myself think.

But he stays asleep, blissfully unaware as the rain grows louder outside, a murmur building into a relentless drum, masking the sound of my breathing, hands tightening around the wood. I think about what he'd say if he knew. If he had even an ounce of understanding of how his words lingered, how his inaction poisoned me, drop by drop.

I lean forward, the bat hovering over him, my chest heaving with the weight of things I can't say. Every muscle in me is tensed, a coiled spring ready to release. His chest rises and falls, oblivious, mocking, like he doesn't know he's earned this. Like he'll go on sleeping through it all, through me.

My arms tremble as I steady myself, the bat suspended high above him. I picture her again, my mother's silhouette etched into my mind, just beyond his shoulder. The bat feels alive now, humming with the weight of my anger, my betrayal, everything he's forced me to swallow over the years. Every tear, every scream buried down deep.

The thought of what comes next fills me with a strange calm, almost a relief, as if the act will empty me of this sick heaviness that's been sitting in my stomach for so long. My hands tighten further around the bat's worn handle as I inhale sharply, the rush of air catching like a stone in my throat.

I bring the bat down.

The wood cracks against him with a sickening, dull thud, the shock of it vibrating up my arms. His body jolts, a groan escaping his mouth before he even registers what's happened. But I don't give him a chance to react, to open his eyes, to ask me why. Before he can make sense of it, I'm bringing the bat down again, harder, feeling the splinters bite into my palms as the sound fills the room. Each impact drowns out the memories he's left me with, the bitter taste he's planted inside me, one blow at a time.

He's muttering something, words garbled and slurred, hands lifting weakly to shield himself. But his eyes never open. His weakness, the very thing that's let him sleep through every hurt, every wrong in this house, has left him defenceless. It's almost too easy.

I take a step back, my chest heaving, the bat still gripped tight in my hands, heavy with new blood and splintered in places. I look down at him, at the strange, warped reflection of myself in his slack face, and for the first time, I feel something close to peace.

The silence returns, thick and complete, broken only by the sound of the rain and my ragged breathing.

I drop the bat to the floor, watching it bounce and roll a little before settling, its blood-streaked wood catching the faint light from the hallway. It feels weightless now, nothing more than a discarded stick, stripped of purpose, a shadow of what it was just moments ago. My fingers ache as I open and close my hand, the muscles tight and raw. I press the back of my hand to my mouth, wiping away the warmth there, smearing blood across my cheek without caring.

I don't look back at him as I slip out of his room. The door creaks closed behind me, the sound loud but hollow in the quiet. A strange calmness settles over me, a surreal detachment, like I'm watching myself from above, hovering somewhere outside my own body. My footsteps echo down the hall, each step feeling strangely lighter as if a weight I never fully understood has finally lifted.

In the bathroom, I flick on the light, blinking as the bright fluorescent glow spills over the small, cramped space. The mirror catches my reflection, and for a moment, I barely recognise the girl staring back at me. There's something in her eyes, a darkness, a strange, steady look that doesn't belong. The blood streaks her skin like smeared war paint, staining her clothes, trailing down her arms in thin, drying rivers. I reach out to touch the edge of the sink, grounding myself in the cold porcelain, before stripping off my top and letting it fall to the floor with a soft, wet slap.

The shower knob turns easily, and I step into the stream, feeling the hot water pour over me, washing away the blood in thick, swirling ribbons that disappear down the drain. The water stings where the splinters dug in, the small cuts lighting up like tiny fires, but I let the warmth numb it. I watch the water turn red, then pink, then clear again, scrubbing at my skin, wiping away everything he left behind.

The minutes slip by, and I stand there, letting the water pour over me, heavy and hot, a blanket that presses down, easing the last of the tremors in my hands. I take a deep breath, letting the steam fill my lungs, clearing out the stale, metallic smell of blood and something sharper, darker, that clings to me. I close my eyes, pressing my palms against the cool tiles, steadying myself against the waves of something raw and unnamed rising in my chest.

When I shut off the water, the silence returns, as heavy as ever, but different now. It's not the silence of a house suffocating under his presence. It's a new quiet, almost pure, like a freshly erased slate.

I step out of the shower, grabbing a towel and wrapping it around myself, feeling the soft fabric cling to my damp skin. I glance in the mirror once more, meeting my own gaze, searching for any sign of guilt or remorse in the girl staring back. But there's nothing, only that steady, unblinking look, a quiet satisfaction that settles in my stomach like a warm stone.

It's over now. Finally, truly over.

All I have left to do now is work out what I do next.

FEBRUARY 18TH

Owen walked towards the doctor's office, his footsteps echoing down the narrow, sterile hallway. He felt small in the space—surrounded by white walls that were somehow both clinical and oppressive, the faint scent of antiseptic mingling with the underlying chill that clung to the air. His reflection flashed in the polished metal of a nearby cabinet, and for a moment, he barely recognised the man staring back at him.

His face was pale, etched with worry lines that seemed to deepen every day. The stubble he hadn't bothered to shave made him look worn, weary, haunted even. His shoulders were tense, his suit hanging loosely from weight he hadn't noticed he'd lost, and his once steady hands now trembled slightly. He shoved them into his pockets, trying to conceal the signs of his own fraying edges as he reached the doctor's office.

The room was small, cramped but somehow cosy, like an oasis of warmth amid the cold, impersonal corridors. A small, mustard-coloured lamp cast a gentle glow over the room, its light glinting off the polished oak of the doctor's desk and the shelves lining the walls, filled with thick medical textbooks and worn folders.

Doctor Patel sat behind the desk, his expression calm, composed, the epitome of a man who had seen all manner of human suffering and had learned how to keep it from etching itself into his own soul. He was an older man, with salt-and-pepper hair neatly combed back and warm brown eyes that softened the otherwise stern lines of his face. His glasses perched low on his nose, and his hands—strong, thick-fingered—rested calmly on a folder labelled with Lila's name. His suit, crisp and neatly pressed, bore a faint scent, like he'd dabbed cologne just under his collar before beginning the day.

Doctor Patel gave Owen a slow, understanding nod as he gestured for him to sit. Owen settled heavily into the small leather chair, its surface worn and cracked, feeling as if it might swallow him whole. He leaned forward, elbows on his knees, his hands still shaking slightly despite his efforts to steady them.

"How are you holding up, Mr. Wellington?" the doctor asked, his voice gentle but firm. His accent was soft, his words precise, as though he chose each one with great care.

Owen forced himself to meet the doctor's eyes, though he felt unsteady, unfocused. "Honestly? Not well. I barely recognise her." His voice cracked, and he looked away, swallowing the emotion that threatened to surface. "She's like a stranger."

Doctor Patel nodded, allowing the silence to settle before responding. "Lila has been through a lot," he said softly, his voice barely above a whisper but resonant with empathy. "Her condition is complex, and it's not something that developed overnight. What we're seeing now is the culmination of prolonged stress, trauma, and perhaps undiagnosed mental health issues that have built up over time."

Owen shifted in the chair, running a hand through his thinning hair. "But... she was okay before," he murmured, his gaze drifting over to the shelves. His eyes settled on a diploma framed in dark wood, hanging slightly askew on the wall. The creases around his mouth deepened as he struggled to make sense of what he was hearing. "She was strong, resilient. This doesn't make sense."

The doctor leaned back in his chair, resting his hands calmly on his lap, his fingers lightly tapping the surface of Lila's file. "Mental health can be complicated, Mr Wellington. It's often hard to predict when someone will reach a breaking point." He spoke slowly, clearly, and with compassion. "From what we understand, Lila experienced a series of traumatic events recently, correct?"

Owen nodded, his mind drifting back to the past months—the paranoia, the affair, the outburst at Molly's party. The memories felt like weights dragging him down, each one settling heavily in his chest. "Yes," he murmured. "A lot has happened."

The doctor shifted in his chair, his eyes narrowing with thought. "It's possible that Lila was dealing with these pressures in ways that weren't visible to others. Sometimes, people bury their emotions, compartmentalise their pain. Over time, that can lead to a build-up that's too much for the mind to process. When that pressure reaches its peak, a psychotic episode can be triggered."

Owen clenched his jaw, staring down at his hands. He hated how fragile they looked, veins bulging beneath the skin, as though they were as frayed as he felt. "So... this psychosis... is it permanent?"

The doctor leaned forward, folding his hands together in a gesture of assurance. "Psychosis is a symptom, not a lifelong sentence. It can be managed, sometimes even overcome, but it requires the right treatment and, most importantly, time."

Owen swallowed, nodding, though he struggled to picture Lila—the woman who had always been the backbone of their family—being helped by medication and therapy. "What kind of treatment?" he asked, his voice hoarse. "What are you doing to help her?"

Doctor Patel's finger drummed on Lila's file as he spoke. "We've started her on a regimen of antipsychotic medication. The sedated state you see her in now is largely due to these medications. It's necessary in the early stages to prevent further distress and to help stabilise her mood." His stare was steady, as though he wanted Owen to understand that Lila's stillness wasn't a void, but a bridge to healing.

The room felt smaller with each word, as though the reality of Lila's illness was closing in on Owen, forcing him to confront it. "Will it help her?"

"It can, if she's willing to engage," Doctor Patel replied, his tone cautious but hopeful. "She'll also undergo cognitive behavioural therapy once she's stable enough. It will help her process her thoughts, her emotions, and gradually make sense of the experiences that may have contributed to this episode."

Before Owen could respond, a loud clang from the hallway made him flinch. Both men looked toward the door, and for a brief moment, the doctor's calm demeanour slipped, his eyes flashing with concern. He quickly turned back to Owen, resetting his expression into practiced composure.

"It's nothing to worry about," he said, though his eyes betrayed a flicker of unease. "We occasionally have disturbances here, but our staff is well-equipped to handle them."

Owen nodded slowly, his eyes lingering on the door as his unease continued to build. The noises outside were muffled but persistent, the faint sounds of raised voices and hurried footsteps creating a sense of barely contained chaos. The world beyond the walls of the office felt fragile, unsettling.

Doctor Patel's voice drew him back to the moment. "As I was saying, Mr Wellington, this is a long process, one that requires both time and patience."

Owen looked down, his hands twisting together, the weight of the conversation settling on his shoulders. "She told me something earlier. She said it was all a set-up. That… she's innocent."

The doctor sighed softly, leaning forward, his expression sombre. "That kind of delusion isn't uncommon with psychosis, Mr Wellington. It's possible that Lila truly believes she's being persecuted. For someone in her state, creating a narrative is often a way to cope with feelings of powerlessness."

"So, she really believes this?" Owen's voice was barely audible, his mind racing.

The doctor nodded. "To her, these thoughts feel very real. But with time, medication, and therapy, we hope she'll be able to see beyond them."

A sense of helplessness washed over Owen as he absorbed the doctor's words. He had come here seeking answers, some sign that Lila could come back from this, but all he felt was the weight of uncertainty. As the doctor explained the treatment, the room seemed to grow dimmer, the once warm light casting deep shadows across the walls.

Doctor Patel leaned back, his expression both kind and resolute. "This will take time, Mr Wellington. And it won't be easy. But we'll do everything we can for her."

Owen rose from his chair, feeling the ache of exhaustion settle into his bones. "Thank you," he whispered, his voice hollow.

As he turned to leave, the earlier guilt of keeping this visit from Cass resurfaced, gnawing at him with renewed intensity. The doctor began sorting through Lila's file, but Owen lingered by the door, his mind a storm of doubt and guilt. He wanted to tell Cass, to share the weight of what he'd seen, but the fear of shattering the fragile stability they'd built held him back.

Stepping into the cold hallway, Owen felt the shadows of

guilt, secrets, and the reality of Lila's condition strangle him. And as he walked away, he wondered how long he could keep carrying it all alone. He no longer understood her, but he had loved her once, more than anything, and he started to wonder when and why that changed.

SHE

I stand at the top of the stairs, my bag slung over my shoulder, watching as shadows lengthen across the walls, filling the empty spaces in this place that was supposed to be my home. It should've been warm and alive, filled with laughter and love, but there's nothing here. Every corner, every room is haunted by the things that were promised and never delivered. It's a shrine to all the things that could have been—and I can't stand to look at it.

My eyes wander to the family room, with its stiff, lifeless furniture, untouched and unloved. I can still picture it—the way it looked when we first moved in, the bright, hopeful walls, the fresh paint that smelled like new beginnings. It's faded now, yellowed and cracked, just like the promises they made to me. Promises of family dinners, of late nights and whispered secrets, of a life that felt safe. Instead, it's been nothing but a prison, a place where love was rationed like scraps, doled out only when they wanted something in return.

I walk down the hall slowly, each step a dull thud against the floorboards, like I'm hammering in the last nails on the coffin of this life. The photographs line the walls, rows of smiling faces frozen in time, hollow and staged. I glance at them, the fake smiles and empty eyes, and feel a heat crawl up my spine. How long have they been lying to me? How long have they pretended that this house, this life, meant anything at all?

My fingertips brush against the frame of a family photo—me, standing between them, looking up with that stupid, trusting smile on my face. It's laughable now. The girl in the picture, naive and hopeful, thinking they'd actually be there. I yank the frame off the wall, watching as it drops to the floor and shatters, glass splintering across the hardwood. Good. Let it break. Just like they did to me.

I move to the kitchen, the bag on my shoulder growing heavier with each step. This was supposed to be the heart of the house, where we'd cook together, share stories over dinners. But I can't remember a single real conversation happening here, only icy silences, sharp words cutting through the air like knives. I open a cabinet and stare inside—perfect rows of cups and plates, the ones we never used. They're as cold and lifeless as the people who collected them. I want to smash them all, feel the satisfying crunch of glass and porcelain under my feet, but I hold back. Let them sit there, unloved. Just like me.

The hallway to my room feels like it stretches out in front of me, as if it doesn't want to let me go, like this house itself is trying to trap me here. But I push forward, my heart hammering in my chest, each step stoking the anger that's burning inside me. It's a rage that's been simmering for as long as I can remember, buried under fear and disappointment, but now it's raw, alive, filling me with a bitter kind of strength.

My room is the last stop, the place that was supposed to be mine but always felt like it belonged to someone else. I look around, taking in the lifeless decorations, the walls painted in colours they picked, the furniture they arranged. It's a room built for show, for their idea of who I should be, not who I am. I grab a few last things—a book, a photo, a bracelet my mum bought on a *whim and never actually noticed if I wore. These things are meaningless, but I take them anyway, just to leave the place a little emptier. Just so they know I was here and now I'm not.*

I stand in the middle of the room, breathing heavily, letting the memories of every careless word, every broken promise, every single way they failed me wash over me like a wave. They think they can leave me here, forgotten, invisible, while they play house and pretend they didn't tear me apart in the process. But I won't stay here, not anymore and if I can't have the life I deserve, no one will have it.

With one last look around, I turn and walk back down the hall. The house feels like it's watching me, judging me, but I don't care. Let it try to keep me.

I walk out the front door, letting it slam behind me, and I feel the anger in my chest shift to something different—something like freedom.

The air outside is thick with the quiet of midnight, the silence so deep I can hear my own heartbeat as I step onto the street. I drop my bag there, just out of reach of the house, and look up at the dark, empty windows, the silent walls that held me like a prison. They look back at me, unfeeling, just like they always have.

The street is empty, not a soul in sight. The streetlamp casts a cold, pale glow over everything, and for a moment, I feel like I'm already a ghost, slipping away from a life that was never really mine. I take one last glance at my things lying in a heap on the pavement, then turn back towards the house. I know what I need to do.

The back yard is overgrown, weeds tangled and thick, reclaiming the land that's been ignored just like everything else here. I push through the knee-high grass toward the small shed in the corner. Its door creaks as I pull it open, the smell of damp wood and rust filling my nose. The jerry can is just where I remember, tucked behind a stack of cracked flowerpots. I pull it out, feeling the heavy slosh of fuel inside, the weight solid and real in my hands.

With the can in hand, I head back towards the house, the night folding around me, silent and watchful. I step inside and stand in the quiet, letting it wash over me. This place has been silent for so long. Now it's time to give it a voice.

I twist off the cap and pour the fuel slowly, deliberately, watching as it soaks into the carpet, spreads across the floorboards, fills the room with that sharp, oily smell. I walk through each room, spreading the fuel over the furniture, the cold spaces that have held nothing but disappointment. Each step feels like a release, like I'm leaving a piece of myself behind with every drop.

When the can is nearly empty, I go back to the hallway, pulling a rag from my pocket and shoving it into the mouth of the can. I hold it there for a moment, staring at it, feeling the roughness of the fabric. Then I pull out a lighter, flicking it until a small, steady flame dances at the end. I watch it for a second, mesmerised by its warmth, before I lower it to the rag.

The flame catches, creeping up the cloth until it's a bright, hungry light. I stand there, just outside the front door, watching the fire eat its way down, and then, without a second thought, I throw the can inside and step out, pulling the door closed behind me for the last time.

I walk away, the night cool against my skin, my feet steady on the pavement. Behind me, I can hear the faint crackle as the flames take hold, growing louder, faster, spreading with a ferocity that surprises me. I don't look back, but I can see the glow stretching out across the street, casting a long, red shadow that follows me as I walk.

By the time I reach the end of the block, the flames have grown high, licking at the windows, reaching for the sky. The *smoke curls into the night, dark and thick, and the air is filled with the smell of burning wood and fabric. The whole house is alive now, more alive than it has ever been. It's like it's finally releasing everything it held, all the broken promises, the shattered dreams, the lies.*

I keep walking into the night. Behind me the sky begins to turn red, glowing with the light of the fire. A signal that I have been reborn, and my new life is only just beginning.

FEBRUARY 21ST

Cass strolled along the cobbled streets of Cambridge, her heels clicking rhythmically against the stone as she moved from one boutique to another, a picture of urban elegance, without a care in the world. Dressed in a sleek, black dress that hugged her frame, her heels adding inches to her statuesque figure, she turned heads effortlessly. Her make-up was heavy, with a dark eyeliner that accentuated her striking brown eyes. She was aware of every glance, every whispered compliment, and it made her glow with a quiet, self-satisfied confidence.

She stopped in front of a small jewellers, its window filled with glittering displays of gold and diamonds. The light of the early afternoon cast a soft glow through the glass, making the jewellery sparkle enticingly. Cass walked in, her stride languid as she approached the nearest case. The assistant behind the counter—a young man in his twenties with a perfectly pressed suit and an eager smile—immediately took notice.

"Good afternoon, madam," he greeted, his eyes lingering a moment too long on her as she leaned over to examine a pair of diamond earrings.

"Afternoon," Cass purred, returning his smile with a playful glance. "I'm looking for something special. Perhaps... diamond?" She glanced up, her eyes gleaming with interest as she indicated the earrings.

"An excellent choice," the assistant said smoothly, reaching into the case to retrieve them. "Diamonds are timeless, aren't they? Would you like to try them on?"

Cass nodded, allowing him to fasten the earrings for her. She admired herself in the mirror, tilting her head slightly. "Stunning," she murmured, casting a glance at the assistant. "I'll take them."

After paying, she sauntered out with her purchase, slipping the small velvet box into her designer handbag. She made her way down the street, dipping into a few more shops—each one carefully selected for its exclusivity. In a luxury cosmetics store, she was met with a more reserved assistant, a woman in her forties with hair pulled back into a severe bun.

Cass pointed to a lipstick display. "I'm after something bold."

The assistant nodded, taking her time to suggest a few options, though Cass's air of impatience was clear as she inspected each one. She settled on a vibrant scarlet, swiping it onto her lips in the shop mirror before smiling at her reflection.

"Perfect," she said, admiring herself. "I'll take two."

With a flick of her hair, she exited the store, the familiar, heady scent of Chanel No. 5 following her. She felt in control, revelling in the small indulgences, her self-assured smile lingering as she strolled through the city. She made her way to a high-end perfumery, where she chatted with another eager shop assistant about the nuances of top notes and base notes in the latest designer scents. After selecting a bottle of expensive perfume, she watched as the assistant carefully wrapped it in layers of tissue and placed it in a glossy shopping bag.

Cass found herself in a children's boutique, the interior

awash in soft pastels. Rows of tiny, delicate clothes were folded in pristine piles, and plush animals stared down from their shelves with painted eyes. Cass ran her hands over a rack of outfits for newborns, her face softening momentarily as she picked out a few gender-neutral onesies in soft greys and whites. She approached the saleswoman—a friendly, older lady who cooed over the baby clothes as Cass handed them over.

"When are you due?" the woman asked warmly, ringing up the items.

"August," Cass replied, a touch of pride in her voice. "It's my first."

The woman smiled. "August babies—brave little souls, they say."

Cass left with a satisfied smile, laden with more shopping bags. She felt a thrill at each transaction, each piece she selected building a sense of a life she was crafting with precision and care.

As she made her way into the Grand Arcade shopping centre, her heels clicking on the polished marble floors, she felt her confidence waver slightly. The sprawling space was crowded with shoppers—families with children, couples strolling arm in arm, students rushing with textbooks in hand—and yet, Cass felt an odd sensation prickling at the back of her neck, as though someone's eyes were fixed on her.

She glanced over her shoulder, searching the faces around her. Still, the feeling persisted, a faint, uneasy sense of being watched. She forced a smile, dismissing it as nothing more than nerves. After all, her life had taken on a heightened intensity lately, with Owen's troubles, the issues with Molly, and the strain of maintaining a picture-perfect façade. It was only natural, she told herself, to feel on edge.

Cass continued her stroll, but the sense of unease lingered, shadowing her movements as she drifted in and out of more boutiques. By the time she reached John Lewis, she felt her confidence beginning to slip. The store was bustling with people, yet the feeling of being followed only grew. She passed a mirror and caught a glimpse of herself—a vision in black, striking and almost out of place among the families and casual shoppers.

In the baby department, Cass picked up a soft, cream-coloured blanket, running her fingers over its fabric. She felt her shoulders tense as she looked around, although she found nothing out of place. Despite the ordinary scene, the strange feeling persisted, an irrational fear creeping over her skin.

She moved briskly through the remaining aisles, her movements no longer languid but tight, controlled. She paid for the blanket with a clipped nod, her eyes darting from one side of the store to the other as she left, clutching her bags more tightly than before. She knew it was silly, but she couldn't shake the sensation that someone was watching her.

As she descended the escalator, she resisted the urge to look over her shoulder. She reminded herself that she was being ridiculous—no one was watching her, no one cared. But by the time she reached the bottom, her heartbeat was faster, her hands clenching the handles of her bags tightly.

She made her way out of the Grand Arcade and hurried to the car park, her heels echoing loudly in the dim, cavernous space. Shadows loomed around the parked cars, the fluorescent lights casting an unnatural, cold glow over everything. Her eyes flickered from side to side, watching for any movement, her nerves on edge. She reached her car—a sleek, black Audi convertible Owen had bought for her—a symbol of the new life she was constructing, shiny and alluring.

As she slid into the driver's seat, she exhaled, realising she'd been holding her breath. She shut the door and turned the key, the engine's low hum a comforting sound in the silence of the car park. She cast one last, wary glance around her, scanning the dimly lit space for any sign of movement.

Nothing. Only the shadows, still and unthreatening.

With a sigh of relief, she pressed down on the accelerator, eager to leave the unsettling feeling behind her. She navigated the winding levels of the car park, the neon EXIT signs glowing eerily as she drove past, until she emerged onto the street. The city lights blurred beneath the darkening sky as she sped away, but the unease remained, a shadowy presence she couldn't quite escape, a reminder that her carefully constructed world wasn't as solid as it seemed.

FEBRUARY 26TH

Owen sat at his desk, tapping his pen against the polished glass surface, his eyes scanning through the columns of numbers that seemed to melt into one another. The conversation with his accountant earlier that morning had been both tense and worrying, and his mind kept circling back to the implications of those ominous words.

He picked up his phone, reluctantly dialling his accountant's number again. After a couple of rings, John, a man with years of experience in financial scrutiny, answered with his familiar gravelly tone.

"Owen. I hoped you'd call back," John began, his voice carrying an edge of concern. "I've been reviewing the accounts again. We need to talk about these anomalies. This is getting serious."

Owen clenched his jaw, his frustration simmering. "All right, John. Lay it out for me. What's going on, exactly?"

John sighed. "There are substantial gaps in cash flow from the last quarter—large transfers that don't add up, expenses logged that we can't trace back to anything. We've accounted for your usual overheads, payroll, and operational costs, but these expenses... they stick out like a sore thumb."

Owen frowned, flipping through the spreadsheets on his computer, each line a reminder of the supposed wealth that seemed to be slipping through his hands. "Are you saying we're in trouble here? How bad is it?"

"If HMRC catches wind of these irregularities, Owen, it won't be a simple slap on the wrist," John replied, his tone grave. "They'll launch an audit, and believe me, they'll dig through every piece of paper, every email, every bank transaction. If they suspect tax evasion, fines are the least of your worries."

Owen ran a hand through his hair, feeling the weight of John's words settle on him. An audit would mean exposure, not only to the tax authorities but to the whole financial world—a scar on his business's reputation. "There must be a mistake," he muttered, half to himself. "I don't remember signing off on anything like this, but I'm the only one who could. I will check with my team."

"That's the problem, Owen," John pressed, his voice steely. "These transfers are signed but none of the documentation seems to line up with legitimate business expenses. If we don't get a handle on this fast, we're looking at potential fraud allegations. You need to get to the bottom of who's been authorising these payments. It's not a small amount we're talking about here."

The possibility of fraud clawed at Owen's stomach, his grip tightening on the phone. "How much are we talking about, exactly?"

John hesitated, the pause almost unbearable. "Upward of a quarter of a million. Enough to attract HMRC's attention in a heartbeat."

A cold sweat broke out across Owen's forehead. A quarter of a million pounds missing. His mind raced, trying to reconcile the lavish spending and apparent security his life with Cass had afforded him with this looming threat. If this went public, it would shatter not just his business, but everything he'd worked so hard to maintain.

"Owen, I'd suggest a full internal audit before HMRC comes knocking," John continued, his voice hard and unyielding. "Something doesn't add up. Either way, if HMRC gets involved, they'll assume you're complicit unless proven otherwise."

Owen sat in silence, the gravity of John's words hanging heavy in the air. "All right," he managed, his voice barely a whisper. "I'll look into it. But, John, what happens if I can't explain these… gaps?"

"If you can't account for it, Owen, HMRC will assume tax evasion or fraud, both of which come with serious legal consequences. We're talking not only about fines and penalties but, in the worst-case scenario, prison time."

Owen's stomach dropped. "Right. Thanks, John," he said, his voice tight.

He ended the call, his hand lingering on the phone as he tried to process the severity of the situation. He glanced around his office, at the polished glass and pristine décor, all symbols of the success he'd meticulously built. And yet, all of it felt like a façade.

MARCH 13TH

Owen took a deep breath as he followed Doctor Patel down the corridor to his office. His mind was still spinning from the visit with Lila, her hollow, distant stare, the way she seemed to sink further into herself every time he saw her. The sterile smell of the hospital filled his nose, mingling with a damp chill that seemed to cling to his clothes and skin, and an uneasy feeling began to settle in the pit of his stomach.

When they entered the doctor's office, Owen felt a pang of familiarity mixed with dread. The small room, with its walls lined with shelves of worn medical books and folders, felt almost claustrophobic. The doctor's small desk lamp cast a warm but dim glow over the space, contrasting sharply with the harsh fluorescent light of the hallway.

"Please, Mr Wellington," Doctor Patel said, gesturing to the chair across from his desk. "Take a seat."

Owen lowered himself into the chair, feeling its worn leather crack under his weight. He ran a hand over his face, trying to steady himself. "Doctor Patel, I'm... I'm not seeing any progress with her. She's silent, unresponsive, like she's...

disappearing. I need to know what else can be done. Is there any other treatment, any other therapy that might help?"

The doctor watched him carefully, his hands folded on top of Lila's file. He nodded, his face softening with sympathy, and Owen could see the weariness in the doctor's eyes, the strain of years of difficult cases. "Mr Wellington, I understand how difficult this must be for you, seeing Lila in this condition. I assure you, we are doing everything within our capacity to help her. However, in cases as severe as hers, conventional treatments can take time—and may not always yield the desired response."

Owen's jaw tightened. He felt a surge of frustration, his hands balling into fists on his lap. "So... what are you saying? That she might not recover?"

Doctor Patel held his gaze, his tone calm but direct. "There is one additional option we could consider," he said, his voice carefully measured. "It's called electroconvulsive therapy, or ECT."

The words hit Owen like a punch. He had heard of ECT, but only in the vaguest, most unsettling terms. "ECT?" he repeated, his voice thick with uncertainty. "Isn't that... extreme?"

Doctor Patel nodded, his expression both serious and reassuring. "It is a more intensive treatment, yes. ECT involves administering a brief electrical current through the brain to induce a controlled seizure. This process can help reset certain aspects of the brain's chemistry, particularly for patients who are unresponsive to medications or suffering from severe, treatment-resistant conditions like Lila's."

Owen felt his mouth go dry. "And... and the risks? What kind of risks are we talking about here?"

The doctor leaned forward slightly, his gaze steady. "The most common side effect of ECT is memory loss, particularly for events surrounding the time of treatment. Patients may experience temporary disorientation or confusion. However, these effects usually diminish over time. ECT today is administered under anaesthesia, with muscle relaxants to prevent injury, and it's far more refined than it was in the past."

Owen struggled to process the information, his thoughts swirling as he tried to picture Lila undergoing such a procedure. The idea of her lying on a hospital bed, electrodes attached to her temples, jolted by electric currents, made him feel sick. "But... will she remember who she is? Will she still be... Lila?"

The doctor's expression softened, though his voice remained calm and clinical. "There is no guarantee, Mr Wellington, but in many cases, ECT has proven highly effective in restoring some semblance of stability and clarity to patients who were previously unreachable. And quite honestly," he looked down at his notes, frowning, "it's not clear now, exactly who she really is."

Owen swallowed hard, his throat tight. The possibility that ECT could help Lila was tantalising, but the risks were terrifying. "And... would she have to agree to this? Could you administer it without her permission?"

Doctor Patel's face grew sombre, his brow furrowing slightly as he carefully chose his words. "Typically, ECT requires the patient's consent. However, in cases where the patient lacks the mental capacity to make an informed decision, there are legal avenues to proceed. For patients deemed unable to consent, next of kin or a designated decision-maker can authorise the treatment on their behalf. In extreme cases, if it's deemed in the patient's best interest, a court order can be obtained to proceed."

Owen's hands tightened on the arms of the chair, the weight of the decision pressing down on him. The thought of signing off on something so invasive, so drastic, made him feel like he was betraying Lila. But he couldn't ignore the possibility that this might be the only way to reach her.

"Is there no other way?" Owen whispered, his voice barely audible.

The doctor shook his head slowly. "We're doing everything we can, Mr Wellington. But ECT may be the best option we have left. This can only be performed with the consent of a doctor, if Lila is not fit to consent for herself."

Owen nodded absently, but remained unsettled by the creeping sense of dread that had been building since he'd arrived. He felt trapped, cornered by decisions that seemed both impossible and inevitable.

The doctor shifted slightly in his seat, his expression thoughtful. "Mr Wellington, there is something else I should mention, as it could be relevant to Lila's treatment."

Owen looked up, his brow furrowed. "What is it?"

The doctor took a deep breath, folding his hands together. "It has come to our attention that, prior to her being admitted, the police received an anonymous call. The caller described Lila as unstable, violent, and... a drug addict. This was why the police went to visit her in the first place. They have a duty of care to anyone who might be a danger to themselves or others."

Owen's stomach twisted violently, a wave of horror and anger flooding through him. "What?" he managed, barely able to process the words.

Doctor Patel nodded, his face unreadable. "The caller suggested that Lila had a history of drug use and that her behaviour had been increasingly erratic. This information influenced the police's approach to her case, and, ultimately, the decision to have her sectioned. I understand this might be difficult to hear, but we need to know if there is any truth to this. A history of substance use can be crucial in determining the best course of treatment."

Owen's mind raced, his thoughts a chaotic jumble of disbelief and fury. "No," he said firmly. "Lila isn't an addict.

There was... there was one incident. She dabbled at university, but that was..." He hesitated, a memory flashing in his mind—the night Cass had brought drugs into their home, the night everything had begun to spiral out of control.

Doctor Patel's expression remained neutral, though his stare was probing. "So you're saying there's no history of substance abuse? How well do you know your wife's history, Mr Wellington?"

Owen shook his head, the anger simmering just beneath the surface. "Doctor Patel, Lila isn't an addict. This accusation... it's absurd. Whoever made that call has got it wrong."

As he spoke, a disturbing thought crept into his mind, unbidden but insistent. The anonymous call—Cass had been there when Lila had tried cocaine. She knew the details of that night, knew the chaos that had followed. She was the only one he could think of who could have painted that picture for the police.

A part of him rejected the thought. Cass had been so supportive, so understanding. She had stood by him through all of it. She wasn't capable of doing anything so damaging, so underhand. And yet...

The question gnawed at him, a seed of doubt taking root in his mind.

"Are you all right, Mr Wellington?" The doctor's voice cut through his thoughts, his tone tinged with concern.

Owen blinked, forcing himself back to the present. "Yes. I... I'm okay," he said, though the lie felt heavy on his tongue.

Doctor Patel watched him closely for a moment, then nodded. "If you think of anything else that might be relevant, please don't hesitate to reach out. Our goal is to support Lila in every way possible."

Owen managed a tight nod, though the unease twisted deeper into his gut as he rose to leave. As he walked down the corridor, the sterile walls seemed to close in on him, amplifying his sense of dread with every step.

He couldn't shake the lingering suspicion, the sickening thought that Cass might have been the one to make the anonymous call. But the more he thought about it, the less sense it made. If she'd been the caller, wouldn't she have told him? Would she act without consulting him first?

By the time he reached his car, the doubt had twisted itself into a knot of fear that refused to leave, leaving him haunted by questions he wasn't sure he wanted to answer.

MARCH 22ND

Cass and Owen walked through the playground at dusk, the evening light casting long shadows over the brightly painted swings and slides. Children's laughter rang out as they darted across the worn rubber matting. Owen's lips curled into a faint smile as he watched them, but Cass remained unimpressed, barely glancing their way as she strode ahead, her heels clicking on the path.

Inside the school, the warmth of the hallways contrasted with the March chill outside. Colourful drawings and paper garlands adorned the walls, but while Owen found the atmosphere comforting, Cass's expression betrayed her disdain. She walked stiffly, ignoring the friendly chatter of the parents queuing outside the classroom. When she perched on the tiny plastic chair, her irritation was palpable.

"Hi, you're Molly's dad, aren't you?" a mother nearby said, turning to Owen with a smile. "She's so lovely—my daughter adores her."

Owen's face softened. "Yes, we're really proud of her."

Cass said nothing, her eyes darting to the family photos and children's 'Star of the Week' charts. She shifted in her seat, her diamond ring catching the light as she crossed her arms.

Once inside the classroom, the teacher greeted them warmly, but her attention was clearly focused on Owen. "Molly's a bright student," she said gently, "but I've noticed she's been a bit withdrawn lately. She's sitting alone more and seems unsettled. Is everything all right at home?"

Cass stiffened, cutting in before Owen could reply. "I'll soon be Mrs Wellington," she said triumphantly, ignoring the teacher's question. "Molly's mother isn't exactly up to the job, but that'll be sorted soon enough."

The teacher's expression cooled, but her professionalism didn't falter. "I see," she said, her tone neutral. Her eyes flicked briefly to Cass's stomach. "Congratulations are in order, I hear."

"Thank you," Cass said, her voice bright. "But we'll be sending our child to private school. I want somewhere that meets our higher standards."

Owen shifted awkwardly as the teacher directed her next words to him. "We truly care about Molly, Mr Wellington. If there's anything we can do to help, please let us know."

Cass's expression hardened as they left the classroom. Outside, Owen walked ahead, his tension visible in his shoulders. When they reached the car, he spun to face her.

"Did you have to be so dismissive?" he said, his voice low but brimming with anger. "Molly's struggling, Cass. Do you even care?"

Cass folded her arms, her tone icy. "Why should I be sentimental? She's got her mother's temperament. This school isn't good enough for our child. I'm entitled to an opinion."

Owen's face darkened. "She's a child, Cass. She's hurting. I hope to God you show more care for the baby than you've shown Molly."

Cass's lips curled into a sneer. "I know what's best for our child. And it's not *this*."

Without another word, Owen yanked open the car door and climbed in, his movements sharp. As soon as Cass sat beside him, he started the engine and pulled out of the car park in tense silence. The air between them was thick with anger, the sound of the engine the only thing breaking the quiet as they drove into the night.

Ella stood looking up at the front of Granta Hall, and the old, familiar unease settled over her. The grand structure loomed above them, its large, imposing silhouette cast in the dim light of the early evening. The windows reflected the grey, overcast sky, and Ella couldn't help but feel as though the house itself disapproved of her presence. The curtains were drawn in the sitting room, a faint glow of light spilling from beneath them, casting an almost ghostly aura over everything. The house, for all its grandeur, felt cold and unwelcoming, its elegance hollowed out by the unhappiness it contained.

Molly needed her, needed someone steady in her life—someone who wouldn't walk out on her. The thought gave her a surge of determination as she reached for the front door, feeling a slight tremor of unease as her hand hesitated on the handle. She pushed the door open.

A waft of unfamiliar scents hit her as soon as she crossed the threshold—garlic, lemongrass, and the unmistakable richness of Thai spices. Ella's mouth tightened; the smell was out of place in a home she'd come to feel was partly hers. She wasn't used to the presence of Cass here, this stranger who had invaded their world, reshaping it in ways that felt wrong, even threatening.

As she stepped into the kitchen, Ella's hardened expression

softened immediately at the sight of her little sister. Her arms, which had been tightly folded across her chest, dropped to her sides, and for a moment, the strangled atmosphere in the room seemed to melt away. Molly's face brightened, darting over to Ella, who wrapped her in a tight hug.

"I missed you," Molly murmured, clinging to Ella.

Ella gave her a reassuring squeeze. For a few fleeting seconds, the kitchen felt welcoming.

But as quickly as the warmth appeared, it dissolved, coldness seeping back in. Cass cleared her throat, turning to face them with a slight smirk, stirring the pan with exaggerated calmness. "Nice to see you two reunited," she said, her voice cool and detached, breaking the quiet peace with an edge that brought tension rushing back into the room.

Ella's expression hardened instantly, her arms moving back across her chest as she stepped protectively in front of Molly, her eyes narrowing. The warmth of that brief, touching reunion was now swallowed by returning coldness, like a fragile flame snuffed out.

She loathed Cass, felt it like a sickness in her stomach, but she held it in, determined to keep the peace for her little sister.

"It's a lovely surprise to see you here," Cass said, her tone carefully neutral, hiding the resentment that simmered beneath.

Ella kept her arm around Molly's shoulders, giving her a reassuring squeeze before letting go. She glanced at Cass, then back to Molly, determined to ease the atmosphere in any way she could.

"So, how long will you be staying?" Cass asked, her voice light, hoping to steer the conversation into easier territory.

Ella hesitated, her gaze flickering briefly to Cass before she answered. "I'm only here to see my sister. I have no intention of staying under the same roof as you or my father."

Her heart swelled with a strange satisfaction at her own

words. She felt a fierce protectiveness over Molly, a feeling that had grown even stronger over the months, turning into something she struggled to define. She wanted to be more, to give her the stability and warmth she deserved, and she was willing to do whatever it took.

Cass barely looked up, an indifferent smirk tugging at the corners of her mouth as she continued cooking, seemingly unfazed by Ella's statement.

But Cass's indifference was short-lived. She cast a quick, scornful glance at Ella, her expression shifting as she spoke with mocking disdain. "Well, that's sweet of you, Ella," she said, her tone dripping with sarcasm. "I'm sure your brief visit will really cheer her up."

Ella's anger flared as Cass's mask cracked. She set the spoon down with a sharp clang, her voice cold, laced with a bitterness that made Ella's stomach twist with unease. "You are more than welcome to leave," she said, her tone carrying a faint sneer, her eyes locking on Ella with a hard stare. Ella felt a chill run through her, but she met Cass's gaze unflinchingly, refusing to let her see the vulnerability lurking beneath.

Just then, the kitchen door swung open, and Owen stepped in, his expression darkening as he registered Cass's words. His eyes immediately narrowed, flicking between Cass, Ella, and Molly. The warmth that Ella had briefly tried to rekindle vanished entirely, replaced by the icy tension that seemed to follow Cass wherever she went.

Ella's mind raced, calculating her next move, the bitterness radiating from Cass only fuelling her resolve. She wasn't about to let Cass ruin it, wasn't about to let this woman tear apart her fragile family.

A deep bitterness radiated from Cass, Ella thought, watching her carefully, her eyes narrowing. The calm façade Cass wore had fractured, revealing a cold edge that Ella hadn't fully seen until now. She looked directly at Ella with biting contempt.

"You can leave. Honestly, I don't need this stress, in my condition," she said, her voice smooth but dripping with venom as she glanced between Ella and Molly.

Owen's gaze flicked to Cass, his expression a thunderous storm of emotions. Ella felt a flicker of satisfaction, hoping he would see Cass's true nature, that he would understand the threat she posed. She glanced at him, her heart sinking as his silence dragged on, as the weight of all that had been unspoken settled around them like a shroud.

Ella turned to Molly, giving her a gentle nudge. "Let's go, Mol," she murmured, casting one last look of disdain at Owen.

APRIL 4TH

It was a bright afternoon as Zara came and sat beside Lila on a bench in the hospital grounds.

"Hello, Lila," she said gently. "I thought today would be a nice day for a visit."

Lila turned her head, managing a small smile. "It's good to see you, Zara," she replied softly.

Zara took a deep breath, letting the peacefulness of the day settle around them. "The girls are doing all right," she began, hoping to lift Lila's spirits.

Lila nodded, her gaze slipping toward the ground, a flicker of pain in her eyes as she processed Zara's words.

"You know I'd do anything for them." Zara reached out and gave her friend's hand a gentle squeeze. "How are you doing? Is the medication helping?"

Lila shrugged slightly. "It's... helping, I suppose. I don't feel as... as lost."

"Well, that's a good sign," Zara said, her voice soft and encouraging. "It means you're turning a corner, which is exactly what they want to see."

Lila's eyes widened and she stared at Zara, panic flickering over her face. "They want to give me ECT. I heard them talking about it." Her voice was hushed now. "No one asked me—not my doctor, not... not even Owen." Her voice was thin, laced with quiet disbelief. "They didn't tell me." She began to sound frantic.

Zara looked at her sympathetically. "I'm sorry, Lila. You must keep focusing on recovery, all right? The girls need you. We all do. You have to get out of here."

Lila nodded slowly and looked away, a slight tremor passing over her as she drew in a shaky breath. Lila's suddenly calm voice broke the silence.

"She's expecting, isn't she?" Lila's tone was even, almost too composed, but her eyes were dark with a mixture of shock and hurt.

Zara nodded reluctantly. "Yes, she is. How did you know?"

Lila remained calm, but was aware that Zara could see the pain painted on her face. Lila's heart ached as Zara squeezed her hand again, watching her struggle to hold herself together.

"Ella," Lila replied with no emotion.

"One step at a time. You'll get there." The two sat in silence, the peacefulness of the spring afternoon a quiet contrast to the turmoil that was bubbling inside Lila.

Lila took a deep breath, her expression hardening. Slowly, she rose from the bench, standing tall, her shoulders squared as if she were gathering strength from the earth beneath her feet, a fire rekindled in her eyes.

"I'm getting out of here. I won't let that woman get her claws any deeper into my family," she said firmly, her voice more powerful than it had been in months. She paused, her hands clenched at her sides, her whole body radiating a new-found resolve.

"That's what I want to hear, Lila," Zara said quietly, rising to stand beside her friend. "You have every reason to get well.

Focus on that and you'll be out of here in no time. I'll help you. Just tell me what you need me to do."

Lila's gaze drifted out over the hospital gardens, her eyes sharp and focused.

"Cass thinks she can just slip into my life, take my place, claim my family as hers," she continued, a chill edge to her voice. "But I'm not letting her win."

Zara nodded, giving Lila's shoulder a reassuring squeeze.

"You're stronger than you think. Just keep pushing forward, and soon enough, you'll be out of here."

Lila's face softened just slightly, but her determination remained clear.

"Thank you, Zara. For being here, for keeping an eye on everything. For protecting me."

As they walked slowly through the hospital gardens, an uncomfortable silence hovered between them. Lila eventually spoke, her voice hesitant but resolute. "Zara... I need to say something about that day," she began. "At Molly's party..." She shook her head, the memory bringing an unwelcome flash of pain. "It's all muddled in my mind now, but I remember you, Cass, seeing the earrings and feeling... angry."

Zara took a deep breath, letting the words hang in the air for a moment before responding. "I know, Lila," she said softly, her tone steady. "You were having a difficult time. I was there. I saw it all."

Lila's mind spun, trying to piece together fragments from that chaotic day. She swallowed, feeling a shiver down her spine, an unshakable sense of something dark and hidden beneath the surface.

Zara walked alongside Lila in the hospital gardens, her hand resting lightly on her friend's shoulder. The breeze rustled the budding branches overhead, and a few stray cherry blossoms drifted down, their delicate pink petals brushing against the ground. As they reached a quiet corner, Zara stopped and turned to face Lila, her expression carefully composed, her voice soft and understanding.

"Lila," she began gently, "I think it's important to talk about what really happened."

Lila looked up at her, confusion clouding her gaze. "I don't know what to believe anymore," she admitted, her voice shaky. "That day at Molly's party... everything just snapped. I wasn't myself."

Zara nodded, her eyes narrowing thoughtfully, as if she were piecing together a puzzle that only she could see. "I know, Lila. It was so out of character for you. You're not violent. That's not you. I know that."

Lila's brows knitted in confusion, her mind struggling to connect the dots. "Who am I?"

Zara took a deep breath, her face a picture of gentle sympathy mixed with restrained conviction. "Lila, you are you. And I am Zara. I'm your friend. I'm here for you. Cass, she is the danger. She is the threat. She put you under this stress. She pushed you over the edge."

A flicker of doubt passed over Lila's face, her eyes clouded with a mixture of pain and anger.

Zara tilted her head, a small, knowing smile tugging at the corner of her lips. "That's why you ended up here. She made you look unstable, unfit, like someone who isn't in control. It gave her an opportunity to step in and take your place."

Lila's face paled as Zara's words began to take root in her mind. The notion felt insidious, worming its way through her thoughts, weaving a web of suspicion. She clenched her fists, her body tense as the memory of that day resurfaced, clearer now than it had been in weeks. She could see Cass's smug smile, the glint of the sapphires as she'd turned to look at Lila, almost daring her to react.

"I thought I was imagining it... the way she looked at me," Lila murmured, a chill creeping into her voice. "But now..."

Zara's hand squeezed Lila's shoulder, her voice soft and reassuring. "You're a wonderful mother, a loyal friend. You've been through hell and back. She's trying to replace you."

The words settled heavily on Lila, her expression hardening as anger began to bloom in her chest. "She manipulates everyone," she whispered.

Zara leaned in slightly, her tone conspiratorial, almost soothing. "You're stronger than she is, Lila. You just have to stay focused. She wants you to fall apart, but if you hold on, if you keep your wits about you... she won't win."

Lila looked at Zara, a flicker of gratitude mingling with the pain in her eyes. "I don't know what I'd do without you," she said quietly, her voice raw. "You're the only one who understands me, who sees through her."

Zara smiled, a hint of satisfaction glimmering in her eyes. "Of course, Lila. I'll always be here for you. I'd never let someone like her come between us."

As they walked on, Zara continued, her voice soft and persuasive. "When you get out, we'll make sure things are right. I'll help you rebuild everything—your relationship with the girls, your place in their lives. It'll be like she was never there."

Lila nodded, her determination rekindled, but beneath her gratitude, a seed of doubt lingered. She knew Zara was offering her the lifeline she needed, but a part of her couldn't help but wonder if there was something off. But as quickly as the thought entered her mind, she dismissed it, too grateful for her friend's unwavering support to question it.

They continued walking, neither one voicing the darker thoughts lingering in their minds, the spring sun feeling suddenly cold against their backs as something dark and hidden lingered between them.

APRIL 25TH

The garden at Granta Hall was radiant, a colourful display of spring, every inch meticulously designed and maintained. Rows of lavender and rosemary lined the stone pathways, their earthy, sweet fragrance drifting gently in the air.

The swing hung from a thick branch of an enormous oak tree at the far end of the garden, where the perfectly manicured lawn softened into a more natural, almost wild border. Molly sat alone on the wooden seat, her small feet dangling above the ground as she gently swung back and forth. Above her, the tree's branches reached wide, filtering the sunlight in patches that dappled her face and danced across the ground. The leaves rustled softly in the breeze, adding a quiet, soothing sound to the warm afternoon.

All around her, the garden was alive. Flower-beds edged the lawn, vibrant with tulips in shades of deep purple, pink, and bright yellow, their colours nearly luminous against the green backdrop.

On the terrace Cass lounged comfortably in her designer dress, her large sunglasses reflecting the garden as she sipped from a glass of chilled white wine. Her gaze wandered across the landscape in lazy sweeps, taking in the garden's flawless perfection, but never lingering on Molly. Next to her on the metal table was an open maternity magazine, the glossy pages catching the light. She occasionally glanced at it, the edges of her lips curving in a faint, almost self-satisfied smile.

Molly swung quietly, casting occasional glances back toward Cass, her small face a mix of longing and hesitation. She slowed her swing until she stopped, her feet now flat on the soft grass. She watched a few birds flutter down near the flowerbeds, pecking at the ground, their feathers ruffling as they moved.

After a moment, Molly called out, her voice hesitant but hopeful. "Cass, can I go in and get some bread to feed the birds?"

Cass turned slightly, her glass halfway to her lips, and waved a dismissive hand without really looking at her.

"Fine," she replied, her tone light and disinterested, as she placed her glass of wine down on the magazine, using it as a coaster before returning to her carefully curated peace.

Cass waited until Molly disappeared into the house, her small figure swallowed by the shadows in the hallway. Once she was sure the girl was out of earshot, Cass removed her phone from her pocket and glancing around the garden to make sure she was truly alone. Her polished nails tapped the screen lightly as she dialled, holding the phone close to her ear.

When the call connected, her demeanour shifted instantly. She leaned forward, her voice a low murmur but laced with a quiet intensity, harsh and clipped. "Yes, it's me," she said, glancing around again. Her eyes narrowed, the calm mask slipping to reveal a sharp, calculating expression. "Everything's moving forward as we discussed. Better than expected, actually."

The voice on the other end replied. She listened, her lips

pressing into a thin, satisfied line. "No, no complications so far," she continued in a whisper, casting a quick look back at the house. "I've taken care of any potential interference."

Cass chuckled, making a sound devoid of warmth. She spoke again, her voice tinged with something darker, a hint of satisfaction veiled in menace. "All that's left is timing. We need to be patient, let things unfold naturally. People are so predictable when they think they're in control."

Her fingers tapped rhythmically against the glass of wine, as if in time with the invisible clock ticking down toward an unseen climax. "Just keep to your side of things, and I'll handle the rest," she said, her tone firm.

There was a pause, her face hardening as she listened to the response. Then she nodded once, more to herself than anyone else. "No. No one suspects a thing. It's all going to plan perfectly." She put her hand on her belly.

She ended the call and tucked her phone back into her pocket, settling into her seat with a faint, satisfied smile as she took another sip of wine. Around her, the garden remained serene, but the air felt charged with something unspoken, an ominous tension woven into the tranquillity. Cass leaned back, basking in the sunlight, a sense of satisfaction radiating from her. Whatever her plans entailed, there was an unmistakable sense that she was winning—and the pieces of the puzzle were all falling into place.

What she didn't realise was that Molly, who stayed crouched behind a large California lilac plant, had heard everything.

APRIL 26TH

Owen's home office was a sanctuary of calm, an oasis within the storm of his life. The walls were painted in deep charcoal grey, accented with elegant, framed art—prints of abstract shapes in muted colours, chosen for their subtlety and sophistication. A large mahogany desk sat at the centre, polished to a dark gleam, with neat stacks of papers and a leather blotter pad. A tall bookshelf lined one wall, filled with hardbacks and leather-bound volumes, the spines facing outward in order. The room was his own, designed and curated without Cass's input—a place he could think, and reflect.

But tonight, as Owen paced the floor, the calm of the office seemed to mock him. He pressed his phone to his ear, as his accountant's voice crackled through the speaker, each word tightening the vice around his chest.

"I'm sorry, Owen," the accountant said, his tone grave, "but the numbers don't lie. The discrepancies in your finances... they're extensive, and I'm talking hundreds of thousands here. This isn't something we can sweep under the rug."

Owen closed his eyes, taking a deep, shaky breath, and lowered his voice, almost a whisper. "There has to be a mistake. Maybe... maybe a miscalculation? I don't know how this happened." He threw a glance at the closed door, listening for any sounds from upstairs, acutely aware that Cass was in the bath and that her hearing anything now would be disastrous.

"No, Owen," John replied firmly, "this isn't a simple miscalculation. Funds have been moved; expenditures logged under false accounts. It's all there in black and white, and frankly, it's not just a financial issue—it's fraud."

The word hit him like a punch to the gut. "Fraud?" he whispered, feeling the weight of it sink in. He paced faster, rubbing his temple, his voice a strained hiss.

There was a brief pause, then the accountant's voice came back, hesitant but blunt. "Given the amounts, the way these books look now, prison is a possibility. Look, Owen, I need you to be honest with me. Did you authorise these transactions? Is there something—someone—you're not telling me about?"

Owen felt his throat go dry, his mind racing as he tried to piece together the impossibility of it all. "I didn't authorise anything. I don't even know where the money's gone! Everything was supposed to be in order..." He broke off, his voice cracking. "I've been... distracted."

The accountant's tone softened, but only slightly. "We need to get to the bottom of this, fast. And you need to consider your options. There may still be a chance to negotiate, to make amends, but only if we act now. Otherwise..."

Owen nodded, a futile attempt to ground himself as the walls seemed to close in. "I understand," he whispered, fear thick in his voice. He tried to swallow, his gaze falling to the polished desk, but he saw no reflection, no stability in anything around him.

John cleared his throat, the finality in his tone chilling. "This is serious, Owen. If you don't figure out where the money went, and if you can't explain how this happened, you may very well lose everything.

"You understand, don't you, what the implications of fraud are? The charges you could be facing—embezzlement, falsification of records... it's not a light matter. If the authorities get involved, they'll be looking to make an example."

Owen gritted his teeth, barely managing to keep his voice low. "John, please... I've done nothing wrong. There must be some way to prove I didn't authorise any of this. I wasn't even aware it was happening!" His pulse thudded painfully as he waited for John's reply.

"Intent doesn't always protect you from liability in cases like these," John pressed. "Once the paperwork suggests wrongdoing, any investigation will look at your entire financial history. Your assets, your business deals, even personal accounts—they'll scrutinise everything. You could be looking at more than just fines or bankruptcy; prison time isn't out of the question, Owen. And if they bring charges of aggravated fraud or conspiracy..."

Owen clenched the edge of his desk, his knuckles white. "There must be some way out. Can't we negotiate or... or arrange some settlement? Pay the fines, cover the discrepancies... anything to avoid dragging this into court?"

There was a brief pause before John spoke again, and this time his voice was a touch softer, almost reluctant. "We may be able to work on a settlement, Owen, but that's if they believe you were unaware of these transactions. If you go to court and they find even a shred of evidence tying you knowingly to these discrepancies, any negotiation might fall apart. And the penalties, Owen, they won't just affect your finances—they'll destroy your reputation, your business... possibly your entire life."

Owen's head spun, the weight of it all pressing down on him

like a vice. "John, I swear to you, I don't know where the money went. This isn't my doing. There must be another way."

"There is only one other option," John replied bluntly. "Without something concrete that proves you had no hand in this, you'll have a hard time convincing anyone in court. My advice? Be prepared for a battle, or start moving your money. Transfer your savings to someone you trust. That's the only way I can see to protect any of your assets."

The line fell silent for a long moment, the reality settling over Owen like a dark cloud. His entire world was crumbling.

Owen remained frozen, his hand still gripping the phone tightly, John's words echoing in his head. If he couldn't fix this, if the investigation went public, if the authorities came after him with full force... he could lose everything. It wasn't just his reputation or his wealth. The stakes were far higher than that.

But worse than losing the house or the business was the growing realisation of what this would mean for Molly and his unborn child. Owen felt his stomach tighten painfully, his mind racing through scenarios he hadn't allowed himself to imagine before now. If he went to prison, Cass would be left to raise their baby alone. And Molly—his sweet, sensitive Molly—she'd lose another parent, just as she was starting to rebuild some stability in her life.

A chill settled over him, and he could feel his pulse pounding in his ears. "John," he managed, his voice barely above a whisper, "do whatever is necessary. I have to protect my family. Someone is stealing from me. There has to be a trail that leads to them."

John's voice softened slightly on the other end. "Owen, I know this is hard. But right now, you have to focus on survival. If we can get out of this cleanly, your family's future remains intact."

The words cut into him. He could picture Molly's face, her

wide eyes, her cautious smile. She was still so young, so vulnerable. And the baby—what kind of life would it have without a father present? Cass wasn't the maternal type, not with Molly, and he feared she'd be even more detached with the child if she were left alone to raise it.

Owen felt a wave of desperation wash over him, an almost choking realisation that his mistakes, his blind trust, had brought them all to this. He had always believed he could protect them, that no matter what happened, he'd be there to shield his family. But if he was forced away, locked behind bars, who would Molly turn to? Who would teach his new child to walk, to speak, to be kind?

"John... do it—" he stammered, his voice cracking as he struggled to hold back the panic.

There was a pause, and then John spoke, his tone gentler now. "I will send you something to sign that allows me to transfer the funds. You need to provide me with the right bank account details and a scan of your passport."

As the call ended, Owen was left standing alone in the room, the silence pressing in on him, his entire world teetering on the brink of collapse. The quiet of his office felt oppressive now, the sophistication of his surroundings empty and hollow, as though mocking the precariousness of everything he'd built. He forced himself to breathe slowly, realising that one wrong word, one hint of what was unravelling, and everything he'd hidden from Cass might come tumbling out. He could lose everything, but it was the thought of Molly and the unborn child that terrified him most.

APRIL 26TH

Molly curled up on the edge of her bed, knees drawn to her chest as she held the phone in both hands. Her little face, still round with the softness of childhood, was drawn into a frown, her lips pursed in a way that looked too old for her. Wisps of her dark hair fell loose from her braid, sticking to her cheeks. Her eyes, big and grey-blue like her father's but edged with something darker, stared at the screen as she waited for Ella to pick up.

Finally, her sister's face appeared, fuzzy at first, then clear as she leaned closer to the camera. Ella looked a little different— maybe older, maybe just worn down, Molly couldn't tell. But seeing her sister's face made her feel like she could breathe for the first time in days. Granta Hall was beautiful but empty in ways that words couldn't fill, and sometimes Molly thought even the walls themselves seemed unhappy.

"Hey, Moll," Ella said softly, her voice breaking through Molly's worried thoughts. She sounded tired, too, like maybe she didn't want to be talking about this, but she was here anyway. Ella always showed up, even when it was hard.

"Ella," Molly whispered, her voice barely loud enough to carry through the call. "I hate it here. I want to come home."

The words tumbled out, and she felt the weight of them settle around her like a heavy blanket. Molly glanced around her room—the room that was hers but didn't feel like it at all. The furniture was sleek and modern, all whites and blacks and polished metal, chosen by Cass in a style that felt more suited to a hotel than a little girl's bedroom. There were no stuffed animals or messy shelves with books and crayons spilling over, just empty, cold space.

Molly could hear her father's voice from down the hall. He'd been in his office for hours now, his tone strained, low, clipped. Sometimes he sounded angry, sometimes sad, but mostly he just sounded tired. Like he was the one locked up in this house instead of her.

"Can't you just come get me, Ella?" Molly's voice was a hushed plea, her heart squeezing tight. "Please. It's so awful here. I heard Dad... he was talking to someone, and he sounded so... so sad."

Ella's face softened, her sharp eyes dimming. She didn't speak right away, and the silence on the other end made Molly's heart skip a beat. She felt like she'd said something she wasn't supposed to, something Ella might not want to hear. But she couldn't take it back now. She just wanted to be anywhere else.

"Ella, please," she whispered, holding the phone so close her nose nearly touched the screen. "Can you take me to see her? I just want to see Mum. She'd know what to say, she'd make everything better. Even if she's not... well."

Ella let out a sigh, brushing a strand of her wild, curly hair out of her face. "Moll, you know it's not that easy. It's... it's complicated. I can't just take you. Dad would—he'd freak. You know that."

Molly bit her lip, her hands trembling as she hugged the phone close. "But why? Why can't I see her?"

"She's really sick right now, Molly," Ella said, her voice gentle but with a seriousness that Molly wasn't used to. "They're helping her, okay? That's why she's there."

"But I miss her," Molly whimpered, her voice cracking. "Dad's not the same either. He's so... different. And Cass..." She trailed off, not wanting to say what she was really thinking. Ella hated Cass, and it was easy to see why.

"Yeah, I know," Ella replied. "That house... it's all wrong." She paused, looking away from the screen for a moment, then back, her eyes sharper, more determined. "Look, I'm trying, okay? I'll... I'll see what I can do."

Molly let out a shaky breath, relief mixing with the ache still knotted in her chest. Just hearing that Ella might try was enough to dull the edge of it, to make her feel a little less alone in that cold, sprawling house.

Molly leaned closer to the phone, her small face filling Ella's screen.

"Ella," she murmured, her words barely above a whisper, "I'm really scared of Cass. She... she's not like Mum. Sometimes she's nice, but other times..." She glanced toward her door as if expecting Cass to be listening, then whispered, "She makes me feel like I'm in her way. And when Dad's not around... she drinks wine."

Ella's expression turned fierce, her brows knitting together. "Molly," she said, her voice carefully low, "she drinks *wine*? Have you told Dad?"

Molly shook her head quickly.

"How about I come and visit this weekend? Get some things together in a rucksack but don't tell Dad or Cass I'm coming." Ella's mind was whirling now as she paced up and down. "It can be a surprise."

"Really? You promise you're coming?"

"I promise, sprout." Ella used to call her that when Molly was little. It was a name she'd not heard in a long time, but it felt like a hug.

APRIL 30TH

Lila sat in Dr Patel's office, her back straight, hands resting in her lap. The room was quiet except for the ticking of a small clock on the doctor's desk, marking time in steady beats. The air was soft, comforting even, and she breathed it in slowly, the scent of old leather calming her nerves.

She had changed in the months since she'd first entered this room, hollow and haunted. Her cheeks held a trace of colour, her eyes no longer shadowed with fear, though they held a certain guardedness. Lila looked down at her hands, tracing the edge of a new scar from where she had scratched herself during the worst of it, before the new medication had started working. The numbness had lifted, little by little, replaced by a sharpness she hadn't felt in years. She could think again, see herself clearly, even if she didn't always like what she saw.

Dr Patel sat across from her, his face kind and steady, his gaze as attentive as always. "How are you feeling today, Lila?"

She met his eyes briefly, giving a small shrug. "Better, I think. The medication... It's different now. Less foggy. I feel more like myself."

Dr Patel nodded, taking a few notes before looking back at

her with an encouraging smile. "That's good to hear. Progress can be slow, but you're moving forward." He paused, leaning forward slightly. "We've covered a lot in these sessions—your relationships, your role as a mother, your feelings about Owen and Cass. But one thing we haven't touched on much is your past, your childhood."

Lila's body stiffened. She looked down, the urge to retreat folding over her like a shadow. Her hands tightened in her lap. "I... don't see why that's important now. It was a long time ago."

"Those early experiences are the ones that stay with us the longest," Dr Patel said gently. "You've made a lot of progress, Lila, but the path to real healing often involves revisiting things we'd rather leave buried."

She shook her head, her mouth tightening into a thin line. "There's nothing to talk about, really." Her words were clipped, her gaze hardening as she looked out the window. "I learned not to miss people who didn't want to stay."

Dr Patel watched her carefully, his eyes gentle but unrelenting. "That sounds like a difficult thing for any child to go through. Growing up without the stability that parents should provide—it often leaves scars, ones we carry without realising it. The important thing is to talk about the past. Your childhood. What happened. What you did."

Lila's face flickered, just for a moment. "My childhood was difficult. You know that. It's in your notes."

Dr Patel nodded, encouraging her to continue, but she clamped her lips shut, swallowing hard. Talking about her past stirred something sharp and painful, a bitterness she thought she'd left behind. It was strange to her how she felt nothing toward her childhood now—just the faint sting of a past wound left too long to heal.

"Lila," he said softly, "I know this isn't easy. But if you keep those memories bottled up, they'll only weigh you down again.

Childhood experiences can shape our relationships, our sense of self. Revisiting those memories doesn't have to be painful; it's part of the process of understanding why we react to things the way we do."

She felt her shoulders tense, a flicker of anger sparking beneath her skin. "What difference does it make now? I have children of my own, I... tried to be different with them. Better. I never wanted to be anything like my parents." Her voice grew quiet, her eyes fixed on her hands as if they held answers she couldn't see. "But even when I tried, I don't think I knew how."

Dr Patel let her words settle, not pushing, just holding space for the silence. When he spoke again, his voice was soft, as if coaxing her to let go of something long clutched too tightly.

"Sometimes, facing our past can help us break cycles we don't even realise we're caught in," he said gently. "And those cycles often continue with our children. We owe it to ourselves —and to them—to face what's buried. Healing yourself can be a way to help them, Lila."

She looked at him, the words landing like small stones in her chest. She wanted to argue, to tell him he was wrong, that she was different, that her childhood had nothing to do with the mistakes she'd made as a mother. But the truth gnawed at her, that uncomfortable realisation that she still carried her childhood with her.

Her throat tightened, a dull ache swelling in her chest. She hadn't cried in months, maybe longer. But the thought of her daughters—of Molly's small, hopeful face and Ella's guarded, watchful eyes—dredged up an ache she couldn't ignore.

"Maybe... maybe next time," she whispered, her voice barely audible. "I don't think I can... not yet."

Dr Patel nodded, his expression understanding, patient. "That's okay, Lila. We'll take this one step at a time. I'm here whenever you're ready."

She managed a small nod, though inside, she felt a weight deep in her chest, pressing down with each breath. The memories she'd fought to bury rose faintly, ghosts she wasn't ready to face, yet somehow she sensed she couldn't avoid them forever. The path to healing wasn't what she'd thought—it was longer, harder, and it led back to places she'd rather not go.

Lila sat up straighter, her hands clasped tightly in her lap. Her voice was steady, almost too calm, as she looked at Dr Patel.

"Do you think..." she hesitated, her eyes dropping momentarily before lifting again, "... do you think I'm getting closer? To being... well, to being able to leave?"

Dr Patel leaned back, the kind look in his eyes unchanged. "You're making significant progress, Lila," he said gently. "I can see the difference in you from when we first met. You're more grounded, more open to facing the parts of your life that have caused you pain."

Lila's hands tightened around each other, her knuckles whitening. "But is that... enough? I mean, I can feel myself getting better, at least sometimes. I don't feel as... lost. I want to go back to my life, my children. To make things right."

Dr Patel nodded slowly, his expression thoughtful. "I understand, Lila. And I think your desire to make things right is a sign of your commitment to healing. But recovery is a process, and we're not quite there yet." He paused, watching as Lila's face fell slightly. "What I can tell you," he continued, his voice gentle, "is that we're close. I hope this is a conversation we can have in the very near future."

Lila's eyes lingered on the doctor, searching his face for signs of certainty. "I just... sometimes I feel ready. I want to believe I can be a good mother again, that I can be okay with my girls and not..." Her voice trailed off, the words slipping away as her gaze fell to the floor.

Dr Patel leaned forward, his voice reassuring. "These are

very natural feelings, Lila. And it's good that you're able to look ahead with hope. The more you build on that strength here, the better prepared you'll be for the challenges of going back to that life. Take it one step at a time, without rushing yourself."

Lila nodded, though her face held a glint of frustration, tempered by the calm she'd learned to rely on. She glanced toward the window, the sight of the sky outside filling her with a longing she could barely contain. But beneath it was a small but powerful hope, a fragile light she hadn't felt in years.

"All right," she said softly, as she met his eyes. "One step at a time."

Lila offered a small, grateful smile to Dr Patel, as she rose to her feet. "Thank you," she murmured, her voice soft but filled with genuine appreciation. "For... for listening. And for not giving up on me."

Dr Patel nodded, his expression warm. "You're doing the hard work, Lila. Keep holding onto that strength."

With a nod, she left his office, the click of the door closing softly behind her as she returned to the quiet of the ward. The air felt different here; it always did after her sessions. Somehow, the walls seemed closer, the sounds sharper. She took a slow, steadying breath, clutching her phone in her hand.

This small piece of freedom had come back to her just days before, a sign of the trust she was beginning to rebuild, proof of the progress she'd fought for. Lila had been tentative at first, as though the phone were some relic of her old life, something that might vanish if she looked at it too closely. But now, as she sat on her bed, alone in the silence of the ward, she felt a rare warmth as she turned it on and watched the screen come to life.

The photos were there, untouched since the day she'd last seen them. Her thumb hovered over the screen, a mixture of anticipation and hesitation making her pause before she opened the album labelled *My Girls*.

The first image made her ache inside, a pang of longing striking her with the force of a wave. It was Ella and Molly, both smiling wide, arms slung around each other on a sunny day at the park. Ella's hair was wild, tossed by the wind, her expression filled with that familiar look of fierce independence. Molly's face was turned up to her big sister, eyes filled with adoration, her cheeks still chubby, her smile innocent and wide.

Lila swiped to the next photo, then another, each one bringing back memories she'd locked away. Molly on her birthday, holding up a brightly coloured gift bag, her face aglow with excitement. Ella stood beside her, a rare, soft smile on her face as she leaned down to help her sister open the present.

She traced her finger across the screen, as if by doing so she could somehow bridge the gap between her and her daughters. She felt a bittersweet tug inside, a mixture of joy and regret. They'd grown in her absence, changed in ways she hadn't been there to witness. But looking at their faces, she felt a quiet resolve harden within her—a determination to be a part of their lives again, to be the mother they deserved.

Lila paused at a photo of herself with both girls, her arms wrapped around them tightly, her face pressed close to theirs, all three of them laughing. She barely recognised herself in the photo—bright-eyed, happy, full of warmth. But maybe, she thought, she could discover that version of herself again. It felt far away, unreachable at times, but the seed of hope was there.

She closed her eyes for a moment, her hands wrapped around the phone as she sat in silence, holding onto the image of her girls, the memory of their laughter filling the quiet.

"I'm coming home. I promise you both, I am going to get out of here and I am coming home to look after you. I will never leave you again," Lila said, catching a glimpse of her reflection in the window close to her bed and seeing a stranger looking back.

MAY 2ND

Molly sat on the edge of the couch, clutching the remote in her small hands as the TV flickered in front of her. But she wasn't watching. Her eyes darted to the hallway every few minutes, her mind on Ella's arrival. She'd been counting down the hours, her little overnight bag tucked under her bed, carefully hidden.

Cass sat across from her, leafing through a magazine with her legs crossed, tapping her foot in a rhythm that felt like nails on a chalkboard. Her eyes flicked up from time to time, occasionally drifting to her phone where she typed out texts in short, clipped strokes, a faint smirk playing on her lips as she replied to whoever was on the other end.

Molly didn't know who it was, and she didn't care. She just wanted Cass to stay distracted until Ella came.

The sound of Owen's footsteps echoed from down the hall, and Molly's stomach tightened. She knew her father's footsteps well—how they changed with his mood, how they told her what to expect before he even walked into the room. And right now, they were the clipped, frustrated steps she'd come to dread.

When Owen entered, his face pale, he barely glanced at Molly before his eyes landed on Cass. His voice was low, but there was an edge to it. "Cass, the fridge is empty. We've got nothing in the house. What have you been doing? I know we agreed you'd quit work for a while, but that's what you said you wanted. You said you wanted to be a mum to our baby, to Molly."

Cass looked up from her magazine, arching a brow with a smile. "I've been busy, Owen. And besides, I have a designer coming over soon to help with the nursery." She flipped the page dismissively, as though this conversation were nothing more than background noise.

Owen's eyes narrowed. "A designer?" he said, incredulity creeping into his voice. "Cass, we don't need a designer. We can't be throwing money around like that. Just decorate it yourself."

Cass's smile faded, her hands gripping the magazine as she met his gaze, her eyes steely. "So now I'm supposed to do everything around here, is that it? Maybe if you bothered helping a little more, Owen, I wouldn't have to hire someone."

Molly could feel the tension building, the words sharp and heavy. She shrank back on the couch, trying to focus on the TV, but it was useless. The show she'd chosen to watch, something light and silly, barely registered over the anger simmering between her father and Cass.

"You don't need help, Cass," Owen said, his voice cold. "You're just lazy."

Cass's face flushed, her mouth twisting into a sneer. "Lazy?" she shot back. "Maybe I wouldn't be if I didn't have to deal with all of your mess, Owen. Maybe if you were more responsible, I wouldn't have to pick up the slack."

Molly's heart raced as the shouting grew louder. She could barely hear her own thoughts, and the room felt like it was closing in on her, her skin tingling with the uncomfortable heat of it all. She wanted to cry out, to tell them to stop, but her voice felt trapped, locked somewhere deep inside her chest.

Unable to take it anymore, she bolted from the couch, running past them with her hands pressed tight over her ears. She didn't look back, didn't want to see their angry faces. She ran through the hallway, feeling tears prick at her eyes as she dashed up to her room.

She slammed the door behind her, muffling the noise from downstairs, and let out a shaky breath. Her hands still pressed to her ears, she paced around the room.

It wasn't fair. None of it was fair. She hated the way they shouted, the way they seemed to forget she was even there. She thought of Ella, her sister's strong arms around her, her calm, quiet voice telling her it would be all right. Just a little longer, she told herself. Ella would be here soon.

Downstairs, Owen's face went white, his mouth opening and closing like he was trying to process what he was hearing. He stared at Cass, barely recognising her as she spat out words sharper than he'd ever heard from her before.

"Cass," he managed, his voice low and shocked. "She's a child. You're upsetting her. Can't you see that?"

Cass let out a short, cold laugh, dropping her magazine onto the coffee table with a snap. "Upsetting her?" She raised an eyebrow, her face twisting in disgust. "Upsetting her, Owen? Maybe if you were a decent father, she wouldn't be such a tragic little loser. She's fragile, she's weak, and she's *just like her mother*."

Owen's eyes narrowed, but he looked more hurt than angry. "That's... that's a vile thing to say. She needs support, not—"

"Oh, please," Cass interrupted, her voice slicing through the air like a blade. "Let's not pretend this isn't entirely your fault. You can't see it, can you? You ruin everything you touch. Look at how you've let your family fall apart around you. Look at how you abandoned Lila when she needed you most."

Owen stared at her, gobsmacked as he took in her words. He'd seen glimpses of this side of Cass before, but nothing like this. She was unrelenting, venomous, like she was taking years of frustration and dumping it all on him at once, ripping through his every flaw with ruthless precision.

"You know what, Owen?" she continued, her voice dropping to a vicious whisper, her eyes narrowing. "You're not the noble father you think you are. Trying to keep this family together when you can't even keep yourself together. Well, I see it. I see right through you. And I know you're going to let me down too—me and this baby." She put her hand on her stomach, her lips curling in disdain. "It's only a matter of time."

Owen's face fell, his expression crumbling under the weight of her words. He looked down, his shoulders slumping as he fumbled for his car keys on the table. "I'm... I'll go to the supermarket. Is there anything you want?" He was too tired to fight.

Cass didn't even look at him, her eyes fixed on some invisible point across the room. "A man with a spine," she said dismissively. "I can't expect you to know what that is." She picked up her phone, her attention already elsewhere.

Without another word, Owen walked out of the room, his head down, his steps heavy as he headed for the front door. The weight of Cass's words hung over him, pressing down like a lead blanket, as he disappeared into the hallway.

Cass watched through the window as Owen's car finally disappeared. She waited a moment, then let out a slow breath, her face shifting from irritation to a steely, calculated calm. Holding her phone, she scrolled through her contacts until she found the number she was looking for.

The phone rang once, twice, before a deep voice answered, clipped and professional. "Why are you calling me? We agreed, you wouldn't call from this phone."

Cass let the silence settle for a moment before she spoke again, her voice lowering to a more familiar, intimate tone. "I really can't take much more of this," she said, her words laced with a quiet frustration. "Being around him is... intolerable. We need to bring our plans forward."

There was a pause on the other end, then a soft chuckle, rich and knowing. "Cass," came the reply, "I thought you said you could hold out a little longer?"

Cass sighed, pressing her fingers to her temple. "I thought I could, too, but things are getting complicated. He's watching the money now—he's been more cautious lately, and if he starts looking too closely, it could... interfere."

"I see," the voice said, turning serious. "Then perhaps it's time we finalise everything. Make sure that by the time he realises anything's off, it's too late for him to react."

"Exactly," she said, her voice growing firm. "I want him out of the picture entirely. And I need to know you're still committed. We've both invested a lot in this."

The response was immediate, steady. "Of course, Cass. You know I wouldn't have stayed in this mess if I didn't think we could pull it off. Just tell me what you need."

She allowed herself a smile, feeling the weight of the past few months begin to ease. "The fewer decisions he makes, the easier it'll be to..." She paused, searching for the right words, "to take control when the time is right."

"Understood," came the smooth reply. "I'll handle the adjustments you requested and send you the details privately. Just be careful, Cass. Owen's not a fool—if he gets any hint of who is behind this..."

"He won't," she interrupted, her tone crisp and confident. "I can handle him, John. Just do your part, and we'll be done with this soon."

John chuckled softly. "Then here's to new beginnings."

As she ended the call, Cass's expression softened, her usual mask of irritation and impatience fading into something more satisfied, almost gleeful. She glanced around the room, feeling, for the first time, like this house and everything in it might soon be hers entirely—and Owen, nothing but a distant memory.

MAY 2ND

Lila sat on the edge of her bed, the sterile sheets pulled tight beneath her, her heart pounding in a steady beat. She had practised the routine so many times in her mind it felt almost effortless. She'd earned their trust; she'd played the part of the compliant patient, taken her medication, attended every session. She'd smiled when she was meant to smile, kept quiet when expected. She was the model patient now, so much so that the nurses didn't even glance at her twice when she moved around the building. No one thought of her as a threat anymore. Just as she planned.

She looked at the clock on the wall—just after 7pm. The evening shift had begun, and this was the quietest time, the time when no one would think twice if she wandered the halls, maybe stepped out for a bit of fresh air. She took a deep breath, pressing her hands to her stomach, feeling the nervous flutter there settle into something sharper, stronger.

Her hair was tied back neatly, looking every bit the part of someone well enough to be trusted with a bit of freedom. She stood, slipping her small overnight bag—no more than a few essentials—over her shoulder. She took one last look around the room, noting the pale-blue walls, the clean but suffocating sterility of it all, and let herself feel a moment of satisfaction. This would be the last time she saw it.

Without hesitation, she walked down the corridor, moving with purpose but not haste. No one looked twice as she passed the nurses' station. One nurse nodded at her, offering a friendly smile as Lila gave a small wave in return. She walked steadily, feeling the weight of each step growing lighter as she neared the door, the exit where the fresh evening air was just within reach.

Outside, the lights were dim, the familiar grounds stretching out under a hazy early evening sky. Her heart hammered, but she kept her pace steady, breathing in the air that felt like freedom on her skin. She moved toward the edge of the car park, blending in with the few others who were out for their evening stroll, some visiting with families.

Lila made her way across the grounds to a hedge on the far west side of the gardens and found the hole in the fence that gave direct access to a large supermarket car park. On many occasions Lila had watched other patients climb out through the gap. Some were sneaking out to buy alcohol, some collecting drugs and others, normally the manic women, had escaped so they could get their kicks with an old flame, or anyone who would oblige.

Lila scanned the area. The car she was looking for was waiting in the farthest row, headlights off, but the faint rumble of the engine was unmistakable, a quiet pulse in the stillness of the evening. She could barely make out the figure in the driver's seat, but she knew it was them, knew that everything was in place as promised. She took one last glance behind her, ensuring no one had followed her, no one was watching. They weren't expecting her to go anywhere, not tonight, not yet. By the time they noticed her absence, she'd be far from here. Far from Cambridge. Far from all of it.

Lila slipped into the car, closing the door softly, her breath held as she met the driver's eyes. She didn't say a word. The figure gave a curt nod, and in the next moment, they were pulling away, merging onto the narrow lane that led from the hospital and disappearing into the quiet of the night. The lights of the hospital grew smaller and smaller in the rear-view mirror until they were nothing but a distant glow on the horizon.

"Are you ready, Mum?" Ella asked, putting the car into gear.

As the car picked up speed, Lila felt a strange lightness fill her chest, the weight of months spent in confinement lifting away like fog.

MAY 2ND

Cass moved frantically around her bedroom, yanking open drawers and sweeping her belongings into an open suitcase on the bed. She barely glanced at what she threw in—handfuls of clothes, shoes, and cosmetics tossed in among the jewellery she'd stuffed hastily into her leather make-up case. She paused only to pull a stack of cash from her bedside drawer, stuffing it into a zipped pocket with shaking hands, then reached for her perfume bottles, and expensive trinkets that had sat untouched for weeks. The room was in chaos now, her usual neatness abandoned in her haste.

Her breath came quickly, shallow and panicked, as she grabbed another pair of earrings from the bedside table, her fingers clenched around them tightly. She muttered to herself under her breath, trying to remember what she'd need, what she couldn't bear to leave behind. Each item she packed felt like a piece of herself she was trying to salvage, a collection of things she'd gathered to construct the life she wanted. And now, she was dismantling the illusion piece by piece.

Just as she reached for a stack of folded dresses, a voice cut through the silence behind her, freezing her in place.

"Going somewhere?"

Cass whipped around, her hand clutching a silk blouse, her expression flickering from shock to irritation. Ella stood in the doorway, her arms crossed, her eyes narrow and unreadable as they took in the room, the mess, and Cass's frantic state. Cass's mouth opened and closed as she tried to gather her composure, her grip tightening on the blouse in her hand.

"Ella," she said, her voice dropping to a forced, brittle calm. "I wasn't expecting you." She couldn't quite control the quiver in her voice.

Ella raised an eyebrow, glancing around the room, taking in the open suitcase, the scattered clothes, the pieces of Cass's life being packed up in a hurried frenzy. "Looks to me like you're in a hurry to leave."

Cass's jaw tightened, and she turned back to her suitcase, stuffing another shirt inside as she struggled to regain her composure. "Owen's gone to the supermarket, and I thought I'd... take a little time for myself. Is that a crime?"

"No, not at all," Ella replied, her voice casual as she leaned against the doorframe, watching Cass with an expression of mocking curiosity. "It's just interesting, that's all. Convenient timing, don't you think?"

Cass shot her a glare, her lips pressed into a thin line. "Not that it's any of your business, Ella, but I don't need permission from you or anyone else to leave this house."

Ella's smirk widened slightly, her eyes never leaving Cass as she stepped into the room, folding her arms as she took in each detail. "No, you don't," she said softly. "But you might want to think twice about running out on Dad. He's not as stupid as you think."

Cass let out a laugh, though it was brittle, her hands trembling slightly as she shoved more clothes into the bag. "Owen is clueless. You think he notices anything? He's too busy playing the tragic father to keep an eye on what's really happening around him."

"Maybe." Ella's gaze darkened, her voice dropping a notch. "But you don't fool me. And you won't fool him forever."

"What exactly are you accusing me of, Ella?"

Ella took a step closer, her face a mask of cold amusement, her voice calm but cutting. "I'm not accusing you of anything. I'm just saying that running won't make this go away. Dad's going to see through you eventually, Cass. And when he does..." She let the sentence hang, the implication sharp and unmistakable.

Cass's face darkened, her grip tightening on the handle of her suitcase. "Listen, you spoiled little brat, you don't know anything about what's going on here. You think you're so clever, playing spy, trying to be your father's little protector." She gave a bitter laugh, shaking her head. "But you're just a kid, Ella. You don't understand anything."

Ella tilted her head, unfazed, her eyes meeting Cass's with an unwavering steadiness. "I understand more than you think," she said quietly. "And I know you're not as untouchable as you want everyone to believe."

Cass stared at her, a flicker of doubt crossing her face before she smothered it, her voice turning icy. "Well, you'll find out soon enough that this is none of your concern."

Ella shrugged, stepping back toward the door, her face relaxed but her eyes hard as steel. "Suit yourself, Cass. But if you think you can just walk out of here without consequences, you're in for a surprise. Dad won't just let you leave with his child."

"Clearly, he doesn't care about his children."

Cass could see her words stung like an arrow to the heart. Ella turned and left, her footsteps echoing down the hall heading for Molly's room, leaving Cass in the silent, tense room, gripping her suitcase handle with white-knuckled fury.

Cass nearly stumbled as she descended the grand staircase, her luggage banging against each polished step, her pulse hammering with each hurried footfall. She glanced back over her shoulder, her face twisted in a mix of urgency and fear. She just needed to get out of here before Owen returned.

Reaching the bottom, she paused to catch her breath, adjusting her grip on her bag, and then turned towards the front door—only to stop dead in her tracks.

Lila stood there, half in shadow, her figure still and composed, her face unreadable as she watched Cass. The overhead lights cast a soft glow on her, illuminating a face Cass hadn't seen in months, a face that looked both familiar and strangely distant. Lila's hair was pulled back, her clothes simple, almost casual, like she'd just come in from a walk rather than a psychiatric ward.

Lila's gaze didn't waver, her eyes scanning Cass, the suitcase, the wild, panicked look on her face. Then, a faint, almost amused smile touched her lips, as if she were savouring this moment, letting it settle between them like a secret.

"Going somewhere, Cass?" Lila asked, her voice smooth, calm, and unshaken.

Cass's face twisted with fury as she hissed, "Get out of my way, you mad bitch." Her voice was low and venomous, laced with the fear she could no longer hide. She dropped her suitcase with a heavy thud, her eyes darting around wildly before landing on a heavy decorative vase on a nearby bookcase. In one swift movement, she seized it, her grip tight, as she brandished it towards Lila.

But Lila didn't flinch. She remained still, her calm unsettling as she stared back at Cass with an unwavering, almost detached expression. "Really, Cass?" Lila said, her voice barely above a whisper, yet somehow cutting. "You think that's going to make me leave?"

Cass's hand shook, her grip on the vase tightening as she felt her options narrowing, slipping through her fingers like sand. "I swear," she spat, her eyes flashing, "I'll do whatever I have to. Get. Out. Of. My. Way."

But Lila took a step forward, her face close to Cass's, her expression cold and unwavering.

Cass's eyes widened, her lips curling back in a snarl as Lila's words cut deep, hitting something raw and vulnerable beneath her anger. With a sharp, wild motion, she raised the vase, bringing it down towards Lila with every ounce of strength she could muster.

But Lila moved quickly, dodging to the side as the vase smashed against the floor, sending shards flying across the marble tiles. Cass let out a frustrated cry, her fingers curling into claws as she lunged at Lila, her face twisted in a mix of desperation and rage.

Lila met her head-on, grabbing Cass's wrist and wrenching it away, her expression fierce, a strength in her that Cass hadn't anticipated. They struggled, locked in a grapple, each pushing and pulling, stumbling against the walls, knocking into furniture as they fought. Cass's nails dug into Lila's skin, scratching and tearing, but Lila held on, her grip steady, fuelled by something darker, deeper.

"You think you can just take everything and walk away?" Lila hissed, her voice low, filled with a quiet fury as she shoved Cass back against the wall.

Cass twisted out of her grip, shoving Lila back, her breaths coming in quick, shallow gasps. "You have no idea what I'm capable of," she spat, her voice thick with rage and defiance. She charged again, this time slamming her shoulder into Lila, knocking her off balance.

But Lila recovered quickly, grabbing hold of Cass's arm and twisting it behind her back. Cass let out a sharp, furious scream, struggling against the hold, her face contorted in pain.

"I know exactly what you are, Cass," Lila whispered, her voice laced with a cold, terrifying calm.

With a sudden surge of strength, Cass jerked free, spinning around to face Lila, her eyes flashing with pure hatred. "You're nothing but a pathetic, broken woman," she sneered, her voice shaking as she backed towards the door, her gaze darting between Lila and her escape route.

Lila's eyes narrowed, but she didn't move, her posture steady as she watched Cass inch towards the exit, her chest rising and falling with measured breaths.

"You may think you can just leave after all the damage you've caused," Lila said, her voice soft, deadly, "but I promise you, Cass..."

Cass hesitated, just for a moment, and in that second of uncertainty, Lila lunged again, grabbing her by the shoulders and slamming her back against the door. Cass struggled, her fists pounding against Lila's arms, her voice shrill and panicked as she twisted, but Lila held firm, her grip unflinching.

They stood there, locked in a vicious, breathless standoff, the air around them thick with months of resentment, betrayal, and simmering rage. The house around them was silent, the echoes of their struggle filling the empty hall.

As the fierce struggle continued, a sudden, piercing scream broke through the chaos, slicing through the atmosphere like a knife.

"Mum, stop! Stop it! Please!" Molly's voice trembled with fear and desperation. She stood at the top of the staircase, her small frame dwarfed by the banister, her face pale, eyes wide. Next to her was Ella, who held onto her sister tightly, her own expression cold.

At the sound of Molly's voice, Lila froze, her hands loosening on Cass's shoulders. She turned, breathing heavily, her face softening as she looked up at her daughters, her chest heaving with a mixture of exhaustion and shock.

"Ella, take your sister to her room. Now!" Lila boomed with the strength of a tigress.

Cass seized the opportunity to tear herself free, staggering back a few steps, clutching her arms, her expression livid but shaken.

"I... heard Cass on the phone yesterday," Molly whispered, looking at her mother with wide, tear-filled eyes. "She was talking about plans... about money. She didn't know I was there."

Cass's face drained of colour, her mouth opening as she took a step back, her gaze flicking to Ella, who was watching her with icy disdain, her arms protectively around her sister.

"Molly..." Cass began, her voice trembling, desperate.

"No!" Molly interrupted, her voice stronger now, her little face filled with a strange certainty. She looked straight at Cass, her eyes fierce, unyielding. "I heard you. I heard you say there's no baby."

The silence that followed was suffocating, the air full of disbelief and horror. Lila's face twisted in shock, her mouth opening as she stared at Cass, who was frozen, her eyes darting wildly, trapped under the weight of Molly's revelation.

"You lied," Molly whispered, her voice breaking, tears spilling down her cheeks. "You lied to all of us. There never was a baby."

Cass's face contorted, eyes flashing as she turned back to Lila, who stood motionless, her expression hardened, a fierce protectiveness radiating from her.

Ella's voice cut through the silence, low and razor-sharp.

"She's a fake. Nothing about her is real. Look at her." Her eyes flicked to Cass, cold and accusing.

Lila stepped forward, her eyes never leaving Cass, who now seemed small, cornered, her bravado drained.

Cass opened her mouth, her lips moving, but no words came out. She was caught, and the realisation hit her like a blow. Her mask shattered, and all that remained was raw, naked fear.

Molly began to cry, her small sobs cutting through the air and echoing around them like a trapped ghost.

MAY 2ND

Lila took a deep breath, steadying herself, her face an unreadable mask. She looked up at Molly and Ella, her voice calm, almost gentle, as she spoke.

"Girls, go to Molly's room," she said, her tone firm but softened by a protective tenderness. "Stay there. I'll come and get you soon."

Molly sniffed, wiping her eyes with the back of her hand, but she nodded, clutching Ella's arm as her sister led her away. Their footsteps faded, leaving Lila alone with Cass, who stood trembling, her face twisted in an expression somewhere between shame and desperation.

Cass's knees buckled, and she sank to the floor, her hands grasping at Lila's hem, her face contorted with misery. "Please, Lila," she whimpered, her voice barely more than a rasp. "Please let me go. I... I'm sorry. I didn't mean for it to go this far. I just... wanted a family. I wanted someone who would... who would love me. That's all I ever wanted." Her voice cracked, her words spilling out in a pathetic, broken mess.

Lila stood over her, her eyes cold, unreadable, her face

showing none of the sympathy Cass was desperately pleading for.

Then Zara appeared in the doorway. She stopped abruptly, her eyes widening as she took in the scene: Cass on the floor, Lila standing above her like a sentinel of judgement. Zara's eyes moved from Lila to Cass, her mouth opening in stunned silence.

Cass looked up, her face pale. Her hands shook, her breaths coming fast and shallow as if she knew there was no way out now. She began to speak, her words tumbling out in a chaotic, frantic confession.

"I... just wanted him to love me. I knew he would stay if he thought there was a baby..." Zara didn't flinch, her expression remaining impassive, cold.

Lila's hand flew to her mouth, a gasp escaping as she took in the confession, her eyes wide with horror. She stepped back, pressing herself against the wall as if needing its support to process the torrent of Cass's guilt.

Cass didn't stop; she seemed unable to now, the words pouring from her as if some dam had finally broken. "I called the police. I told them you were... unstable, dangerous. I made it sound like you'd hurt someone, like you'd hurt the girls." She sobbed, wiping her tear-streaked face with trembling fingers. "I had to make it look real... to keep you out of the way. Owen was finally mine, it was all going to be mine and... and I couldn't stand the idea of losing it."

Lila's eyes flicked to Zara, her face frozen in disbelief. But Zara didn't so much as blink, her eyes hard as stone.

Cass reached out, her hands trembling, her voice pleading. "Please, Lila. You have to understand—I never meant for it to go this far. I was desperate. You have everything—family, love... even now, you have it all." She slumped, tears streaming down her face. "I just wanted something of my own."

Lila stared at her, her face etched in icy calm. "You tried to destroy everything I had," she said, her voice low, controlled, almost detached. "You tore through my life, my family... because you felt entitled to something that was never yours."

Cass opened her mouth, but no words came. She crumbled, her hands falling to her lap as she shook, a hollow, broken figure on the floor. Lila, who had found her voice, stepped forward, her gaze flashing with a sudden, fierce anger.

"After all you put us through..." Lila's voice shook with fury, her fists clenched at her sides.

The truth lay between them, a dark, heavy, weight that settled over the room like a suffocating blanket.

Cass straightened, her voice low and sharp, her eyes hard as they fixed on Lila. There was no trace of warmth, no mask left to hide behind. She'd been waiting to say these things for far too long. Finally, the real Cass would be revealed to them, and all her dark and bitter ugliness could rise to the top and bubble over, splitting like lava and burning everything in its wake.

"You know, Lila," she began, voice dripping with disdain, "people like you make me sick. Always bending over backward, letting others push you around, handing out chances as if they're charity. Weak men and pathetic women, always tripping over their own feet and looking for someone to catch them."

She laughed, a harsh, hollow sound. "Do you think I feel bad for any of this? Do you think I spent a second regretting the things I've done, the people I've left in the dust?" She shook her head, the smirk on her face dark and cruel as she got to her feet. "No. I saw what I wanted, and I took it. You have no idea how sick I was of watching everyone else get what they wanted while I was expected to smile and wait patiently on the sidelines, grateful for whatever scraps life decided to throw my way. Well, I'm not grateful, Lila. I'm owed. And I decided to collect."

Her eyes narrowed, glinting with satisfaction. "You think I'm ruthless, and maybe I am. But at least I'm honest. Honest about what it takes to survive, to win. Because in this world, there are takers and there are those who get taken. And I chose my side."

Cass straightened, folding her arms as she looked at Lila with barely concealed contempt. "I took the life I deserved. Do you have any idea what that feels like? To step into the shoes of someone who's stronger, more powerful, more capable than the pathetic excuse of a person you used to be? I reinvented myself. I became someone who doesn't flinch, who doesn't stumble. Someone you admired. Someone you wanted to be. Someone your husband wanted."

Her lip curled, and for a moment, she seemed almost to relish Lila's stunned silence. "So don't look at me with that wounded little expression, like I'm some kind of monster. I simply did what all of you were too weak to do. I built a life, a life where I don't have to beg or wait or play by anyone else's rules. I'm done watching people like you land on your feet."

Cass's voice softened, almost a whisper now, her tone venomous and unyielding. "And if you're thinking of standing in my way... don't. Because I'll do it all again, and I won't think twice."

In one last final desperate attempt to run, Cass lunged towards the door before she felt the sharp tug on the silk scarf around her neck, the force pulling her backward, her feet slipping out from under her as she stumbled, helpless against Zara's grip. She tumbled to the floor with a sickening crack, her head slamming against the polished hardwood, her vision swimming as pain shot through her skull.

Zara loomed over her, her breathing ragged, her eyes blazing with a fury Cass had never seen before. She barely had time to register the glint of glass in Zara's hand—the heavy paperweight, solid and cold, its edges catching the light as Zara lifted it high above her head. For a moment, Cass saw her own reflection in it, small and terrified, before Zara brought it down with a scream that belonged to a feral dog.

The paperweight struck Cass's ribs with a dull, sickening thud, her face twisting in pain, her hands scrambling to shield herself. But Zara didn't stop. She raised the paperweight again, her grip tightening, her eyes wild, every scream, every silent moment of agony pouring out in release, the rage pulsing through her like a tidal wave.

Zara stood over her, hands still clutching the blood-smeared paperweight. She looked down at Cass, her face and body an unrecognisable mess of blood and bone, a pool of crimson spreading beneath her. In the distance the sound of Owen's car returning could be heard on the gravel driveway.

Lila stood staring at the body in shock as he entered the room.

JUNE 28TH

The warm afternoon light filtered gently through the tall windows of Granta Hall, casting a golden glow over the polished wooden floors and soft furnishings that Lila had carefully chosen. The house, once shrouded in tension and secrets, was now a refuge of laughter and love. The laughter of her daughters drifted from the kitchen, interspersed with the sounds of Molly's high-pitched giggles and Ella's more controlled, older-sister tone. The home felt like a haven, yet shadows lingered in the quiet corners, waiting.

Lila was seated by the large bay window, her fingers lightly tracing the rim of her teacup, lost in thought. Weeks had passed since Cass's sudden, violent exit from their lives, but the memories were stubborn, surfacing unbidden in moments like this. Her peace was fragile, sustained by her daughters' well-being and the routine they'd rebuilt together. She'd worked tirelessly to create a new life for them, one of calm and stability. But even in this sanctuary, she could feel the weight of that day still pressing on her, like an injury that hadn't quite healed.

A knock at the door stirred her from her thoughts, and she rose, already knowing who it would be. Zara had kept her distance over the recent weeks, her visits sporadic, her eyes watchful, searching. Now, as Lila opened the door, she saw that same wariness etched in her friend's face.

"Zara," Lila greeted her, her voice steady, though a flicker of tension tightened her mouth. "Come in."

Zara nodded, stepping inside with a slight hesitation, her gaze flicking around the room, as if assessing how much it had changed. Lila led her to the living room, where they settled across from each other, Zara perched stiffly on the edge of the armchair, her hands clasped tightly together in her lap. The weight of their unspoken words filled the space between them.

"How are you?" Lila ventured finally, her voice stiff, as if the words were foreign.

Zara gave a tight smile, but it didn't reach her eyes. "I'm... managing," she said, a hint of sarcasm in her tone. She glanced around the room, taking in the neatly arranged furniture, the calm Lila had tried to create in the weeks since. "Granta Hall looks... different," she said, the tension between them deepening with the unsaid things beneath her words. "You've finally made it... yours."

They exchanged pleasantries, brief and almost formal, before silence settled again, thick with memories. Finally, Lila broke it, her voice low, carrying a note of something darker. "I still can't quite believe it."

Zara's gaze hardened. "She was a shadow, nothing more. She didn't really exist," she replied, her tone clipped. "Cass was a chameleon who fooled us all." Her voice caught, a bitter edge creeping into her words. "She was a monster, Lila."

Lila shivered, her hands tightening in her lap. "She wormed her way into my family." She swallowed, glancing up at Zara with haunted eyes. "And the lies—the heart attack, the cancer... she was even more twisted than we realised. She didn't even have a husband. Mark didn't exist. It was all something she concocted. Who does that? Who invents a person? And the pregnancy. It's sick. How could Owen have been so stupid?"

Zara nodded, a grim expression settling on her face. "It was all a game. The lies were a way to gain sympathy, to manipulate everyone around her. The girls... you... Owen. He only saw what he wanted to see. Some people can't acknowledge the truth." She paused, her gaze dropping to her lap. "She'd mastered the art of deception. I doubt she even knew who she was herself."

Lila shifted, the unease in her posture sharpening. She hesitated, then spoke, her voice soft but edged with accusation. "We need to talk about what happened that day... before Owen arrived."

Zara's shoulders tensed, but she held Lila's gaze, her voice firm. "I did what I had to do, Lila. She was dangerous. I couldn't let her destroy your family." Her eyes blazed with a quiet fury, a fierce protectiveness. "She left me no choice. Like we said to the police, it was self-defence."

Lila studied her, her expression torn. Her voice was laced with a mixture of disbelief and mistrust. "There isn't a day that goes by when I wonder if we did the right thing."

Zara's jaw tightened, her voice dropping to a near whisper. "She left me no choice, Lila. She taunted you, gloated about it... she wore your suffering like it was a trophy to her. And then she attacked you. I was protecting you. Like I always have. Like when we were kids." She met Lila's gaze, unflinching. "I don't regret it. You would have done the same for me."

They sat in silence, the confession hanging between them, raw and charged. Lila's expression softened, but there was a flicker of something darker in her eyes—an unease that refused to be quelled. Yet, after a moment, she nodded slowly, her voice steady but cold. "I promise no one will ever know it was you. I will keep that secret. Always." She spoke the last words carefully, as if convincing herself.

Zara felt a pang of relief but sensed Lila's lingering doubt, like a thin veil that wouldn't lift. She chose her next words with care, her voice calm.

"Thank you. I did what you needed me to do. You and your girls are safe now."

Zara glanced toward the kitchen, where the laughter of Ella and Molly drifted through, a gentle reminder of innocence reclaimed. But when she looked back at Lila, her face was pale, her mouth set in a thin line, a spark of something unreadable there.

Lila met Zara's eyes, feeling the challenge there, the doubt that hadn't faded in all these weeks. "The girls are safe," she replied, her voice firm.

A heavy silence settled over the room, the deadlock of emotions that had piled up between them. The sounds of Ella and Molly laughing in the kitchen drifted through the tension, innocent and unaware, a small reminder of what had been at stake and what they both had fought to preserve.

Lila took a slow breath, her voice softer now, almost pleading. "I'm working on myself. I am going to be a better mother, a better person."

Zara's expression softened just slightly, but the wariness remained, a rift that couldn't be bridged by words alone. She leaned back, as she released a heavy sigh.

"She'll always be there, in the background. Just like I will," Zara said, her voice barely above a whisper as she rose, her body tense as she took a small step toward the door, her face pained yet resolute. She turned before leaving, with one more question, that appeared more like an afterthought. Their eyes meeting again. "How is Owen?"

"He's coping, I think. The divorce will come through soon.

I'm selling Humberstone Road. He's renting a flat. All that business with his finances has been cleared up now. John is behind bars, where he belongs and Cass... well." She blinked again and continued. "He's building bridges with the girls. I'm encouraging them to forgive him." Lila looked down at her hand where her wedding ring used to be.

"Thank you for coming, Zara," she said softly, her voice steady, though sadness tugged at its edges. "You always have been there for me."

Zara looked back one last time, her gaze lingering on Lila with a mixture of sadness and disappointment.

"And you've always been there for me." Without another word, she turned and walked to the door, stepping out into the fading light, leaving Lila behind, alone.

Lila moved back toward the laughter and light that filled Granta Hall, determined to leave the darkness behind—even as it clung quietly in the corners of her mind, a reminder of the price she'd paid to keep her family safe, and as she passed a mirror and looked at her reflection, she saw Zara staring back. In that moment she knew the shadows of that day would always be there, just beneath the surface.

She headed into the kitchen, determined to build something pure out of the fragments they'd been left with, but acutely aware that the past, like Zara, would never be too far behind.

SHE

The last rays of the sun dipped below the horizon as I stood outside Granta Hall, the shadows stretching long over the old stone walls. I stared up at the house, its grand façade bathed in twilight, my face carefully unreadable. Slowly, I reached up and brushed a strand of hair behind my ear, a faint smile tugged at my lips, knowing and deliberate. Lila never saw me—not really. No one ever did. But she did now. She couldn't ignore me now.

When Cass had arrived, sliding into Lila's world with that charm, that too-perfect smile, wrapping herself around Lila and the girls like ivy choking a tree, my anger had simmered, quiet and cold, as I felt myself being replaced. Ignored. And then, without even thinking, I'd done it—I returned. I'd been dormant for so long. She thought she could get rid of me, dispose of me. But I was always there, just beneath the surface, waiting to return.

When she was a child she would call on me. After she killed her little brother I was the one brave enough to remove her father from her life, like the disease he was. I was the one who burnt her house down.

And when the hospital came to cart her away, I was the one they put in the hospital. I took her place, like I always did. I stood *up for her and did what was needed. I paid the price for the darkness inside her. I hadn't expected the fallout to be quite so explosive, but, if I'm honest, some small part of me had relished it. Killing Margaret, that old bitch who was so belittling, disposing of Owen's precious dog, to punish him for turning his back on her. On them. On us. The chaos that had been created and now owed me again. It is a dark, bitter little victory that I will cling to.*

As I stood there, staring at Granta Hall, the win felt hollow. The house was peaceful again. Warm. Full of life. Through the bay window, I could see Ella and Molly in the kitchen, their faces glowing in the soft light. They were laughing, their world calm and untouched by the storm that I had stirred. For a moment, I raised my hand in a small, friendly wave but no one saw me.

My smile slipped, replaced by something sharper as I took in the scene inside. Lila thought she'd rebuilt her life. Thought she was safe now. That the past could be tidied up and buried. But I knew better. I'd seen the cracks, the darkness still clinging to the edges of her carefully constructed world. Cass's death had been brushed aside. But I knew the truth. I'd kept it close, the little details no one else had seen, the ones I could share if I chose. It sat between us like a thread I could pull at any moment, unravelling everything.

As I remained there, the knowledge of it settled over me like a cloak. The quiet power I still held. The power I would always hold. I turned away eventually, my gaze lingering one last time on the warm glow of the house. As I walked down the gravel drive, the weight of my presence clung to the air behind me, a silent reminder to myself—and to Lila, whether she realised it or not—that I wasn't going anywhere. I would always be part of their lives. Part of her.

ME

I stand in the doorway of my kitchen, leaning against the wooden frame, watching my daughters as they slice vegetables and argue over the right amount of garlic for the sauce. The air is warm, filled with the comforting scents of basil and tomatoes, laughter mingling with the sounds of clinking knives and spoons. The smell of summer and a fresh start in the air.

It's strange, how easily I've fallen back into the role of mother. I am different now. I tell myself this every morning, every time I look at my reflection and feel the calm settle over me. I am better, whole again. The things I did, the secrets I buried... they belong to another life, another version of me. They are gone, swept away by the tide of time and distance, and all that's left is a woman who has survived it, who has fought her way back to this quiet, precious moment.

But sometimes, in the stillness, memories drift up like smoke. I remember the look in his eyes—my father's eyes—as he finally realised what I was capable of. That single moment when he understood everything, the horror dawning on his face. I stood there, watching him, and I felt nothing. Not fear, not regret, only the certainty that he had to be stopped. After he was gone, I let the house burn. I will never forget the warmth from the flames. The inferno that erased who I had been and gave birth to a new me. The fire took everything, the rooms where I grew up, the walls that had held me in. I watched it burn, watched the flames lick at the windows, reducing everything to ash.

And then, when it was over, I left. I left that life, left her—the girl who did those things—behind. She went away. She went into the hospital and didn't come out. Not until I needed her again.

I built a new life where no one knew what I'd done, where no one could see the blood on my hands, the troubled girl I had been. The girl who killed her brother. The girl who had been locked up for many years before being released back into the world. I shed my past like dead skin, like the shell of someone I no longer needed. I couldn't keep being that person. So, I removed her and waved her goodbye, closed the door on her. I shut her away, back inside the corners of my mind.

I became someone else and it felt good. It felt right. For a time. Until Cass came into our lives. And then that jealous girl, the one full of bile and rage, she came back. She crawled out from under my skin like a larva hatching from an egg.

Sometimes, in the darkest hours of the night, I still feel her, the girl I buried. She lurks in the shadows, just behind my reflection, whispering that no matter how far I run, she's still part of me. And as I watch Ella lift her knife, laughing at something Molly says, a familiar sensation stirs, cold and dark, hidden beneath the warmth of this perfect scene. It's the feeling that it's all too fragile, that there are cracks in the foundations, hairline fractures that might grow if I'm not careful. I am different, I repeat to myself. I am good now, steady, in control. And then I notice a flicker outside the window and turn. No one else is there.

But something inside me waits, silent and patient, watching with quiet satisfaction. Sometimes, when the night is dark and *the world falls silent, I wonder if that girl—the one who killed before and burned her life to the ground—is now, finally, really gone after all. Or if she's just biding her time, waiting for me to need her again.*

THE END

ALSO BY BETSY REAVLEY

Carrion

Frailty

Murder at the Book Club

Murder in the Dark

Pressure

The Quiet Ones

The Optician's Wife

A NOTE FROM THE PUBLISHER

Thank you for reading this book. If you enjoyed it please do consider leaving a review on Amazon to help others find it too.

We hate typos. All of our books have been rigorously edited and proofread, but sometimes mistakes do slip through. If you have spotted a typo, please do let us know and we can get it amended within hours.

info@bloodhoundbooks.com

Printed in Great Britain
by Amazon